IAN McDONALD is Antiguan b[y] birth, Guyanese by adoption, an[d] Indian by conviction. After gaini[ng a degree in] history at Cambridge, where he [founded the West] Indian Society, he returned to the [Caribbean to work] in the then British Guiana where [he has lived ever] since. As a world class sportsman, he played in and captained the West Indies Lawn Tennis team in the Davis Cup for many years. He is well known as a devotee of cricket and is one of the best regional writers on the subject.

During a distinguished career in the sugar industry, Ian McDonald has also contributed greatly to the Caribbean literary scene, not least as editor of one of the leading West Indian magazines, *Kyk-over-al*. He is a fellow of the Royal Society of Literature, and in 1991 was appointed Editorial Consultant to the West Indian Commission.

Many of his own works have been published, including two widely acclaimed collections of poems, *Mercy Ward* (1988), and *Essequibo* (1992), both from Peterloo Poets. *The Humming-Bird Tree* (1969) won the Royal Society of Literature Prize. Ian McDonald is also a regular contributor of newspaper articles on current affairs, literature and sport.

In 1986, McDonald received the Guyana National Honour, the Golden Arrow of Achievement.

IAN McDONALD

THE HUMMING-BIRD TREE

HEINEMANN

Heinemann International Literature and Textbooks
A division of Heinemann Educational Books Ltd
Halley Court, Jordan Hill, Oxford OX2 8EJ

Heinemann Educational Books Inc
361 Hanover Street, Portsmouth, New Hampshire, 03801, USA

Heinemann Educational Books (Nigeria) Ltd
PMB 5205, Ibadan
Heinemann Educational Boleswa
PO Box 10103, Village Post Office, Gaborone, Botswana

LONDON   EDINBURGH   PARIS   MADRID
ATHENS   BOLOGNA   MELBOURNE   SYDNEY
AUCKLAND   SINGAPORE   TOKYO

Series Editor: Adewale Maja-Pearce

British Library Cataloguing in Publication Data
A catalogue record for this book is available from the British Library.

ISBN 0435 989340

Printed and bound in Great Britain
by Cox & Wyman Ltd, Reading, Berkshire

92   93   94   95   10   9   8   7   6   5   4   3   2   1

For my son, Keith

When we walked up the cool and gleaming river we used to pass a big cassia tree at a lovely bend in the path. It was cool and green in its shade. On certain months of the year its heavy silvery branches were laden with golden blossom. It was like a high, green-sailed ship freighted with ingots and yellow coin. Then the humming-birds came to suck in the sweet-blossom bells of gold. They glittered and gleamed like showers of flame. Sometimes there would be twenty or thirty humming-birds darting and flashing around the tree. In the morning as we walked up to the mountains we saw the humming-birds around it and they gave delight to the whole day. We clutched the immortal morning in our hearts and knew there could be no sourness or disaster or stale disgusts in life while the jewelled birds flew in the air and made lovely bracelets around the cassia's branches. But in the evening when we returned the dark was coming like a great black pig and the humming-birds had flown away. It was sad and menacing to see the big tree stripped of its decoration, and suddenly the day had died.

🎋 The Marbleus

I

The scent of hog plums lay in the ground. Their fragrance was sweet and subtle and a person who didn't know better would have thought for sure that each one of the deep orange plums scattered under the river trees must prove a delicious, juicy thing in the mouth, fruit as good any day as a mango or a rich purple governor plum. Yet only bats would eat them, they were so acid. I remember once Kaiser fooled me. It was my first adventure up the river with him. He had picked one of the plums up and offered me it.

'Man, tas'e dat if you really want to know what fruit tas'e like.'

I bit into the plum, for it smelled as sweet even as sugared cherries, the kind we bought in the tall glass bottles and which the servants used to put in gin-and-orange drinks when friends visited. I actually shuddered with the shock; the acid juice set my body on edge. I spat and spat on the ground and looked fiercely at Kaiser.

'Ha! Ha! Boy, I bet you never tas'e fruit like that before! What you is at all, a bat or what?'

'That's not funny. Perhaps it's poisonous.'

Kaiser laughed again. Ever since that time I had wanted to play the same trick on some other innocent who didn't know about hog plums and important things like that. But I never got the chance.

At that moment, I was not thinking about hog plums. In front of me lay a treasure so great that my eyes dazzled in the sight of it. Not more than two yards away two marbleus were settled on the wet black rock. These are the rarest butterflies and for a boy they were worth more than toy soldiers (like those I had with miniature black busbies on at home), an electric train or bow and arrow, even more than the pirate gold I hoped to find one day in the garden. And they were there so close that my net on the long bamboo pole would easily reach them with one wide swoop. I noticed they were stuck together at the ends of their thin brown bodies and I couldn't understand this. But it didn't matter, the main thing was that the posture made them so easy to catch. I had never seen a marbleu settled before. Generally they flew high and fast down the middle of the river and so were impossible to catch. Only one of my friends had a specimen, and that was old and battered; we teased him that his grandfather had given it to him, that it was out of date. Now two of them had settled clumsily on an open rock face, like a special sacrifice to me. Their deep blue wings lay against the black stone, like fragments of linen tacked on to black sugarcloth. I knelt watching them, in one of boyhood's trances. Sometimes their wings moved lazily upwards and gently down, as if a delicate wind disturbed them; then the little light there was under the trees gathered in the wings and they shone in my eyes like triangles of blue glass reflecting a cloudless sun. It was the most beautiful thing I ever saw.

I knelt forward, almost in worship. But as I raised the bamboo pole ever so carefully, slowly (if I had done it quickly, with vehemence, I think I would have caught them), my knee slipped on the wet rock and my hands went sprawling, with the net, to save myself. The marbleus were disturbed by this gross fall and carefully, still together, they lifted themselves off the rock and flew down over the river where it rushed white and dangerous between the black rock walls.

Their blue wings moved languidly as they dipped and floated away from me. I recovered quickly and, standing up, made wide and desperate sweeps at them as far as my reach went over the edge of the rock. I had tears in my eyes, and as it became plain that they were escaped for good it suddenly came to me that nothing crueller might ever happen to me in life. The hurt struck me into marble stillness on the edge of black rock. I stood as if I would never move again unless it was to hurl myself in a fury of frustration into the sharp-rocked tiger water raging beneath me. I had

2

left my large poison bottle under the leaves of a tough mountain lily growing higher up the rock where it held a little earth, and now I fetched it down (it contained a coffee, a lady slipper and two donkey eyes) and flung it into the water. That gave me some satisfaction and I stood less hurt then.

I didn't stand there for long. I heard a shout from lower down the river:

'Hey, man! Come and see what I get!'

I went down to where Kaiser was squatting on a fat stone. He looked pleased with himself. A few minutes before I had left him chasing a kingfisher butterfly hell for leather. I saw he had caught it. The kingfisher had a thick, unlovely body and big eyes like beads. I think it must have been a sort of moth, and not a real butterfly. Anyway, its wings were truly beautiful, glossy brown, fringed delicately with purple, and in the centre of each a star of scarlet. It was almost as good a catch as the marbleus would have been.

'You know already how fast these things does fly, eh, boy? Well, he settle just one time on a lily leaf back there and pap! I pick he off like a bird, man!'

He grinned and flung his hair backwards.

The butterfly lay dead in his poison bottle, resting on the white camphor. I could see that Kaiser had crushed its head between his fingers to make quite sure of his catch. He was smiling so that it hurt to think of the marbleus I had lost.

'I tell you, you know, Kaiser, I nearly caught two marbleus just now.'

'You only boas'ing. You is jealous, man. What you jealous for? I is giving this one here to you for keeps anyhow.'

If there had been nothing else I would have accepted joyfully— an offer like that wasn't to be expected every day— but now I was intent only on convincing him that what I had said about the marbleus was true.

'But I'm telling you, really, Kaiser. They were joined together and almost as if they were asleep there on the rock, just up there.' Out of desperation I was much more convincing.

'Join together! But, man, what you telling me! You don't know yet that you mus' never whatever you do in this worl' try catch

3

two but'flies who join up like that. You well lucky, man. You well escape. You don't know if you had catch them you would ha' pee your bed all nex' week and maybe worse things than that even. Talk 'bout ghosts haunting; man, those marbleus'd've haunt you' backside off for you. You well lucky.'

This dark knowledge surprised me. I now thought myself rather as sweet in the eyes of God than cursed by a demon of ill-luck. What good fortune not to have caught them! Another thing puzzled me though.

'But why were they joined together at all?'

'You mean you don't know why! You really green as grass, boy. You' Mam and Pap join up jus' so when they making you, boy, the same way as dem but'flies. It's the same t'ing they was doing.' He paused, appreciating my innocence.

'But don't worry your head 'bout those things,' Kaiser went on with a dismissing gesture. 'They is only grow-up people business. You don't have to bother wid that at all. As Ol' Boss up in the village say, "ignorance does live dam' happy!"'

'But why should I be ignorant? It's something to do with love, isn't it? I've read some books you know.'

'What books know 'bout that, eh? But don't bother your head at all, boy.'

It was coming on to rain. It was getting darker than ever under the trees that leaned over the black rocks. The roar of the river came to our ears ominously like thunder now. A small wind breathed in the branches over our heads. It was prophesying a sudden lash of rain, I was sure.

'Where d'you think we could shelter, Kaiser? It's going to rain.'

He must have known the rain was coming but he hadn't moved an inch. He had a peeled tamarind stick in his hand and with it he dug at the hard earth as he sat forwards, forearms on knees, on the fat stone. His butterflying pole lay beside him. Its mosquito netting bag was coloured red. He had told me that butterflies couldn't see red very well, but I had not yet got my mother to dye my net that efficacious colour and the white heap of it lay in contrast a few yards away. Now Kaiser grunted a little sourly.

'You all right, man. I don't min' a dam' if I get soak right through in the dam' rain. It only because you got a nice shirt that you want to run and hide from a little bit o' water. I could be a fish here. I don't mind one dam'.'

I looked at the thin tropical shirt I was wearing. It was made of a fine blue poplin material. I had rolled the sleeves up past my elbows untidily, the tails had long ago crept out of the khaki pants I wore, but despite its dishevelment anybody could see it was a good shirt.

Kaiser wasn't wearing a shirt. The only clothing he had on was a pair of khaki pants, like mine but much shorter (and the legs were different lengths), much more tattered and torn, much dirtier. It was belted with a piece of yellow string. I envied him.

'Oh, I don't mind getting wet. Once down the Islands I stayed out in the rain and got wet. It was much wetter than just having a bath. It smelled better too. Mother was vexed though. You might catch pneumonia, that's the thing. You spell it with a pee.'

'Ha! Ha! Boy, how you could spell it with a pee!'

'Oh, blast, Kaiser, you know I didn't mean that.'

'Anyhow, boy, you know what; you too soft.'

'All right then, I'll just go and put my shirt away, then you'll see. Who's afraid of rain?'

I scrambled up the rock, pulled off my shirt, rolled it up carelessly, and put it in a hollow trunk of immortelle where it was almost dry. Then I slid back down, smiling, gay, and said:

'I don't mind a dam' about the rain now!' Suddenly I felt such freedom. The bones in me were looser. My body surged with confidence. Joy abounded in me. I felt I could do anything in this new, exciting, uncomplicated world. I leaped around Kaiser exclaiming. Again and again I shouted:

'I don't care one dam', see!'

Kaiser grinned up at me. He flicked some earth over my legs with his tamarind stick.

'You is a hero, boy!'

When the rain did come we stayed there and danced in it. It began with a scattering of huge drops that cracked like bullets on the leaves overhead and on the rock.

5

If one hit you it stung hard. Then a stillness in which we hardly dared to draw a breath. Hush. The rain streamed down and the world was wet, the earth soggy, in a minute. It ran over the black rock so that it glistened like a cape. The rain poured on us as if we were under buckets and we laughed and laughed. I closed my eyes and tilted up my face to the rain. I opened my mouth and drank the rain; I thought it tasted like blood, blood from the sky; perhaps it was dripping from hurt flamingoes. We tossed our heads and the water sprayed out of our hair; we tried to fling the water into each other's faces from the long, wet locks, his black as a blackbird's wing, mine fair, almost flaxen. The smell of rain new on the baked ground, in it the fragrance of fresh nutbread, of salmon pools, of green-fern roots dug out of the ground, seemed to make us drunk. We leaped like monkeys around a hoard of bananas.

'We is fish!' Kaiser shouted. 'We is fish! We don't give a dam', we don't give a blast, we don't give a fuck!'

I repeated what he said, delirious with the joy of rain. We shouted and laughed and danced about. It was a wild glory of boys. We were near to each other in the joy. We touched hands and spun about in crazy waltzes. The rain pelted down and the trees groaned with the bigger wind. We vowed to be friends forever. For sure, which of us will dance like that again.

2

The difference between us was that I was white and he was dark brown. That, I suppose, was the major difference. But there were other differences. He was older than I, fourteen he said, though I think he may have been more than that; I was not quite twelve. And yet I was as tall as he and my limbs and body as big as his. Not half as tough though. One of the first things he had done when I met him was ask me to feel his muscles. They were hard. When he pressed mine with his stubby, powerful fingers they gave like rubber. He laughed at me:

'You have muscle like a fairy, boy, or what!'

I did not speak to him for days after that, but secretly punched the pillows in bed at night, tested the puny and despised muscles almost every hour. If it was possible I wanted to be as strong as he was.

Kaiser was strong and hard all over. He had a heavy neck, a deep chest and his slightly bowed legs were thick with firm and bulgy calf-muscles. In comparison with him I was altogether flabby. Just to look at him I felt soft. My big bones were covered with tender, pampered flesh, and in contrast with his brown and shining skin my milky complexion seemed to proclaim a sickly weakness. Sometimes he called me White Cockroach, terrible insult! His skin was fine, smooth as silk and dark. When he ran or otherwise exerted himself it rippled evenly where the good muscles tightened and relaxed underneath.

He could run faster than I and was more active in every way. One day we ran a race from the old samaan tree up the pitch road to the plum tree near the railway line. He beat me by twenty yards and I was sobbing with lack of breath when I came up to him. He then swung into the branches of one of the plum trees; he did it with all the ease and assurance in the world. Then I was not expert at the happy art of climbing trees and I watched him enviously. I got laboriously up with him, and from our perch we looked out for adventure. After a few minutes we saw old Ramlal, the village rum-dealer, coming down to fill a bucket from the water-pump further on.

'Let we pelt he. He only a dirty coolie t'ief!'

'I don't think we should, you know, Kaiser. You should have respect for old people like that.'

Kaiser wasn't listening. He picked a handful of green hard plums and pelted Ramlal as he passed. I tried to stop him but at once I saw the thrill of the game. I tossed one plum tentatively at the old man; it landed square on his thin nose! I was delighted and shocked. This was a terrifying adventure for me. I quivered at the thought of showing such disrespect to a grown-up. But Kaiser only bawled with laughter as the surprised old man looked about to see what had hit him so hard in the head. He shook his greasy hat at us, cursed us roundly.

'You dam' little boys playing your arse all the dam' time! Who you think you is? You think you is badjohns? Come down here and see if I don't beat you up and down. Police should lock all you up.'

Kaiser only laughed. I felt guilty and ashamed. I stopped throwing the plums.

'And as for you, Master Alan, what happen to you at all, pelting a old man who only minding he own business. I bet I tell your Mam here today and she lick your backside off for you!'

He went off, mumbling angrily and clanking his bucket. His last threat had sobered even Kaiser, though in defiance he stubbornly continued to force a laugh until the old man was out of earshot. He knew that any complaint about us getting back to my parents would mean his dismissal. He was certainly afraid of that. He had then been with us only a few weeks.

Kaiser was the family yard-boy. He cut the lawn, kept the flower beds tidy, looked after the fowls and ducks, tended the fruit trees, cleaned and polished the car (that was the work he liked). He did all sorts of odd jobs about the house, cleaning the shoes and washing floors, killing chickens for lunch, polishing the silverware, picking lemons for Alice, the cook. The spare time he had he played with me. We had become good friends from the start. I was shy, I did not make friends easily, but with him I felt contented.

A few weeks before my father had taken him on for the job. He was very conscientious and I could never tempt him to come and play when he was engaged in some work for my mother. I remember hearing her say that she had never known a better yard-boy, one that worked harder. My father had said something about a new broom sweeping clean, but he too said that Kaiser worked hard enough, and soon he trusted him with more and more important jobs. Kaiser badly wanted to keep the position. He was getting better pay than he would get anywhere else as well as food and often, if he was lucky, some of the old clothes I had discarded and the tennis shoes that had holes in them. Kaiser played a big part in supporting his family. They lived in the village, cramped into a small mud hut. One of that family was his sister, Jaillin, a young girl who also worked for us in the house. She and Kaiser were good friends and so we three were together often. She had come with us today butterflying but had left us long before, even before we had got to the dark river where the excitement of chasing began. She had said something about going to see Mother Gawmy, an old woman who cooked bakes for sale and lived near where the path up the hill ended.

I never thought of domineering it over Kaiser, though at first I sometimes took pleasure at home in ordering him to clean my shoes, sharpen my boy scout's knife on the whetstone so that it shone, clean the bicycle I owned. He never disobeyed me, or made any comment at all, in the course of his work, and it gave me a feeling of power. But as time went on I took less and less advantage of my position as master in relation to him. It didn't seem much fun any more.

The truth is that there was another difference between Kaiser and myself, and it became more and more marked as I got to know him better. He was a hero; I became his disciple. I soon saw that he was better than I in all the ways that really mattered. He was strong and active, a very good athlete. He knew how to climb trees to perfection. I saw him go up a coconut palm once like lightning, without a loop of rope, like the copra workers used, to help him; on my part I slid back down the trunk almost as soon as I started and had badly grazed hands for my pains. He could milk a cow. He did things which I would never dare to do. He shot humming-birds off the telephone wires when they settled there, an accurate master with his limewood catapult. I was horrified at this not only because I didn't like to kill birds but also because it was against the law to shoot humming-birds at all. They were talismanic in the island and rare and beautiful, and I was under the impression that you could go to prison for years if you killed one. I was timid. Kaiser laughed at the law. He shot them down and carefully collected their rainbow feathers, some like sunset in water, some a shimmering metallic green, some pale gold, others deep-sea blue, into match-boxes, just like a jeweller. He had many match-boxes full of humming-bird feathers. He offered me one of them once, ironically, I thought.

'What you 'fraid for? You 'fraid they going put you in jail or what!' He was always scornful when I showed I was timid.

'No,' I said, untruthfully, 'but I don't like them much. I prefer butterflies.'

9

'Go to hell then!'

And he pushed the match-box out of its cover with his fore-finger and emptied all the lovely feathers on the ground. It was amazing how many there were crammed into the one small box. Now they scattered on the pitch road where we were outside the house like so many brilliant leaves. The gentlest of winds blew them yards they were so light and delicate. A few floated by chance into the gutter beside the road and, landing in the sluggish water there, moved slowly away like petals drop-ped from the samaan tree above us. I couldn't understand why he had done this. It seemed a little thing to get so annoyed about.

'What are you so vexed about, Kaiser?'

'Go to hell, eh! You white people too scornful, boy.'

'I don't understand what you mean at all.'

'It always so. You never going understand we. You is all right you know, boy, but you is white.'

'All right, I'll take the feathers. Really and truly I like them you know.'

'I not giving you a nex' box, boy. If you want, go and pick up in the gutter.'

He wasn't often like that. I looked on it just as a bad temper, a natural hazard. I would have to go easier if I wanted to learn from him all the things he had to teach.

Kaiser knew everything about birds. He knew their different songs and where they were used to lay their eggs. He showed me how to preserve their delicate and many-coloured shells intact for collection: at both ends you pierced each egg with a pin, then you blew out the contents, so that the eggshell was left dry and felt light as air in the hand. This was an operation which required extreme delicacy and many times, before I learnt properly, I shattered the eggshell while blowing it clean. As a result I had to practice on doves' eggs, which were the commonest (those of a mountain dove were a different matter), before Kaiser allowed me to try blowing a treasure like the egg of a humming-bird or a bluebird. When I could do these I was very pleased, put on many airs with my other friends. But Kaiser said with a great and healthy sneer:

'You still making you' pin-hole too dam' big. What you think you doing at all, boring wid a gimlet or what?'

One kind of bird he warned me about was the cassique. These were beautiful birds, some all yellow, some with scarlet backs. It was a temptation to raid their nests. But Kaiser told me the danger. These birds always hung their nests close to a marabunta's hive and seemed to have some contract with those vicious bees to guard against intruders.

'Tek care, boy. Watch out what you do. Cassique nes' an' 'bunta nes' look jus' the same. Don' stick up you han' near one so or you going get bite like a dog. I self had swell eye fo' two week one time fo' doing that same thing.'

After that I admired the yellow and the scarlet cassiques from a distance. He showed me how to make gum traps for birds. He slashed a breadfruit tree with a cutlass so that the white milk oozed out down the mottled grey trunk. He collected the milk in a tin cup, and when it had hardened into stickiness placed it on a twig near to some rich and rotting fruit, an already bird-pecked mango, a bee-sucked shaddock. Often even if a bird was not quite caught it could do no more than fly feebly along, its wings sticky with the laglie, its feet catching in any bush it settled on. Then Kaiser would run it down as it fluttered from place to place and wring its neck at once. For a long time I could not bear to see this; to me it was a hideous and cruel thing to do. As usual Kaiser would mock me for my faintheartedness.

'You is a minor mouse, boy, one minor mouse,' he told me once when I said he was bloodthirsty.

He was brought up with a different feeling from mine about these things. He saw no sense in being sorry for animals, or even in being kind to them unless it was a matter of necessity, like keeping a cow in good condition. He couldn't understand why we pampered and petted our dogs and cats. He was not sadistic in this matter—I never knew him to be cruel for the sake of being cruel, but his attitude was not more than one of indifference. He loved a few human beings, himself especially, and he could not see the point of bothering himself with diluted pastime loving. He was hardened through years of example in this attitude. Animals were beneath him; they were meant for his use and further than that not only he but generations before him in similar villages could not see. Many of the village families had a donkey, all had a cow, some had a dog for hunting; none had the green and talking parakeets of many of our drawing-rooms. So the birds that he caught in the laglie traps were more often than not for Kaiser good food which the same night his family could cook and eat. He told me that his father liked doves in particular. They were tender and their bones so small that he could chew and eat those too. In the end I came to see his point of view, but I could never at any time bring myself to wring a bird's neck, and I killed them only for their pretty feathers.

Kaiser was a deserving hero. He taught me an infinity of the tricks of a boy's trade. He showed me how to make a catapult— the best wood was lime or grapefruit, how to make bamboo flutes, whistles from the stalks of paw-paw trees. I was instructed by him in useful lore, like where to find the best fish-holes in the river, how to peel cane with the teeth. I admired him for his fund of forceful common-sense instruction. If I was attacked by a nest of Jack Spaniards, he told me:

'Screw up you' eye, boy, and get to hell!'

Kaiser's magic exerted a strong hold on me. Sometimes he seemed to be in touch with a power which frightened me. There was one thing in particular I was frightened of. In his locker room at the back of the house he kept a mountain dove's egg, blue as pale eyes, which he had blown himself. Through one of the pin holes he had put a grain of rice about as big as the hole. Once or twice he took me into the room and shook the blue shell for a minute or so, and he told me that the time the rice grain fell back through the hole the end of our world was near us and angels would root up even the Treasury Building in Port of Spain and strangle all the people in the world with their golden fingers. This ceremony of shaking the dove's egg terrified me. It terrified him too. I remember the fear and tension in the dark little locker room. Sweat poured down our faces. Two small boys stood at the centre of the universe controlling God. And even though I felt that the grain of rice dictated what He must do, I prayed God desperately in those minutes to keep the white tiny grain safe in the egg. Both of us sweated the minutes out as if they were the

last before an execution. Then Kaiser would pu
smile and sigh.

'God, Kaiser, why do you shake it at all? Don't shake
be all right. One day you might kill everybody.'

'Boy, you *mus'* shake it sometime. They *expec'* it. What ye
think would happen if we show we 'fraid them, eh? No, boy, we
mus'n't 'fraid them like that . . . I going shake the egg sometime an' put a trus' . . .'

'Where? Where? Where're you going to put a trust? If the
rice comes out it isn't God's fault, it's yours.'

'What you saying? It not my dam' fault. I not going be a
dam' coward for nobody. You could get kill for that too besides.
If you don' want to tes' brave what they want, don't come, eh.'

But I always went. It was a kind of joy to be suspended in
fear. I felt a more important person. Kaiser and I were daredevils,
risking everything. It was better than pretending to fight and
conquer a thousand men.

Kaiser made me absorb certain necessary superstitions. If I ever
stepped on a frog I must keep two of my fingers crossed all day or
evil would befall. On the other hand, even to see a coral snake
and far more to kill one, was the best of luck and I could expect
fortune to smile on me for a long week. I was told, and faithfully
believed, that if I ever found a perfectly smooth and oval stone
I had only to place it in a jar full of water, cut a thumb, put a drop
of blood in, and add one more drop every week: in a year's time
that stone would turn into a beautiful and priceless ruby. Once I
found a stone which I thought sufficiently smooth and round to
try my fortunate knowledge on. I kept it a little over a month,
religiously contributing the five beads of blood. I kept it in a secret
drawer but my mother discovered it all the same. To my fury and
amazement, even though I told her what it was for, how it could
make our fortune, she discarded jar, rusty water, oval stone, all,
where I could not find them again, comforting me with a gentle
smile and two paradise plums. I never found another stone so
round. Nor did Kaiser ever find one at all though he kicked even
more earnestly than I at every river path we walked.

On another occasion he told me, his dark eyes serious and intent,
as they always were when he talked of magic:

13

ou this because I know what I saying.
ıp you'self an' walk seven time roun' the
Godfrey. Befo' you know whe' you is you
nad on you' ches' and get strong as Julius

ess. I didn't grow any hair on my chest and
putty in comparison with Kaiser himself, who
d walked around Mr Godfrey's tamarind tree
more th...   times.

Despite these occasional failures I did not in the slightest lose
faith in Kaiser. He was the fount of all worthwhile knowledge;
he was an initiate in the special mysteries of the world; he had
magic in his fingers. He cursed bravely. He was strong and confident. He was a leader. He was a good friend.

What is more he was the brother of Jaillin. And Jaillin I loved.

3

It was only a lash of rain; it didn't last long. When it stopped we
squatted on the wet black rock again, exhausted with our fun.
The sun now came through the trees in places strongly and made
wide marks of gold on the rock where we sat breathing hard. It
was a new world. Birds began to sing cheerfully, as they always
do after a sharp shower like that. The wind was quiet again. Beads
of water fell down from the trees. Sometimes, if you were lucky,
the sun would here and there jewel a drop high up on a leaf and
you could see there the beads hanging for one moment, glittering
with the colours of the rainbow, before they fell into where there
was no sun. It was one of the peculiar graces of sudden and bright
sun after drenching rain, these necklaces of waterbeads, red and
silver and sapphire and emerald by turn and turn again, hanging
for the briefest instants on a branch in the sun, then losing themselves in shadow, so many pearls dropped into an unfathomable
sea of pitch. Even though I was that young I delighted in this
decoration after rain. Kaiser did not see eye to eye with me here.
When I tentatively suggested the comparison with jewels he did
not see it at all:

'They is water an' you well know they is water, so what you talking 'bout jewels for? I don' understan' you, man. They not so pretty as a spider eye even.'

'Well, I've never noticed a spider's eye.'

'Anyhow, they prettier than those piss-drops o' water!'

'Where d'you think Jaillin has got to?' I asked, changing the subject. We couldn't agree on poetry and beauty, but Jaillin at least was common ground. She was a pet of his, and I for my part, I could never see enough of her. 'She said she would catch us up after Mother Gawmy's, didn't she?'

'She said that, yes, but I don' believe that chile know what going on in she head from one minute to the nex'. That is the truth. Pap all the time licking she till she bawl because she come home an' forget to buy split pea or green plantain in the market, or something or the other like that. Boy, you could expec' she any time nex' Christmas or so.'

We got up. I got my blue shirt and put it on again. We slid down the smooth black rock to where a narrow path walked beside the river. This led down for a mile, then it left the river and after that you walked through high bush for about a half mile to where the path up Japon Hill begins. This is where Jaillin had left us to go and see the old bakewoman.

We went back along the river path at our ease. Anything could distract us, a spider dangling on a long pearly thread, a big wild fig leaf which we tested for a green umbrella. We looked for oval stones. Often we took time out to wade in the cool river: the feel of the chill strong water against the legs was the knowledge of pleasure. We played tic-tac-toe with flat stones wherever the river became at all wide and smooth; in one place Kaiser skipped a yellow thin stone four times before it hit the other bank:

'That was a master stone,' he said. I never managed more than twice.

At one place, where the river slowed under trees to a sluggish pond, green as a heron-frog's back with the moss which slimed its deep bed, there was a myriad of dragon-flies. It was a lovely concourse. They darted here, there and everywhere looking for mosquito larvae. Some were colourless, stick-bodies and paper wings only, but the delicately veined, transparent wings of others dazzled with colour. There was one sort which had just a spot of scarlet at the root of each wing; this seemed to me the most beautiful, for the contrast was so dramatic that I could make myself believe as it sped along the surface of the pond that this dragon-fly, Arabian messenger, was flying with drops of blood against its side. Some others had half-green wings, some had great purple bodies which they laboured perilously through the air on small wings.

Kaiser swooped his red net into the midst of them, captured two of the pretty dragons. They buzzed furiously in the netting. They tired themselves with beating on the net, then stayed so still we could touch them and they would not move. We looked at them close and saw their big eyes and how transparent their eyes were. Then Kaiser shook them into freedom. They zoomed frantically, high into the trees. They looked like darts used at a bull-fight.

'Blast, look at them go!'

'They mus've t'ought they were going dead. How fas' you think they going, boy?'

'Faster than an aeroplane?'

'What, boy! No! Aeroplane is the fas'est thing in the worl'. When I get big I going drive aeroplane. Brmmm! Brmmm!' And he went whirring away down the path.

At one small strip of muddy ground we saw what Kaiser told me were the hoof-prints of a tapir. He said they were rare roundabouts. If a villager could catch one it was a treasure not only because of its flesh which made good eating, but also because its hoofs were powerful talismans. The scraping of bone from a tapir's hoof were used by older inhabitants of the village against illness or hurt. But you must take care, Kaiser said, to use for men only the female tapir's hoof, for women only the male, otherwise the power of those charms would be quite annulled.

It was near the tapir tracks that I picked a river-orchid which was growing out of a moist crack in a rock. These orchids were quite common and at some times of the year you might see a whole stretch of river-bank stained purple by their flowering. But this one was alone, growing out of the rock as if it had split it. I picked the flower low down on the stalk so that a long green leaf remained to sheath its petals from below. I put the stalk in the neck of my shirt and the flower tossed over my shoulder as I walked along.

As we went on a little, a great rock we were fond of rose up out of the river. We called it 'Mister Big Nose' because one side of it had been broken off so as to make the profile of a man with a mighty Roman nose. It was a beautiful rock. It looked as if it had been glazed with plumbago, and on its steely surface flecks of silver stone caught the sun and sparkled like splinters of glass. We clambered up on it and in our hearts defied lions and bears; at the last moment were saved from a raging flood. It was our magic refuge; when we sat on it Kaiser said it was like sitting on God's head. We had made a rhyme for it which we chanted now:

'Rock, Rock
'Stand any shock
'Blue as the sky
'Mister Big Nose
'He never die.'

A little further on where the river was forded by a line of stones we met a man coming across gingerly with a jute sack slung over his shoulder. He was an Indian with a white beard and white, curry-stained moustaches. He was well known in the district as the Crabman, because he caught and sold mountain-crabs for his livelihood. As he came near us I could hear the crabs clicking furiously in his sack. I had a terrible vision of the monsters tearing their way out, slashing the poor old man to death with their claws. Up the river I had seen mountain crabs. They were huge and brown and ugly; I wondered why God had ever made them. They were so much like stones when they lay still that you could step on one without noticing it, then it would scuttle away fast under wet leaves with a curious noise, as if a thousand damp toenails were all being cut at once. Once, before I knew Kaiser, my father had taken me up the river and we had come across a giant crab lurking near some ferns. After a bit of a chase my father caught it, but he held the crab awkwardly and it succeeded in cutting him sharply on the thumb, before he got it safely tied up in string. The cut bled a little, my father put iodine on it; so we

17

christened the fierce crab 'Iodine, Crab of Crabs', and took him home in triumph. Since then Kaiser had taught me the right way to hold a crab helpless, but still I never dared to take one of them up.

'Boy, he really catch crab today!'

'One day they'll all get out and bite him dead. Look. one of their claws is showing!'

'You really funny, boy!'

The old man came across the line of stones and nodded to us. He asked me if my mother wanted any nice crabs. I said Alice always wanted a few on Sundays because then she made callalloo and crab soup for dinner; it was a custom of the house.

'Right, boss. Dey is the sweetes' crab you ever going want, you going see, boss.'

And he went away in front of us with his burden of brown crabs, all clicking like mad.

'The Crabman Strikes Again! Boy, that could be a movie picture, eh?'

'But, Kaiser, what on earth's happened to Jaillin? Perhaps she's lost?'

'Ha! Ha! Perhaps the crabs catch she already. Look out well fo' she chew-up body, boy!'

I paled.

'That's not funny! She's your own sister, you know.'

'Don' worry, boy. How she going get los'? She was coming up this part helping wash clothes befo' they finish push you in a dam' pram.'

As we walked along I told Kaiser about Livingstone, whom I had just read about in a geography book. He was taken with the idea of the man. Both of us pretended to be that explorer. Crocodiles, quicksands, innumerable other dangers barred our way. We pressed on happily.

Before we had even got to the end of the river path, however, we saw Jaillin coming up to us. She was hurrying. She saw us and shouted quickly:

'I was jus' coming to meet up wid you. All you going down already? Why so quick?'

'Who you think we is, chile, Job or somebody, to have patience fo' you?' Kaiser shouted back. 'Whe' you been all this dam' time, eh? You know it nearly twelve o'clock? Why you didn't hurry you' little arse up?'

I was gentler.

'What've you been doing all the time at Mother Gawmy's Jaillin?' I called out to her.

We came up to her.

4

I suppose the story I really want to tell begins with Jaillin. She was at the heart of all the crises which one by one moulded me. When I first met her I was a child, the last time I was with her childhood suddenly came to an end. Looking back she seems to appear in every picture I have of that short span of life. It is as if in painting the pictures my memory must put her in, dominating the composition perhaps, perhaps just a glimpse, a flash of colour, in one corner, but always there. My manhood is without her. What I am no longer comprehends what she is. I suppose that is the story.

Look at her that day. She was a little younger than I and very pretty. She had the same glowing deep brown skin as Kaiser, her hair was black as a blackbird's wing like his. She wore it almost down to her waist at the back in two long plaits and in front it was skinned off her forehead with a curving tortoiseshell comb. Her face was thin. All its features were shapely, but the glory of that face were the dark eyes. They were eyes of true Indian beauty, soft, dark as night, yet they slept with some cruel fire deep within. I was in love with Jaillin's eyes, just to see them shape and glow with a smile, in vexation, in fear. 'She have Deer Eye,' Kaiser said, and you could see that even he, the critic, was a little startled by their beauty. For my part if she looked at me long I grew taut and shivered as if I was cold, cold in a morning wind.

It is not true to say that the feelings of a young boy don't go as deep as those of a grown man. A boy lives more with terror than a man, that is sure. And it is not right to scoff at what is called calf love. It is difficult for people who are grown up and know how to be passionate to realize that the depth of children's love is as deep as theirs, but that is the truth. The love is as deep but it seems less, unreal, since the ways of giving it and taking it have not been learned. It is a strange and puzzling thing. A child seems to be more in love with its mother than an adult because it is practised in loving its mother: a child knows what to do to show its love, make its mother show hers, in every small way. But this new, strange feeling, what is he to make of that? There is no apparatus for it. What is felt cannot be communicated, or if it is, only in ways that seem laughable to grown-ups, who have the techniques of adult love at their finger tips. In my love for Jaillin there was that despair of fulfilment which lies at the centre of real suffering. The despair was at first calm, not understanding, but accepting the hurt. As time went on it was provoked, charged with anger and fear and the active sense of ignorance. The root of love was as strong, and it grew as fiercely in the heart as it may grow in a man's. All I ever knew to do was to pray every night to God with terrible insistence that I should marry Jaillin when I grew to be a man.

All her body was just about covered with flesh so that there were no ugly bones coming up sharply in the lovely contouring; her body, though, was still thin and undeveloped. Her legs were over-long in proportion to the rest of her. But for me she was perfectly graceful. Sometimes, when the three of us went bathing in the river, I saw her without a dress. Her breasts were just coming up, pointed and small and tight on her body, the teats pale and big compared with them. I stared at her body, and wondered at the attraction I was lost in. She laughed at me when I looked so hard.

'What you looking so fo', Master Alan? You never see me befo' or what?'

I got confused then and said that I wasn't looking at her at all.

I was astonished one day when she told us openly that her breasts were a big nuisance: 'They itch like France!' she said, and rubbed them hard with her fingers. I was unashamed of her nakedness because she was not ashamed, but this shocked me. I had got it into my head that a girl did not talk about her body at all, that it was something sacred and unmentionable.

Today she was wearing no shoes. Her dress, printed with

flowers, was old, faded, much too big for her: clearly it had been cut down from a woman's dress for her to wear. At each ear hung a droplet of silver: they were a lovely decoration; she rarely wore them, I knew, afraid to lose the most precious things she had. At each wrist hung a silver bangle, but these she always wore; I never once saw her without them.

I handed her the orchid I held in my shirt, told her to put it in her hair.

'Yes, what you doing all this time so at Mother Gawmy's?' Kaiser repeated my question. 'Eating all she bake, I s'pose?'

She put the orchid in her dark hair, then replied:

'Well, I stay talking wid she till I can't fin' out anything more in my head to talk 'bout. You know how she lonely whe' she is, an' how she want to know everything what going on. Well I tell you, I tried tell she how Ramlal donkey lie down an' dead an' how Aunty Phyllis washing white people clothes for a living these days. All sort o' thing like that. I talk till my t'roat dry up. It's so I sorry for that ol' woman; nobody want to gi' she all the people news because she a little bit deaf, an' she don't know nothing what going on all 'bout.'

'Don't be too sorry for she, oui. You know how she charge for so for bake.'

Often when Kaiser and Jaillin got talking to each other they seemed to ignore me. On those occasions I felt years and years younger than both of them. They showed they knew things about the grown-up world which I had no inkling of as yet. I listened with wonder and envy to their conversations about people years older than themselves, about things which I had felt must be the prerogative of those who were older.

The truth is that they had been living in a world where they had been forced to fend for themselves like any other man or woman in their village from an age when I was hardly rid of my long, girlish and golden curls and had to look after me, when my mother wasn't there, a nurse continually at my beck and call and eagle-eyed for hurt or mischief. As a result I hadn't lost much of childhood's innocence while they in their compulsorily hard life had lost it long ago. There was something in them which was not childish; I saw that often and could not understand. Kaiser once came and told me that his father's cow had died the night before. He was almost crying.

'We los', man, we los'. Wha' we going do, I asking you? Pap only could get another cow from down by Barataria, an' that cos' fifty dollar widout thinking even. He going have to borrow an' everyone know that if a man borrowing he losing and losing han' over fis'!'

Talk of this kind I couldn't for the life of me understand. What concern was it of his if his father's cow died and he had to buy another one? None that I could see. *I* did not trouble myself over what my father bought or did not buy in our household. When we had a new car it was an excitement; for all I knew it might have cost a million dollars. I hadn't the least idea what borrowing might imply in an Indian peasant family, a heavy drain on the trickle of income, a social stigma. On this particular occasion it was Kaiser who, many weeks later, let me know that my father had paid cash down for another cow, charged no interest and set no time limit on the loan. I wouldn't have bothered to find out myself.

'I t'ought you know that long time, man. Yes, man, you have a dam' good Pap. I don't know another white person who would ha' do that same thing for we poor Indian people. Pap goin' pay back, you know.'

It was a mood which puzzled me. I had quickly changed the subject. He showed me that day as a special secret how to shape and grease with candle a piece of cedar wood so that it would sail straight, fast, buoyant in races down the gutter. And Jaillin for a week was shy and would not speak much.

This morning she was voluble. She owed me nothing. She went on :

'After, I help she make aloo pie till I tired. She tell me she doing big trade wid them these days. She make in the morning an' when afternoon come she fill up a basket wid them an' tek she hot sauce an' go 'way down on the Main Road by Curepe an' all. By the time it dark they all sell. Everybody buying. She say even taxi driver stopping she fo' a aloo pie. I tell you, she making money so fas' she don't know what to do wid it.'

She stopped for a moment to let this information sink in,

then continued with a little triumphant inflection in her voice:

'She gi' me a shilling for helping she today alone!'

'What!' Kaiser shouted. 'She gi' you a whole shilling jus' like that so for nothing, nothing at all!'

'Wha' you mean nothing! I work for so at the table. I work till the bone in my han' feel it going break. I well earn my money. An' I telling you something, boy, you not getting none!'

Kaiser began to wheedle; his voice got as sweet as syrup.

'Ey, ey, chile. What, you vex wid you' brother? Don't vex so. You know I love you too bad, Jaillin, chile, gi' you' brother a penny for sweety in the parlour, a penny out o' all the big shilling. What you saying, chile?'

'Don't try an' sweet talk me at all. I not giving.'

'You selfish as a crow! What, you going eat out all that shilling by you' self or what?'

'Min' you' own business.'

Suddenly Jaillin turned to me where I walked unobtrusively, slightly behind them on the path. I had been admiring her silver earrings which tossed as she walked against her brown ears. I had been admiring her graceful neck and the two dark plaits of hair down her back.

'Master Alan, I could gi' you a bit for sweety if you want tho'!'

My heart leaped with pleasure. Then I wondered whether she did it just to score off Kaiser. Her brother was furious.

'You mad or what, girl! You don't know he have so much money already his mout' chokin' wid it. He could buy up all Ramlal parlour today an' have to spare. You chupid, chile, you too dam' chupid. He only going laugh at you, eh.'

Jaillin was silent. She hung her head, didn't look at me again. I was embarrassed. What Kaiser said was true in that I had five dollars pocket money every week and hardly knew what to do with it all; I had even saved. But that I would have thought of laughing at Jaillin was fifty miles from the truth. Yet I could see that both of them believed it. I was hurt, felt not for the last time that there was a barrier between us not to be broken by the equivalence of childhood and its games.

We went on, careful to avoid the subject of the shilling piece. I knew Kaiser would get at least sixpence of it. I walked beside

23

Jaillin and watched her from time to time out of the corner of my eye. She never looked at me. No one spoke for a long time. When Kaiser broke the disagreeable silence he spoke abruptly:

'We is goin' to be dam' late. An' I have all the fowl yard to clean out today.'

We walked more rapidly. We were not now free to make a pleasant thing of walking; it was all hurry. I saw a Ninety-Nine, a red-winged butterfly with 99 clearly marked in black on the undersides of those wings, but we didn't stop. The cicadas were beginning to shrill in the heat of the day, metallic, insistent, rain-provoking. I showed Jaillin the Kingfisher Kaiser had caught on the lily leaf. And I told her about the marbleus I had missed on the black rock by Aaron Falls. She said:

'What you don't get you not meant to have.'

'Anyway, it's a good thing really. They were joined together and you know it's bad luck to catch them when they're like that.'

I was shy to tell her that I would have wet my bed every day the next week: the disgrace of it was too horrible ever to tell a girl, far less Jaillin. She knew about it though. Inherited superstitions were as firmly in her mind as in Kaiser's, and she knew them all. Instead of walking around a tamarind tree, though, Kaiser told me, if they wanted to grow up with nice breasts and pretty faces girls must say a prayer under a donkey-eye tree when the moon was new: he said Jaillin often did this.

There are times I so vividly remembered afterwards: the day of the birthday party, the cockfight, the time Jaillin pierced her hands, the candle-lit Madonna and the cold rough sea we swam in, the Carnival night at Old Boss's. But I think it was during this walk up the river that I had my first deep impressions of the story. Now they fit into a pattern I can recognize: then I just sensed the peculiar, confusing uneasiness.

As we walked on through the bush Kaiser whacked at the encroaching twigs and scrub of thorn with his tamarind stick. Soon we came to a group of thatched mud huts, whitewashed and square and small, where some peasants lived. Frizzly fowls pecked on the hard earth; some took dust baths in the shade of a big plantain tree. I could smell guavas boiling as we passed one of the huts. Children, half and sometimes wholly naked, played apathetically (the sun was so hot) in the hard-beaten dirt yard. Their playthings were pieces of stick and shiny tin cans; a lucky few had marbles. Their stomachs were too fat for their thin bodies: they had eaten too much rice and too little of anything else. One older girl was having a hard time coping with three small, dirty, obstreperous children. She chased one and caught it and beat its ears; it bawled and struggled. She shouted to the others meanwhile to sit quiet or she would fix them up too. A couple of times she tossed her long hair out of her eyes in an exasperated gesture. She was probably as young as Jaillin but she looked worn and quite old.

In front of the doorway of one hut a fat woman scrubbed clothes in a large grey tub. She bounced like a podgy sponge as she worked her enormous hands vigorously in the water. A baby child hung on to a fold of the sari which enveloped her; the babe tottered about to keep its balance as its fat mother went on scrubbing so powerfully.

A scene like this both repelled and fascinated me: it was a whole world different from the things I lived with in my way of life. I had a deep desire to go into one of those huts and see what it was like there. Kaiser had promised to take me into his one day. I couldn't quite believe that people really lived like that.

Two boys sat against one of the white walls sucking at mango seeds. As we passed one of them noticed us and shouted out. He had a clean, white grin on his face all the time. There was a big sore on his ankle and he scratched at it.

'Ey, ey, look at that! Kaiser an' Jaillin walking bold so wid a white man. They think they is big shot or what?'

Kaiser ignored the sneers.

The other boy shouted, at me, this time:

'Who you think you is walking pas' here so cool so!'

'Yes, white man, I bet we stone you' arse out o' here, eh!'

I felt the nerves in my skin tauten. I blushed. Kaiser bristled.

'Tek care how you speak, boy! You playing badjohn or what? Tek care how you speak, or I bet I come and beat you' little tail like I beat a donkey!'

I pretended not to notice, to hold myself superior to the insults.

25

But I was puzzled and hurt that boys I didn't know from Adam seemed to dislike me so intensely, for no reason that I could see. That Kaiser and Jaillin's friends should jeer at me in front of their faces without any provocation cut me to the quick. Kaiser's quick defence only humiliated me further. I almost cried with shame to think that Jaillin was there to see and hear it all. I felt they were embarrassed for me; that was the worse thing, a matter of pride.

The altercation went on. I suddenly realized that the boy hated Kaiser. It made me feel better.

'How you playing so big and bad, Kaiser, boy! Move 'way, le' me gi' he a little stoning, eh?'

'Boy, I see I going beat you bad here today.'

'Why you bothering wid he at all for? You know what white people is already. What he do mek you sweeten up to he, eh? You fo'get what white people do to Indian or what? You mus' be dam' coward!'

'All right, boy, I really going beat you' arse!'

Kaiser walked across towards him. The boy got up. In a flash he pulled a long, jagged piece of broken bottle from his pocket. His smile was like a curved bone across his face. His friend sneaked away behind one of the huts. Jaillin gasped: 'Oh Gawd, he got bottle!' I tightened my teeth. I wasn't embarrassed any more: we came together as friends on the same level of danger.

Kaiser stopped in his tracks. He looked at us quickly and I caught a glint of fright. Then he ran over to one of the mango trees in the clearing. The boy started to follow him. I noticed with an unreal fascination that the little flies never left the sore on his ankle; he kept shaking it to get them off. As he came up with the evil-looking dagger of glass in his hand Kaiser stooped and picked up a heavy stone under the mango tree. He lifted it threateningly. Both advanced tentatively, then stopped a couple of yards apart. They looked at each other intently, armed hands raised, talked softly to each other:

'I going cut out you' heart fo' you, Kaiser, boy.'

'You only talking! When you get this in you' head, eh . . .'

'I going rip you, Kaiser, boy.'

'When you get this in you' head . . .'

26

'I going tek this bottle to you' balls like a knife, Kaiser.'

'Talk, boy, talk a little more.'

'I going cut yours out like a bull's.'

'Talk. When I fill up you mout' wid stone . . .'

'Oh, yes.'

'Yes, boy.'

Then Kaiser began to go forward ever so slowly. The boy held his ground then he inched backwards. All of a sudden he turned and ran headlong.

I found I had been holding my breath the whole time. Jaillin remembered and took her hand quickly off my wrist where it had gripped to whiteness.

Kaiser threw down the stone, dusted his hands. He grinned at us and came over.

'I know he only full o' big mout'. He playing he one big man. Lord, boy-o, I would a kill he!'

'He's just a hooligan, that's all!' I said furiously.

'Man, don't bother you' head wid those chupid little boys. They only like to show off they big mout'.'

'That boy is Ramlal nephew. Everyone know he is a wotless chile. All he ever going grow up be is a Port o' Spain saga boy. Don't min' he.'

'Anyway, why did he say all that? Why did he shout like that?'

'He don' like nobody. He have a nasty min'.' He turned to Jaillin. 'You know what he do one time? I hear Mam and Pap talking. He lay wait when it dark one night for Aunty Phyllis niece, you know that little chile, and he try an' fuck she. Ha! Ha! Girl, you know what Mam say? She say you well better look out.'

'You t'ink I chupid? I know what he like, oui. Ramlal never bother what he do. From the time he Mam and Pap dead he running wild like dat.'

'They should keep him in an orphanage then,' I said.

'Boy, he bus' out of those place like water.'

We hurried along in silence. My nerves were still jumping. Later I remembered about the parents who had died. I meant to ask, but forgot so I never found out.

'But, Kaiser, tell me, were you frightened when he got out the bottle? Perhaps he meant to kill you.'

'Me 'fraid he! What! You didn' see how I fix he up or what? No chupid little boy goin' play he arse wid me, eh!'

Kaiser began running.

'Le' we hurry. Madam going vex.'

Jaillin and I followed more slowly.

'Master Alan, one thing, eh. I want thank you fo' the pretty flower.'

'Oh, that's O.K., Jaillin. I had almost forgotten about it even. Well, no, not really . . . anyway, it looks pretty in your hair.'

'Fo' true? Kaiser say I have hair like black weed. He rude, eh?' She laughed. 'Master Alan, it true it you' birt'day soon?'

'Well, yes. Why?'

'Something I was thinking. Don't min' tho'.'

We ran faster to catch up with Kaiser. We reached him at the Main Road.

'Oh, ho! So that is the case. Whe' you get? I thought you loss you'self in the bush!'

'You think you're funny!'

On the Eastern Main Road the midday traffic was thick. Pirate taxis zoomed to and from town, their horns blowing. The smell of gasolene, burnt rubber, and asphalt dust suddenly hit you. It was such a contrast. Hardly a mile away we had been walking by the cool dark river, wading in green ponds or from stone to stone through white water. The air had been full of the smell of leaves, earth and hot rock soaked in rain. Full of the scent of hog plums. It had been quiet except for the cicadas and the soothing rush of river fall. Now the Main Road bedlam! It was like the end of innocence.

Kaiser and Jaillin looked a little afraid at being late for their work. I was just hungry.

2

🎕 The Drawing-room

I

It was past the normal family lunch hour when we got back. I opened the gates which swung from green concrete posts and we walked up the gravelled driveway. My mother came to the playroom window which was downstairs and called severely to Kaiser and Jaillin. They were late for their work. Kaiser was to go and sweep the fowl yard at once and afterwards prune the lemon tree which was growing over into the Aikmans. Jaillin was to collect eggs, then go and buy fresh vegetables in the market in Tunapuna. I was to come into lunch right away before it got cold. Kaiser and Jaillin went to the back of the house where the kitchen and storerooms were. I continued up the drive round to the front and came in to the drawing-room by the polished teak door.

I loved the house. My father had built it four years before and it was the loveliest in the neighbourhood. It lay in a great garden and orchard. It faced towards the cool north, towards Japon Hill rising a mile away and Mount St Benedict towering above that hill. At night from the stone veranda upstairs you could see the lights of the Roman Catholic abbey shining on Mount St Benedict, and just above that the north star, unmoving all year. In my mind the house had become a defence against the world. In it I was safe against the insecurity and embarrassment which continually plague a young boy. I wasn't really comfortable anywhere else. In my heart I jealously guarded this fortress against aliens. Sometimes I imagined a thousand men besieging it, and I, the hero, repulsed them every time: it was a game I only played by myself.

In all the house I thought the drawing-room most beautiful.

29

...fortress, a place where I was proud of myself, ... others, Six teak pillars stood up in it to the floor of ... storey where the bedrooms were built. These pillars were carved with many flowers, hibiscus, poinsettia, roses, and birds like the long-legged heron and the humming-bird. A workman on one of my father's estates called Mister 'Carpenter' Townsend had done the carving of the pillars. He had spent months perfecting them, like a true artist. I remember passing him day after day in the morning as he cut with small chisels at the smooth, hard wood. Once I stopped and saw him carve and paint the five petals of a hibiscus into a pillar. I, who was small enough to believe in a miracle, went to the pillar and put my hand on the new flower to see if it was real. He laughed and I ran out in amazement. The pillars now were the connoisseur's admiration. Guests, dropped in for a cocktail or a hand of bridge, marvelled at the extreme artistry of the central pillar which held in its dark wood, captured for a hundred seasons, a bluebird on a branch of immortelle blossoming red as sunset. The colours lit the room like rainbows.

And, like a bed of wild grass, the floor was of stone varnished with green wax. All the floor, that is, except an oblong of parquet tiles let into the stone at one end of the room. This block of parquetry had been designed in a pattern of two fierce cocks in a fight. They were meeting in air, their dangerous spurred feet flashing at each other. The plumes of their tails and their ruffled neck feathers showed deep purple and green and velvety red. They were magical; the tropical colours and fury of them burst up like a volcanic lily at you from the floor. One or two of their feathers had escaped from them in the flurry and hung above like little red new moons. I thought this cockfight marvellous and would step on it tiptoe, softly, full of wonder. Year in, year out, while I was young their fight never lacked fierceness or perpetual beauty.

Over the parquetry a mahogany cabinet with clear glass doors stood against the cedar wall which divided the house downstairs. The cabinet was a showcase of particular family treasures. In it on three shelves was a curious and beautiful collection of heirlooms, old prizes, and rarities. On the top shelf stood the silver cups my father had won for racing and high-jumping when he was young, three Coronation mugs, and a variety of engraved christening spoons. A tea set of most delicate china, willow-patterned and glazed, ages old, was the remarkable centrepiece of the second shelf. This set had come down through four generations of the family. Around it were set cut-glass bowls and decanters and old silver small trays. The sword of a great-uncle who had fought in the Boer War lay at the back of the shelf; faded tasselling hung from the handle. The third shelf was most interesting to visitors and amused us children best. It contained curios collected over a number of years. There was a rosary of jumby beads set on a thread of silver, upon which hung a golden crucifix. Four minute yellow metal drops lay on the Christ's side where the Roman spear had cut him. My mother told me she had found this in a Dominican market. There were three mango seeds shaved and carved and coloured into three dwarf's heads with red cheeks and blue eyes and pointed yellow beards. These I loved best and laughed at their quaint expressions, one dolorous, one very angry, one mightily pleased with life. Kaiser and Jaillin often stuck their noses against the glass with me to look at the three dwarfs. I told them proudly that I would get them when I grew up.

'Only three dam' ol' mango seed,' Kaiser muttered, but I knew he envied me them. They were quite new and not valuable at all. They had been made by a Chinese girl in the St Ann's Mental Hospital, and my mother picked them up for sixpence at a sale there: the girl cried and shouted when they went and they took her away for bad behaviour.

On this shelf also were two bracelets of sapodilla seeds, black as night, a stuffed humming-bird, a number of donkey-eyes with words from the Bible cut on them, a set of chessmen carved from deer's hoofs. Mother-of-pearled shells were fixed in the shape of a palm tree on the shelf and under it a mother-of-pearl fisherman slept, his hat one grey slipper shell bent over his eyes. I wondered if in a hundred years the lazy pearl fisherman would still be sleeping on the shelf, or if one day he would sit up, push his hat back, yawn, get up and go to cast for goldfish in the mosaic lily pond at the end of the garden.

In all three white stone walls of the drawing-room were windows of green lattice-work which let in the cool wind from the mountains. 'The north star breeze makes life bearable,' my father said, and my mother said that the monks in St Benedict's monastery on the mountain prayed for cool winds at special Masses, and they came. At intervals between the windows hung four Chinese prints. One was of a lake scene, green weeping willow trees on an island, a red pagoda, and three yellow sampans with white sails. Another showed a heron standing in brown rushes under a full moon; the heron held a gleaming fish in its beak. A third print pictured a blue bridge spanning a river over which a man with a hoe on his shoulder and lively dog at his feet was leading three yoked oxen. The fourth print showed a bird on a cherry branch; the bird's head was cocked to look at a green caterpillar, humped three times, wriggling along the branch. Every time I saw the print in my mind's eye I played out the tragedy which never took place there: I saw the quick flutter of wings, the green caterpillar gone, the cherry branch shaking gently; then I looked back and the bird's head was still cocked, the caterpillar still wriggled, humped three times, along the branch. It gave me in some way the idea of God's will eternally defied by man's art. For me the Chinese prints and 'Carpenter' Townsend's carving in our drawing-room were the best man could do against God's infinite power, a sense of which was just then forming in me.

In one quarter of the room, alongside one of the green latticed windows and separated from the rest of the room by a long bookcase filled with leather-bound and gilt-titled volumes—*Tristram Shandy*, Macaulay's *History of England, Little Dorrit, Oliver Twist, David Copperfield* and *The Pickwick Papers*, Tennyson's *Poems*, Burke's *Reflections, The Lyrical Ballads, Essays of Elia*, and a hundred more—stood a large mahogany dining-table deeplustred through many polishings. In the centre of it on a white cloth was a bowl filled with the orange flowers of Barbados Pride, clipped from the garden a few hours before. Here my lunch was laid, the steaming savoury food set on a white china plate and covered with a dish to keep it warm. I quickly washed my hands and face in the blue and white tiled bathroom upstairs and came down again. My mother sat down with me at the table to make company. She was still a young and very beautiful woman and even after a full morning's housework she looked neat and cool. I loved the way she looked so pretty and clean and happy. Her dark hair, tinged with bronze, was held at the ear with a silver pin.

'What did you do this morning, son? Did you enjoy yourself?'

'Went up the river with Kaiser—you know, by Japon Hill—catching butterflies. Kaiser got a Kingfisher.. Almost got two Marbleus, Mum. And we got soaked in the rain!'

'Where were Tony and Lee and Tanner? Didn't they go with you?'

'Oh, they were playing . . .'

'Alan, why don't you play with them? Kaiser has work to do and anyway I don't think you should play with him so much.'

'Oh, but Mum . . .'

But I stopped. I knew my mother had fixed ideas about the matter. She thought Kaiser inferior to my other friends, the two Evans boys and Tony Maddox, and she always said the same thing, that I must play with them, my proper friends, and not Kaiser who was a boy from the village and our yard-boy. I knew it was no good arguing so in secret I resisted her disapproval.

In the silence I tucked into lunch hungrily. On the plate was a choice meal of chicken and rice done in pilau, fried plantain, pigeon peas, sweet potato mashed with butter, hot and crisp browned tanya cakes. It was the most tempting food in the world, especially the way Alice cooked it, and I ate ravenously.

'Stop gobbling, and elbows off the table while you're eating,' my mother said. 'Dear, I'm sure you will never learn good manners.'

I grinned at the formula and corrected myself. She smiled at me, rang the bamboo-handled table bell for Alice to bring in more tanya cakes, particular favourites with me. Alice came in wearing a white cloth round her head, 'to keep 'way cold,' she said, and she always wore it, or a rose-coloured variety.

Alice had been with the family as long as I could remember. She was the best cook in all our neighbourhood; for special occasions friends of the family borrowed her to cook for them. She was so faithful, and whenever my mother or I was sick she cried her eyes out. Now she was very old, seventy-five I judged, and many days she would come weeping to my mother and say, 'Oh, Gawd, Madam, I'se going dead soon soon. I'se feel it in my entire body this morning. Pain, pain, Madam, pain too bad.' And my mother would have then to comfort and reassure her. 'Nonsense, Alice, God means you to live for years and years. We all say our chaplet for you.' And she would give her three aspirins which Alice very much believed in.

She was a good Christian and went to Church every Sunday morning, walking two miles there and back, but all the same nothing could shake her belief in demonology. She was convinced that the world was filled with evil spirits. On her right forefinger she wore a wooden ring with two small skulls and two small crosses carved on it, and on this she depended to safeguard her against the innumerable goblins and jumbies, soucayants and devils who all plagued so relentlessly the good world and poor Alice in particular. She was sure that black cats were sin incarnate; she set the dogs on any she saw. Once she had not turned up for work; we discovered, the following day when she arrived looking ill and sleepless, that the reason she could not come was that she had been beleaguered in her room all day and half the night by a host of jumbies with fire-eyes and forked tails like the devil; they had hammered on her door, spat curses at her. The whole time, she told us, she lay in bed, kissing her ring and saying her chaplet over and over: 'That save me, Madam, that save me from hell an' bottomless damnation!'

Alice must have had Carib blood in her. She was tall, lean, and her face was marked like a North American chieftain I had seen in a picture-book, thin, defiant lips, high hawk nose, bones ridging the cheeks, eagle eyes. Jokingly my father called her the last of the Carib princesses. Though she seemed to accept her serving place with no black look or murmur of protest, she lorded it over other servants in the household, tempestuously ordering them to their duties in the absence of my mother's milder control.

Above all she was proud of her art in cooking. She almost never faltered; when she did we all knew then she was dogged by some peculiarly malignant spirit, one only to be exorcised by recourse

34

to the Seven Stations of the Cross in Church and her wonderful ring. In her cooking she thought up perpetual new delights. Today she had clipped a red bird pepper or two into the pilao and the flavouring it gave to the chicken and rice was a joyful new pleasure. I could never resist the tanya cakes she made.

'Eh, eh, you ent eating at all today, Master Alan.' she said. as I refused a third helping of those brown crusted purple succulent cakes done to a turn on her smoky coalpot.

When I finished I fetched a bowl of fruit and chose a banana, a cocoa orange, sweet as sugar, and a pomerack, fruit like a red bell, with white juicy flesh inside. My mother took a golden apple from the bowl and peeled it for herself. She loved golden apples and would eat them if they were green even. I always brought two ripe ones back for her from the market in Tunapuna when I was out that way.

' "Shake golden apples out o' your hair", that's a song Kaiser sings, Mum. It's odd, isn't it?'

'It sounds odd. What does it mean, son?'

'Oh, it doesn't mean anything I don't think.'

'Well, what does it have to do with? Does it tell a story?'

'I can't hear very well the way he sings it. It's kind of religious though.'

'Some of those Indian songs are so beautiful. You know the one about the red cherry that Jaillin sings. How does this one go?'

'Well, a god gives things by shaking his hair. And there's a selfish babu who wants more and more. First the god shakes out of his hair rice for him, then pigeon peas, then red plums. The god begins to get angry but the babu goes on asking more and more. He asks for golden apples, then oranges, grapefruit, pomegranates, and there's a lot more. And at last he asks for a huge green watermelon and the god shakes one out straight on his head and kills him dead.'

'I wonder where Kaiser learnt it.'

'Probably Old Boss, you know. He's always teaching them things. He holds their life in his head.'

'Who said that, son?'

'That's what Old Boss says when he's telling Kaiser and Jaillin anything. He was teaching Jaillin how to make a mat for the temple and he said that.'

'You're often up in the village, Alan?'

'Not very often really, Mum.'

'You'll become a little Indian boy, you know.' She was as playful as a girl. She sliced up a golden apple, dipped a piece pierced on a fork in salt, and handed it to me on the silver tines.

'Thanks, Mum. It's good.'

'Oh, about your party, son. What sort of ice-cream do you want? Vanilla, coconut, strawberry or coffee flavour?'

I chose coconut and coffee. In two days' time I was having a birthday party and preparations were afoot. Twenty of my friends had been invited. A thought suddenly occurred to me.

'Can Kaiser and Jaillin come to the party, Mum? Please!'

'Now, Alan! Of course not! I do not want you to associate with them more than is necessary. That is all. I don't want to hear any more about them.'

'I don't care,' I blustered. 'I like Jaillin. I like Jaillin. And Kaiser's making me a scooter with blue tin wheels next week. Tanner won't even lend me his skates.'

'Alan, those children are not coming to your party. I forbid you to ask them. You won't have any party at all if you go on like this.'

This had its effect. I enjoyed parties and all the presents. So I went into a sulk. I had known from the beginning that my mother wouldn't allow Kaiser and Jaillin to come to the party. Had she said yes, I would have been astonished, a little frightened. I sensed that their presence would bring much embarrassment; I was always shy of them meeting my other friends. But I had asked if they might come, and defended them, to ease an emotion which pressed me to accept them with the whole heart, with no compelled reservations. I did not know my mind very well. So I pretended to be—in a confused, impure way, I suppose, really was—hurt by my mother's uncompromising refusal. Kaiser and Jaillin, I decided, were dear friends, but friends whom I must keep in a separate compartment of my life because of a necessity which I did not fully comprehend, which I did not like at all, but which I much respected since it seemed

36

so securely a part of the attitude towards life of almost everyone that mattered, and in particular my mother and father.

It was a difficult position in which to choose the best thing to do. I sulked now because it was the only compromise between downright revolt on the one hand and rejecting Kaiser and Jaillin on the other. So I finished the orange I was eating quickly, stalked away from the table in a huff. My mother paid no attention to this show of temperament. I was furious with her, ashamed of myself. I felt uncomfortable and helpless.

It was siesta time now. I went upstairs to a cool-sheeted bed, for I was dog-tired after the river walk. Cicadas were singing; it was warm and still; it was sure to rain soon; over the northern mountains a purple castle of storm-cloud was building in the sky. It was easy to sleep. I drowsed off, thinking, strangely, that since I had thrown away my butterfly poison bottle in the river I would have to ask my father to get me some more white camphor in town so that Kaiser could make me a new one.

2

The morning of my birthday party I woke up early. The sun was shining brilliantly on the bed through a gap between the lapis-lazuli coloured curtains which hung down over the wide window from small brass rings. When a wind blew up these curtain rings tinkled merrily together, and the curtains flapped like blue sails. There was no wind now though; there hardly ever was early in the morning like this. The sun, coming in, sifted through the high canopy of mosquito netting on the linen sheets in a fine golden mesh. It was as if the sheets had been worked in petit-point with flaxen thread. Outside the blackbirds fluted to each other. It was going to be a gracious day and my heart was full of it. I could almost see the blue sky spreading for ever over Japon Hill, and the barefoot boys who flew bright kites there on such days as this.

My bedroom window looked on to a cluster of grapefruit trees growing on that side of the house. At this time they were in full dark green leaf and their fruit, mottled green and yellow globes, hung like decorations in their caves of greenery. Those fruit that were bee-sucked glowed with the bloom of impure ripeness more yellow than the rest.

Under one of the trees stood a red see-saw with white bucket seats. It had been a Christmas present for me years ago; I never used it now. It looked much marked by weather and bird-droppings for it had not been cleaned or painted for a long time. One day a few days before this I'd looked out of my window at just about this early time in the morning and had seen Kaiser and Jaillin using the old see-saw. I'd been surprised by the way they played on it; it was as if they were frightened at what they were doing. I'd not waved or called to them because they seemed so different from the excitable, un-secretive, laughing Kaiser and Jaillin I knew when I played with them up the river or in the canefields near the village. They were tense with trying to be unheard as they went up and down on the white seats, and every moment looked towards the house to make sure they were not discovered. I could not understand their anxiety as I peeped at them from behind the curtains: they'd never told me they would like to use it, and I had never suggested that they play on it because the see-saw bored me. I could see now they had always wanted to use it, but had never dared. Then I heard Alice call out fiercely to them from the kitchen in the back of the house.

'Kaiser! Jaillin! What you evil children doing there at all? Using white people thing so bol' so! Off it now; it not yours. You lucky if I don't report you both to Madam an' she pelt you out o' the house. Go on, off it!' She gestured.

And Kaiser and Jaillin jumped like cats from the see-saw at once and ran quickly to the back of the house. I felt like shouting out to them, 'You can use it! You can use it!' But after all I did not, and afterwards never in my life mentioned that I'd seen them there on the see-saw.

I dressed quickly in khaki shorts stained with olive-coloured paint, a favourite ring-necked jersey striped like a tiger, and cool yellow sandals. I tied a brightly coloured scarf as a belt round my waist, and put a red cap with a feather on, for these days I was often Robin Hood, brave vagabond of the green woods.

Downstairs last preparations for the party were already afoot. Jaillin, under severe direction from Alice, was beating up a mass of cake batter in a huge white bowl. At intervals she squeezed a few drops of lemon into the mixture. She was not wearing her silver earrings this morning. On her feet she wore brown clogs, each made from a slab of wood roughly cut to the shape of a foot and two pieces of canvas tacked in a cross over the toes. When she walked on the brown tiles of the pantry in them they made so much noise that Alice frowned at last and made her take them off. To me she looked much prettier with no shoes.

'Good morning, Jaillin. Where's Kaiser?'

'Mornin', Master Alan. Kaiser gone to get ice from Trotter Dairy, ice and milk. Alice tell he to get four poun' ice an' two quart of milk dey so much white ice cream to mek up so. You really eating this afternoon.'

I dipped a finger in the bowl of sweet yellow batter and licked it. Alice scolded me briefly; then she went into the kitchen to begin to prepare lunch.

'Jaillin, you know what. Add little bit an' beat up fo' nother half hour. Don' forget the lemon, chile. An' Master Alan, if you only push you' dirty finger in the cake again I going vex fo' true. You hear me?'

Alice went out and Jaillin and I were left alone together in the pantry. Whenever we were alone there was a strange embarrassment between us. It was always like that. She avoided my eyes. On such occasions she had a quaint trick of tossing her black hair, so long and shining like a blackbird's wing, half over her face, and then brushing it with the back of her hand into place again. She did this now, twice, between vigorously stirring the cake mixture in the bowl. I looked on, shuffling my feet on the brown tiles. I tried to conjure up a daredevil in me but nothing of that was there.

I wanted to tell Jaillin how I would have liked Kaiser and herself to be coming to the party that afternoon. But I could not think of a way of doing this. The subject embarrassed me like the thought of bad disease. I could not think of a word to say.

I put my hand out towards the bowl, thinking to take another

39

dip with the finger at the tempting yellow mixture. But Jaillin slapped my hand sharply down.

'Don' be so boderation at all!'

I was so astonished that I didn't say anything; I took away my hand quickly and stood looking at her, not so much offended as bewildered at what had happened. Her brown cheeks were flushed with emotion; she tossed her hair in front of her face; then without looking at me, very suddenly she said:

'Master Alan, I wanted bad to gi' you Mother Gawmy's shilling fo' you' birt'day, you know the one I get from she fo' helping she mek aloo pie. Dat shilling.'

She paused. I tried to make myself understand what she was saying.

'What, Jaillin . . .' I started to speak feebly.

'But Kaiser say you going scorn it. He say dat. He say a big white man don' want no small-time present at he big party. All the same, I going gi' you, boy.'

Then she thrust her hand, wet with lemon juice, into the pocket of the blue coarse cotton skirt she was wearing and brought out a shilling in her fingers. This she gave to me with a shy smile and turned quickly back to the stirring. I took the silver coin and examined it as if I had never seen one before. I turned it over and over in the palm of my hand. I read the latin words and I was oddly fascinated by the young king's head, and by the intricate crest on the other side of this uniquely acquired treasure. I think Jaillin must have polished it before giving it to me because it shone like a coin newly minted. I looked at Jaillin hard but I could not catch her eyes. I noticed two gold prickles stuck in the hem of her skirt.

'Jaillin, I . . . I love it very much, a lot. I really do. I really like it better than anything else. I really promise you, Jaillin. I'll keep it in my Scottish box for ever.'

This was the utmost I could promise. The box was where I kept all my particular treasures. It was a small, briar-wood box which when you opened it, played 'Auld Lang Syne' in pure tinkling notes. I think it must once have been a miniature cigarette box. It had belonged to my grandmother and one day I had begged her to give it to me as I was so astonished by its sweet musical tune.

She had laughed at the request but all the same had wrapped it up in tissue paper and given it to me with a kiss. It was a pretty curio. On the lid in the middle was a painting of two colourful Highlanders dancing a jig. But at the two long sides of it, in complete contrast, had been hand-painted on more recently rose and milk coral snakes with forked green tongues, their sliding tails just touching two spike-leaved pineapples. These enhanced the magic value of the box. I felt those coral guardians would keep the box and what it held safe always. Kaiser, whom I showed the box to, was certain of their power. Inside the box, on the cover and within the bottom, was a myriad of gilt and scarlet leaves as if they had been captured there in an English autumn. All these fiery leaves whirled on a blue ground. Whenever I looked inside the box I thought of countries over the hills and far away, red diamonds, beards smelling of tobacco and stretches of heather moor.

I kept in it a few souvenirs, mightily precious to me. They helped me to live proudly. They were symbols of a personal and independent love of life which I shared with no one. In the box was a long needle of green glass, polished smooth and cloudy by waves, which I found on the beach amidst pink shells and sea-weed, at Mayaro when we had been on holiday there two Aprils ago. In the box also lay a battered ring of intertwining threads of brass which I had come upon in a dustbin while searching there for stamps on discarded envelopes to add to my collection. I don't know why it took on particular significance for me, but now on special days I wore it for luck, and I intended to pass it on in due time to my eldest son as an important keepsake. In the box too was a mother-of-pearl button, the size of a sixpence, with a tiny blue buddha painted on it, which Kaiser had given me. He told me it had fallen from the robe of the Indian priest who had given blessings at his eldest sister's wedding; he had found it afterwards in the dust outside the bamboo tent. He was slightly afraid to keep it for himself so he gave it to me, telling how holy it was. A fourth treasure was one of my own white teeth which I had pulled out bravely with nervous thumb and forefinger when finding it loose; spat a little blood then, and felt a hero. The same night I put it under the pillow since it was said that a mouse would come, take it to its nest and leave instead a penny or a marble or a sweet. Nothing was left so I had kept the tooth for its own value.

Now, I would put Jaillin's shilling with the other treasures in the box. I had shown both herself and Kaiser the box and the precious articles before, and I think now she was pleased at what I said I would do.

She went on stirring the mixture, her face turned away from me. I plucked up a little courage and said very quickly:

'Jaillin, I wish you were coming to the party, you know. You and Kaiser.'

'Don't min' dat.'

'None of the girls're pretty like you.'

'What chupidness you saying, boy! What you know 'bout pretty so? What you know?'

'It's true, Jaillin.'

'You funny, boy, you too funny. You mek me laugh like a cat. I don' have no pretty clo's like all you' white girl.'

'I like your earrings anyway.' I couldn't think of anything else to say to her.

'My mothers' own an' if I only lose dem I going get hell.' She looked at me then turned away again. It was the first time I had seen her dark eyes directly that morning. Now there was silence except for her wooden spoon mixing the cake in the bowl. I fidgeted around the pantry, opening the bread-bin, taking a ripe orange from a basket under a shelf and dropping it back again, arranging seven eggs in different patterns on a white-pine rack on the sideboard.

At last, to my relief, Alice returned from the kitchen.

'You finish making up dat cake yet, chile?'

'Yes, Alice, it done.'

I slipped out of the room as they talked to each other. I went into the drawing-room. The sun, coming through the lattice windows, made golden oblongs on the green stone floor. It shone on one of the carved pillars and lit up a red anthurium lily, one of the marvels of Mister 'Carpenter' Townsend's deft hands.

I walked over to the bookcase on which a black-boxed gramophone was set beside a porcelain vase containing the big ruby balls of Exora bloom. I put on a record of 'De Camptown Races'. I lay at full length on an old mahogany sofa, my head comfortable on a blue satin cushion on which was embroidered a flowering casuarina tree in whose branches sat three orange monkeys clutching long sticks of sugar cane—it was one of a set scattered on all the chairs around the room—and listened to the rapid thrumming of the guitar music in the tune.

When the record was finished I did not go to change it. I was thinking of the party that afternoon. I was not looking forward to that. The needle on the record went round and round rasping delicately in a groove and I deliberately ignored it.

3

I dressed myself smartly in a short-sleeved white silk shirt, boy's black bow tie, perfectly creased grey flannel shorts, dark blue socks with a line of red diamonds decorating them near their elastic tops, and brown shoes with a dagger pattern of adze holes in the leather at the instep. I even rubbed a touch of brilliantine in my hair. I rather liked dressing up when the occasion suited, though Kaiser invariably mocked my nice clothes, 'girl clothes', and I had grown wary of bringing down on my head his effectual sneers.

Downstairs the drawing-room had been made ready for the party. All the chairs had been pulled back to the wall. The long dining-table was entirely covered by two white table cloths with tasselled fringes. And that table, decorated by two bowls of rosy bougainvillaea, held a fabulous quality and amount of food. In the centre stood a magnificent double-tiered birthday cake. Its smooth blue cream crust was decorated with thin pink ribbons of icing forming extravagant letters which spelled for me 'Many Happy Returns of the Day'. Five crystallized cherries were dotted between the words, and twelve slim small white candles stood in a ring around them. About the great cake was a myriad of sandwiches, lettuce, cheese, crab, egg and ham, on a score of green china plates. Small baskets of dried fruit, oranges and shaddock and raisins, and a thousand multicoloured sweets, paradise plums, strong peppermints, toffees in their gold and silver wrappings, lemon acid drops, were placed everywhere; they were to be staple diet for the afternoon. Small tea-cakes, scattered on top with the minute silver-glazed pearls of the sweets called 'hundreds-and-thousands' abounded. Trays of roasted almonds and cashew nuts were everywhere. Jugs of iced lemonade and orange juice stood waiting on the sideboard. My mother, and Alice, had wonderfully provided.

I brightened at the prospect before me; my early morning depression had now gone. I took a small handful of cashew nuts from a tray and ate them.

My mother was in the drawing-room too, making last minute arrangements, fixing a vase of flowers on the bookcase, stacking beside the gramophone the records needed to play for Musical Chairs, putting away in a safe place the wrapped presents which would be used as prizes for games played later on, counting balloons out, one of which would be given to each child—I had begged to keep the one that blew up like a panda. I knew my mother was anxious that the party should be a success; it was the biggest I had ever been given. It was a social event; my parents were having a number of adult friends and relations in for cocktails afterwards as a sort of epilogue.

My mother was wearing a cool blue dress, fastened at her slim waist with a belt in which at the side a scarlet lily was tucked. At each ear was an emerald earring in the shape of a lizard. I had never seen her wear them before. I told her that I thought she looked pretty.

'Well, son, thank you very much. That's very sweet of you. Are you looking forward to your party?'

'Yes, I really am now, Mum.'

Just then the first guest arrived, golden-haired Judy clutching her present for me, so obviously a book, tightly in her hand.

Soon all my friends had arrived, with their words of good wishes and their various gifts: one brought a bow and arrow and this was the best of all. All the girls were brought by one or other of their parents and these my mother greeted with a smile and had them all sit down and have a drink. Many of them

44

admired the beautifully carved pillars and the cockfight depicted in the parquet tiles, and I could see that my mother was proud of that.

After a while my father too came down. He was a tall and impressive man whose slight stoop faintly damaged what would have been the very strong square of his shoulders. His hair was greying, especially at the temples, and this gave his firmly featured face great distinction. He had amazing grey eyes, kind as heaven. He very, very rarely laughed but often smiled. He had a reputation for kindness and tolerance and for my part I never knew him lose his temper with anyone, though he was stern enough in his convictions, and I deeply respected his firm discipline and will. He never lost his temper, that was the thing. My mother sometimes did, upbraiding Alice or Kaiser or Jaillin or the washerwoman who came on Mondays for perhaps only an insignificant mistake, and sometimes scolding me bitterly when I was stubborn or aggravating. But my father was censorious in another way. He commanded obedience and submission and respect by the cool impression of his voice and face. Once, teaching me to play tennis, he came nearest I ever saw him to real annoyance. I was not playing well and growing disgusted, stopped trying, hitting the white balls I didn't care where. My father walked off the court at once. I remember it so clearly: pink blossoms were drifting down from a high tree which overlooked the clubhouse on to the hot asphalt court. He called me with him. He simply said that if I was not going to try I was never to play the game again; then he told me to go home. I was crying when I got there.

My father was agricultural supervisor of estates belonging to one of the largest companies in the island. Every week he made a number of trips by car to visit these. In vacation time I often went with him. I enjoyed walking behind him and the estate overseer, who wore a cutlass in a cow-leather sheath at his belt, as they walked through groves of citrus and cocoa trees or through occasional patches of coffee, rubber, banana and tonka-bean which scented the air so fragrantly. Once or twice Kaiser came but he enjoyed the drive in the car more than the walk in the estate which seemed so exciting to me. He would put his head out of a window and close his eyes against the rushing wind; sometimes he remained like that for five minutes and more on end, his long blackbird hair dancing in the breeze.

'It feel like aeroplane, chile,' I heard him tell Jaillin once.

At the estates my father was popular with the overseers and the field labourers. Once, when there had been island-wide riots and estates were dangerous to visit, he was the only supervisor to go on his round of trips regularly and unarmed, as if nothing had happened. I remember the time well because my mother had looked frightened and sometimes cried, and I had felt frightened too, though I didn't know why. The men in most cases had not even been sullen. Only a few young firebrands had done any damage to his estates. For the most part they told him their grievances and went on working the fields well.

'It not you, sah, but money scarce scarce roun' dese parts and we want mo'.' Some young men yelled at him insultingly—it was always the young ones who made the trouble, that was the sign he feared. But, it had not lasted long. My father had on the estates men who deeply respected and sometimes loved him, though they were nearly all older men, used to the ways and manners of a less resentful generation.

At every estate my father was given presents of fruit and corn and rice and 'sweet' young chickens to take home. Once when I was with him the overseer had presented him with a bunch of white, waxy river-lilies and a basket of golden apples, 'to bring for Madam'. On another occasion a widow, called Ma'am Sancho, on one of the small estates, to whom my father had arranged a pension to be paid by the company when her husband had died suddenly leaving her penniless, had crocheted with thin bone needles a set of ten doilies, dove patterned, which she had given my father at Christmas time with a little note attached: 'For Mister Holmes, Whume Is Kindness Heself. Blessings from Mam Sancho.' The beautiful doilies were used now by my parents for dress dinners and other important occasions.

But my father, though so tolerant with the men who worked on his estates and though so well liked by them, took care to draw a strict line between benevolence and friendship. On one or two of the larger estates the coloured overseers were men of some education, but even so my father did not regard them in the same way as he regarded ordinary business acquaintances. They did not move in the same social circle. Cocktail receptions for business friends did not include them. Nor did such overseers resent such a situation, I gathered; it was a mutually agreeable relationship, on one side kindness unaffected by airs of superiority, on the other side respect unaffected by frustrated hopes of social climbing. This was the way of life my family and its neighbours had been brought up to, and none of them thought of any other arrangements as satisfactory to either side. Both my parents at times uneasily mentioned that nowadays unnecessary and uncomfortable changes were more and more in evidence; and once they told me that I might have to live in England when I grew up, though they never explained to me why. And my old great-Aunt Ida who lived in Port of Spain was always complaining of the so changed times. She remembered a time when it would have been unthinkable for a Government House Ball to include anyone else but High-Class White and Coloured people. And when she was young the pitch-walk round the Queen's Park Savanna was only used by white people she said; it was never law in her time but it had been a powerful custom.

Certainly, like my mother, my father would have been amazed at my suggestion to invite Kaiser and Jaillin to the party that afternoon. He too would have forbidden it. My life was set on a different tack to theirs by fiercer and more constant winds than I had knowledge of.

My father and mother arranged and supervised the games we played with pleasant charm. You could tell the party was going well by the shouts of excitement and the way the food disappeared so quickly. We played the customary games: 'Musical Chairs', sitting on two lines of rough green cotton-covered cushions which dwindled, one by one, as the game progressed; 'Blind Man's Buff', the competition of pinning a cardboard donkey's tail on while blindfolded.

Then, while the girls, giggling, played 'Truth, Dare, or Consequences' in the drawing-room, the boys went outside on the front lawn for a bow and arrow contest. My father set up three targets under a mango tree at the end of the lawn and we took it in turns to shoot at them with light, but well-shaped and well-balanced, blackwood bows and small blue-feathered arrows. All of us were pretty expert at the sport. One, Tanner Evans, was the best, and he shot with five yards handicap. He wore on his left wrist a tight scarlet leather band with a silver buckle; this mark of true bowmanship was all our envy; it had been given him by an uncle in America who still shot in important competitions, and none of us, though we tried, could get one like it in town. He hit the yellow bull twice and won the contest at my party; his prize was a box of many-coloured arrows.

It was while we were shooting at the targets under the mango tree that I noticed Kaiser and Jaillin. They were standing shyly, half-hidden behind a wall overgrown with bougainvillaea vine of the recently built garage, half a stone's throw from the house itself. They were watching our game silently and with strange concentration. I noticed that Jaillin was wearing a new dress, still far too big for her, and her beautiful silver earrings, and she had combed her hair out carefully over her shoulders so that it shone more than ever. Kaiser wore a clean white polo shirt and a clean pair of khaki shorts and tennis shoes laced up all the way.

I caught their eye but no mark of greeting passed between us. Soon afterwards they became a little bolder and stepped from behind the wall on to the driveway to look at us. They stood silent, serious-faced, and still. When we had finished the archery contest we all came in from the lawn to join the others in the drawing-room. As we passed I noticed out of the corner of my eye that Kaiser had walked back a little way as we came in and now stood leaning against a full, open barrel of corn near the garage. He was looking down and picking up handfuls of corn from the barrel just to let the yellow and red grains drop back in a slow trickle from his fingers. Jaillin, seated a few yards away, on the mosaic stone kerbing of the driveway, was playing with a few white pebbles. She was pretending not to have seen me at all. I went on laughing and chatting with my friends and felt relief when we got back into the drawing-room.

As we went in Tanner Evans asked me who they were. In an

48

offhand way I told him Kaiser was our yard-boy and that Jaillin helped Alice in the kitchen.

'I don't remember them.'

'Well, they only came two months ago, Tanner, and you haven't been around here much playing,' I carefully explained.

'Is he the one who taught you how to blow eggs?'

'Yes.'

'Do you play a lot with him then?'

'No, not very much.' I blushed and tried to change the subject by flattering Tanner about his archery, but he went on.

'My mother says she sees you playing with your yard-boy and she can't understand it. Why do you play with him?'

'I'm telling you, I don't play with him much. Anyway, he does things for me. He's making me a scooter this week.'

'You know, they cook their food over cow-dung.'

I was silent, I did not know what to think of myself, but I hated Tanner Evans then partly because I had been a coward.

After a few more competitions and games and a round of coconut ice cream served in cheap sea-blue glass bowls my friends gathered round to see me cut the cake. The twelve white candles were lighted by my mother who was looking flushed and happy, and I proudly blew them all out with a long, determined puff. My friends cheered and sang 'Happy Birthday'. Then I chose Judy of the golden hair and pretty face to kiss and cut the cake with. Although I had told my mother she was 'soppy' I did rather like her, because she was shy; yet as I kissed her on the cheek I murmured to myself and blushed deeply, 'Jaillin.'

'Look! Alan's blushing like a beetroot!' they shouted. The beautifully iced chocolate cake was handed out in wedges on small china plates. Sandwiches and sweets and almonds were passed around.

Quite suddenly I saw one of the girls point towards one of the latticed windows and say loudly:

'Who're those black children there?'

I looked very quickly and saw Kaiser and Jaillin peeping through the green window. Their heads were together and they were looking at the great cake on the table, half-eaten now. They didn't know anyone had seen them.

'They look nasty. I bet Mrs Holmes wouldn't like them to be looking into her drawing-room.'

'Who do they think they are I'd like to know?'

'Black crow, black crow, peep inside the window!'

There was laughter. General attention was now centred on Kaiser and Jaillin. My friends pointed at them and grinned. All at once Kaiser and Jaillin saw they were noticed and they stared at us, full of shame.

'Go away, you!'

'Shoo fly, don't stain the wall!'

Jaillin fled. Kaiser stayed a while longer, and I could see he was terribly angry. Then he slowly went away from the window too. I saw him through the lattice-work turn around and spit.

'They're Alan's friends,' Tanner said, in the middle of us all.

'They're not!' I denied hotly.

'He showed you how to blow eggs.'

'That doesn't matter.'

The others looked at me in surprise. My mother came over from where she was entertaining the grown-ups and asked what was the matter.

'Nothing's the matter, Mum.'

'What was all the fuss then?'

'Kaiser and Jaillin were looking through the window and we told them to go away.'

My mother looked at me strangely and I was terrified lest she ask me why, since only two days ago I had wanted them to come to the party. But she didn't say a thing about that.

'Ask everyone if they would like another piece of cake, Alan. There's plenty left.' She returned to the corner of the room where the few grown-ups were sitting, sipping cocktails out of delicate, green-stemmed glasses pictured with scarlet ibises around the bowls: my mother's Flamingo set. I cut some more cake and handed it around. I grudgingly helped Tanner Evans last of all.

When the party was over and my guests had left, after thanking me politely with little smiles, I asked my mother a question:

'Can Kaiser and Jaillin have some cake, Mum?'

'Certainly, son, there's quite a lot left.'

'And some sweets?'

'Yes, but remember your father isn't buying any more until next week.'

'All right, Mum.'

I went out to find Kaiser and Jaillin. They were sitting with Alice on canvas stools in one of the servants' quarters at the back of the house. The room smelled strongly of disinfectant and a little of rum and Khus-Khus grass, a bunch of which, to sweeten the room, hung from a nail on the wall by a piece of ribbon. On another wall hung a picture of 'The Sacred Heart of Jesus', and over the thin iron cot set opposite the door, a black crucifix stood on a ledge of poui wood. On both sides of the crucifix a red candle burnt smokily and fitfully. Otherwise the room was almost bare, except for the three canvas stools and a lopsided, unpolished chest of drawers on top of which were an old bible with a gold crest on its faded black cover, a mirror and a dried and stuffed coral snake skin, to keep away evil spirits.

In the middle between the three stools a half-empty bottle of rum stood on the floor; its silver-headed cork lay nearby. Alice, Kaiser and Jaillin all had glass tumblers in their hands; Jaillin had most of the dark rum left in hers. When I came in Alice got up to put away the rum bottle. Then she sat on the cot and began to murmur her Bible out loud. Kaiser and Jaillin looked at me, surprised and sullen.

I asked them if they would like to come and see my presents and eat some of the birthday cake.

'You' dam' frens gone or what?' Kaiser said and finished at a gulp the last drops of rum in his glass.

'They've all just gone.'

'Who de hell dey think dey is, eh?'

'They were very unmannerly.'

'Boy, I could piss on dem.'

I was silent. Then Jaillin spoke, in a sneering voice:

'Eh, eh, so you like de fair-hair girl, Master Alan. You kiss she up too bad, boy!'

I blushed deeply.

'Are you coming or not?' I said.

They got up and came with me. In the drawing-room I showed them my presents. Kaiser tested the red bow I had been given and said that it was a good one. I gave them a large piece of the chocolate cake each and told them to take away a handful of sweets. Last of all, just before my mother came back in to arrange the room for the cocktail party, I took Jaillin by the arm. I whispered that I had something I wanted to give her. I then put in her hand the big yellow balloon that blew up like a panda.

4

When I came out of the drawing-room, after meeting with exact manners my parents' friends at the cocktail party, I went into the pantry for a drink of water. I poured it out in a cup from the big earthenware pitcher that kept water cool even on the hottest of days. I was just going upstairs when Kaiser came in from outside. He stood still, looking serious. He said that Jaillin wanted to see me.

'What for?'

'Don' min' dat. Come go out wid me in the garden.' He turned his back on me and went out without saying anything more. I followed him, very uneasily.

Jaillin was waiting under a grapefruit tree in the garden. Kaiser took me up to her through the dark, then left quickly, without a word.

Out there it was quiet except for the bull-frogs in the gutters; they had just that moment broken into their hoarse chorus. That deepened the silence between us. There was the thinnest of new moons in the sky, like a silver nail-paring, and it gave no light under the grapefruit tree. Thousands of fireflies were about though, glowing for instants everywhere, over the grass in a carnival of sparks, up in the black crystal branches of the samaan tree confused with the north star above Mount St Benedict, tangled in the sweet lime hedge standing between the grapefruit trees and the gravelled driveway. That hedge, in places clipped into the shapes of birds and animals by our expert gardener, was at this time decorated with white buds which gave a most delicate fragrance upon the air. Search for it with the nose, breathe too deeply after it, and the fragrance would disappear, but if you only kept quiet the scent of the buds would lie in the senses subtly all the time and make you think the air was always such a paradise of perfume.

A few fireflies glimmered around us. I stepped a pace away and caught one of them in the palm of my hand; I liked to see its cold green light shine there. I made a fist of my hand to keep it safe, then showed it to Jaillin. She looked at it. She touched me lightly on the cheek with her fingers. I looked at her surprised, and frightened with shyness. I had never touched Jaillin before.

'You don' want to kiss me, Master Alan?' she asked quite timidly.

I had sensed this was going to happen even when Kaiser first called me to come out. I did not say anything. She was leaning against the tree, her eyes turned to the ground. Her silver earrings were bright marks at each ear.

I was something taller than her and to kiss her must bend down. I did not know what to do with my hands. I shut my eyes and leaned to kiss her stiffly. As I did so she put her arms around my sides and clasped her hands at my back. When I put my tightly pursed mouth on hers it gently gave so that I felt the sharp teeth, and with her tongue Jaillin softly rubbed my lips for an instant. Then she took her face away quickly, touched my mouth with her forefinger and ran away in the dark. A firefly had caught in her long hair and I saw it light twice before she was quite gone.

Dazed, for a while I stood still against the grapefruit tree. Then, astonished with excitement, I grasped one of its lower branches and swung myself joyfully up. There I climbed for five minutes and more, daring the very tip in the dark to look at the thin silver moon.

When I came back into the pantry I saw a black-winged beetle crawling on the shelf by the earthenware pitcher. In a certain slant of light its glazed black wings shone with green and gold. I thought it was a marvellous jewelled thing and I swore to myself that I would remember it all the rest of my life.

Upstairs, before going to bed, kneeling on the floor under the mosquito netting, biting my teeth hard, I asked God more insistently than I had ever done before that I might marry Jaillin when I grew up to be a man.

As I lay back on the linen sheets and the duck-feather pillows I found that I was humming to myself an old lullaby song my mother used to sing to me when I was quite small. She had told me it was by a fair gentleman called John Keats. It went:

'I had a dove and the sweet dove died
  And I have thought it died of grieving:
O what could it mourn for? It was tied
  With a silken thread of my own hands' weaving.
Sweet little red-feet why did you die?
Why would you leave me, sweet dove why?
You lived alone on the forest tree,
Why, pretty thing, could you not live with me?
I kissed you oft, and I gave you white peas—
Why not live sweetly as in the green trees!'

My mother had said that really it was too sad to sing to me, and didn't I prefer something happy, but I loved it so much that I used to make her sing it night after night before I slept. She had a pretty voice, small but clear as a bell, and I think her singing of John Keats' song to me at night was a memory probably sweeter than any other of my youngest years.

As I lay half-dreaming before sleep all of a sudden I saw at the dark window a solitary firefly gleam for a second. My body tightened with excitement and pleasure and I was wide awake in a moment. Then it was gone. I could hear the bull-frogs, in the gutters and the rice fields, echoing like horns through the night.

3

❧ The Village

I

I did not see much of Kaiser or Jaillin for the next few weeks. The
school term had started in Port of Spain, and I was down there
in town all week at my grandmother's, only coming home for
the weekends. Once or twice I saw Jaillin when she was working
in the house, helping Alice clean the silver with lime juice and
sapodilla wood ash, scrubbing the tiled pantry, polishing the brass
bedposts upstairs, but I was too shy to speak to her and she would
not say anything either. I wanted to be alone with her, yet I knew
I would feel terribly uneasy unless Kaiser was there too. One
afternoon I wrote a note to her on a page torn from one of my
crown copy books. It read, 'Dear Jaillin, I love you. Do you love
me? Don't show this to anybody except Kaiser. I like your shilling
the best thing in my Scottish box and sometimes just take it out
and look at it. Your affectionate friend, Alan.' I put it in an envelope, sealed it with red wax from my father's desk and gave it to
Kaiser to give to his sister. I was rather frightened at what I was
doing. Then Kaiser laughed and said:

'But what you going give she paper to read fo'? She can't read
a word, boy. Even we Pap an' Mam can't read an' you want she
to read? You think she is big scholar or what?'

'That's true. I didn't remember. Don't bother then,' I said,
almost gratefully, when I heard this. Later I tore the little note
carefully into very small pieces and threw them on the big trash
heap at the end of the orchard.

One Saturday I was at home and my mother gave Kaiser and
Jaillin the afternoon off from work. They were going back to the
village when I asked Kaiser if I might come with them.

'Sure, boy. I got a fresh catapult to show you anyhow. But I throwing dice in Ramlal parlour so you going have to watch on that time.' Kaiser was a good dice-thrower. He won a lot of marbles that way, and sometimes a few pence. Once with a 'master flush' he won a shilling from a boy and the boy didn't have the money to pay. 'I cuff him down. He shoulda say he have no money befo' I t'row,' Kaiser told me afterwards.

The village lay about a mile away from our house. It was not very big, about twenty-five families, hardly more than an impermanent settlement really; the huts were quite new, for the first villagers had only come there about three years back. These had broken off from a much larger village and come to this place where the Government had let them have enough land to graze cows, keep donkeys and goats and fowls, grow rice and ground provisions. The first-comers had been joined by others. They all complained that there was no opportunity in the big village they had come from. 'A man don' like to change whe' he live jus' fo' so but dat place choke up wid people.' The young people couldn't find new land or new jobs. 'Up dere so you never see such idleness in you' life. Saga boy an' small t'ief mounting up like a rage. Why you think I bring me fam'ly right down here so?' Kaiser said that his family had been one of the first to come; his grandfather, Old Boss of the village, had negotiated with the Government for the small piece of land. Not very many others had been as lucky.

The main occupation of the villagers was working in the canefields, which covered rich swathes of land in the neighbourhood. In season they cut the cane and carried it to the small factory in the district. Some of the men worked in the factory; though they did the crudest work there, carting the heavy jute bags of brown sugar, cleaning dirty vats, they proudly called themselves 'engineers', and had a certain prestige in the village. The magic and power of industry and the world of machines touched them. All the young men would have liked to work in the factory.

In the season there was enough work for the village. But in the slack time of the year, when the growing cane needed little attention and the factory was shut down, time hung heavy on the hands of the men there. Petty thieving increased nightly in this off season and there was sure to be a rapid rise in the number of cases of drunkenness coming up before the local magistrate. In all these cases he meted out the customary admonition: 'Why don't you get out of the rumshops and find some work to do, man?' Some did find work. They took odd jobs at rich houses like ours, or at the Government Farm, or at Mr Trotter's dairy. One or two went far afield to find work picking fruit on citrus estates or in part-time jobs on the Port of Spain wharves. Some stayed at home and just spent more time in tending their plots of corn and rice and sweet potato, yams and beans, and in looking after the few cows and donkeys and goats and poultry which they kept. Then perhaps their wives and daughters could sell more vegetables, eggs and milk in the rich houses. But whatever they did, it was still a bad time in the village. Tempers went bad and wives were beaten. There were fights.

Ramlal must have rubbed his thin hands, because his rumshop was always full. However, more often than not even he had to give credit, for pockets were empty at that time of the year. Underemployment made everyone in the village restive.

The most innocent way of relieving this strain of having nothing to do came in epic village cricket matches which sometimes lasted right through the day from early morning until nightfall. They were played on the rough village pasture where in the dry season a dirt pitch, more or less than the regulation length, was hacked out of the grass and smoothed out as carefully as possible. The village didn't have a coconut matting to put over the pitch so at least the menaces with which its uneven surface bristled were visible to the eye. The outfield layout was littered with clots of dung.

I watched one of these big cricket matches once with Kaiser. He was in the village team. They were playing a side from the old village. It was a game hilariously, intensely, and fiercely contested. The day's casualties were high, several bruised heads and broken shins and three fractured noses, but the game seemed to let loose a surge of good humour in the villagers. There was one fight, between a visiting batsman and one of the home umpires, but this was soon over, with the umpire, chosen for his toughness, an easy winner, and the game continued smoothly after it.

Each team consisted of fifteen or sixteen men. I noticed that on Kaiser's side anyway the best batsmen opened the innings and then later, when the opponents could be supposed to have half-forgotten what they looked like, in again at number thirteen or fourteen they strode, wearing different caps. There were complaints, but never successful complaints, about this practice: it was the caps rather than the men who batted.

I gathered these caps were all-important in the game. The team which appeared with the most memorable caps was well on its way to triumph. The village team was pretty well unbeatable, for in its ranks, a Bradman of headwear, it boasted a green Trinidad XI cap. Its authenticity was questioned many times but never disproved. One day at the Oval a great star, as he walked in through a corridor of people applauding a brilliant century, threw his cap nonchalantly to those worshippers, and it had landed straight in the hands of a little boy from the village. He came home with it and sold it to the cricket team for five shillings. Now it starred in every game. In this particular match it made four appearances in the batting order and each of its scores was a highlight of the innings. Kaiser was one of those honoured with the green cap. He let me touch it and examine the treasured emblem on it, the Trinidad crest, the black-masted ships of Columbus in a blue harbour and in the background the trinity of green mountain peaks. Beneath had been sewn the Latin motto of the island: Miscerique Probat Populos Et Foedera Jungi.

'Oh, God, I hope I score big,' Kaiser said fervently as he put it on to go in to bat.

After a nervous start he hit seventeen fiery runs. He hooked one ball into the casuarina tree which grew in the bush in front of Old Boss's hut; the game was held up twenty minutes while both teams searched the undergrowth; the ball was finally recovered from a patch of razor grass into which Kaiser, protesting, was made to go and whence he emerged ball in hand but woebegone, slashed by the delicate, sharp, green blades. The next ball he lifted for another six and hit his mother's cow in the field adjoining; it began to moo disconsolately. In the midst of the cheers for such a fine hit, his mother rushed out into the playing field shouting angrily.

'You crazy or what, boy! Look what the hell you do now! You want to kill we cow or what, er! Come out from dey an' see what I going gi' you here today!'

She advanced towards the pitch; Kaiser retreated from his wicket. The bowler took off his cap and fanned his face. The other fieldsmen flopped down on the grass and took a rest. The two umpires conferred quickly and then told Kaiser's mother she must go. She refused.

'Le' me get me han' on that wotless chile an' I going beat he like I beat a donkey. You hear me cow, you hear it!' The cow was still mooing as if it had all the woes of the world on its back.

Confusion reigned. The umpires conferred again, but could reach no decision. The rest of the village team came streaming out on to the field. A babble of voices and a waving of arms began. In the middle of it all Kaiser's determined mother stood firm, cursing.

'All you big men like baby or what? What you playing this dam' foolish thing for? Why you don' go an' work, eh! You only was'ing you' time wid this chupid little ball an' piece of ol' wood. You' brain mus' be sof'ning fo' true. You think you going stop me bus'ing his little arse fo' him. Look what he do me cow, eh! You hear it?' The cow was still mooing, distraughtly now.

At last they called Kaiser's father. He was in Ramlal's rumshop where he had gone for a rum. He was slightly drunk. He commanded his wife to go off the field when he heard the story.

'Woman, ge' off this fiel' here today,' he said ponderously, 'or I going well beat you. You hear me. Gawd, if you had Bra'man fo' you' son you would vex if he hit you' cow or what! The dam' cow not dead. Go, move, cle' the field, play, play!' he ended, flushed with triumph.

His wife went off crying. Play was resumed. The bowler swung his arms, glared at Kaiser, pounded down and delivered his stock ball, a fast full pitch. Kaiser swung hugely, missed, and was clean-bowled. The fieldsmen clapped the bowler. Kaiser walked away from his wicket, head bowed. As he came to the boundary edge his father caught hold of him and began to beat his ears mercilessly.

59

'Who you think you is, eh, firing shot at we cow like you mad. You don' know cow cos' money or what!'

Kaiser slipped through his arms and ran for his life, the green cap awry on his head; as he ran he straightened it proudly.

The team scored 123 runs of which Kaiser's 17 was top score. This total included eight byes scored when two short-pitched balls had rocketed prodigiously over the heads of both batsman and wicketkeeper and sprung with one leap over the boundary. There was then a chatter of awe amongst the spectators.

The score of 123 was too formidable for the opposing team. The village's star fast bowler, Burnley Hing, a Chinese-Indian who shared a hut with two brothers, who mended motor cars when he wasn't drunk, and who consumed more rum than anyone else in the village, really mowed down the visiting team. He took eight fair wickets and dismissed two other men with broken noses. His fierce slinging delivery was suspect and he was volubly accused of throwing the ball.

'Gawd Almighty!' the visiting captain, a dour, grey-haired old man wearing a flashy, floppy Panama hat circled with a red ribbon, said in an explosion of righteous despair. 'Gawd Almighty! What kin' of game this is! Gawd, man, me di'n' come here to pelt mango, oui! I never see a man pelt so. Eh, what you saying, umpire?'

The umpires shook their heads sadly. The only consolation that the captain had was in scoring ten runs out of their small total of 44, and that ten was top score. Burnley Hing, in whose face lurked a thousand smiles of triumph, was hugely cheered. As he wiped his sweating face with a large silk handkerchief, he expressed himself:

'Where dat rum now, boy? I could drink a barrel o' rum here tonight!'

These matches, especially in the slack season when thirsts were so high were profitable occasions for Ramlal, the richest man in the village. After the game both teams invaded his rumshop. It was now that the glum visitors recovered their spirits.

Kaiser and I slipped in too and had a sweet drink each that evening before I had to go. Kaiser took a Ju-C, I took a 7-Up; I paid for them both.

In the shop the men were laughing, and tossing their fears about as jokes. Tomorrow was another day and perhaps work would come then; meanwhile the cane-scented room was their heaven.

Only Old Boss was serious. He was talking across the table next to us to the visitors' captain. Neither man had a glass of rum to his hand. I heard snatches of conversation.

'How you' people doing up there?'

'Not so good at all, Old Boss. In trut' it's bad times now.'

'It's bad times here too. It's bad times all'bout. You know how it is, the men getting into a way of idleness. I hear one man speak bitter the other day; he say, "This always happen: we can' cut cane all year, so it better we don' cut at all: move off the dam' land somewhe' else, oilfield perhaps." '

'Old Boss, the dam' trouble is too many people living these days. You know how we village choke up when you leave, well it choke up worse now. Man, you know when I was a little chile, long time me Pap an' Mam lose fo', five chile dead so. Only we three grow up safe. Well these days almos' no chile dying nowhe'; six an' seven so in a family. I not saying I want the chil'ren to dead, but how you going expec' all so to fin' work when they grow big so, an whe' all dey food coming from, eh? An' you know something too, I hear enough young people say we ol' people living too dam' long, an' we should dead an' get out the way, eh.'

'You say true, you say true. A gran'father 'e soon get trample in the young herd. But whe' you' people finding work roun' this time, eh?'

'Old Boss, some not finding. Some turn little t'ief, and befo' dey know whe' dey is dey going be big-time Yankee crook, you know how it is. Some lef' the village long time. One come back an' say he driving taxi an' living like a lord. One come back an' say he is waiter in a Chinese restaurant down San Fernando; he say he not even thinking of coming back to the village. Dere is mo' work in the town, that is the trut', Old Boss.'

'You say true, you say true. But you going see the town going choke up worse even. Whe' everybody going live? You see Shanty Town already down by Port of Spain people squeeze

61

up worse than dog, worse than donkey. An' when the women going wit' the men what you think happen to them, eh? Answer me that brief, eh. What you think going happen wit' them so? You well know, I don' have to say, in a week time, in a mont' time, something so, they going sell their cunt to the nearest money. It mek you smell hell in you' nosehole.'

'Old Boss, you right. Dey cunt is the only thing dey have, you right.'

'That is it, man. Whe' they goin' cook their food proper? You know how a woman like she cooking, how she like to hol' a coo-coo stick in she han' or mek up a pilao. She going finish wit' all that big cooking, no mo' four coalpot, oui, an' how she going walk jus' out o' door an' fin' callalloo bush ready so fo' she pot? No, man . . . An' whe' she going grow she rice an' she edoe an' she corn an' she yam an' she sweet potato an' she red heart tomato? Oh, Gawd, man! An' whe' she goin' raise up she chicken an' cow? On concrete or what? An' you know that is what women meant to do in this worl'. An' whe' she going wash she clothes clean as white? Whe' she going fin' to clean she skin in river water an' sing all the time? An' what kin' of place is a nasty concrete street fill up wit' motor car an' wash down wit' beggar piss to raise up she chil'ren, eh? Not a place at all, man. I tell you, it better she dead than a woman go to town.'

The old men were silent, looking down at the table. All around the villagers tossed their fears and uncertainties in the future about as jokes. 'I going pull cart instead of donkey,' one shouted. 'I always would have work then, man!'

'I going sell tadpole in Curepe market!' another roared. When they talked about them at all they talked about their problems playfully that night.

But Kaiser was watching the two old men as if they alone existed. I knew he hung on his grandfather's words always, but I had seldom seen him so intent. The conversation didn't seem interesting to me.

'Old Boss, I hear you speak so many time an' I never hear you say what not true. I always tellin' the young people to tek care befo' they fly into town mad so. But they think money there an' so it attrac' them like molasses attrac' fly.'

'An' in one part it true, there does have money. But Gawd, it not their worl', you hear me, it not their worl'.'

Old Boss paused. With dignity he said:

'I love we village. People these days don't love anything more than themselves. From the time I was small I never love we village so little as that.'

He was silent.

I slipped out into the dark to go home. Kaiser was so engrossed he didn't even notice me go that night.

As in all villages in the island there had to be a rumshop, a general store, a gossip-centre. In this village where Kaiser and Jaillin lived all these were provided by Ramlal's Parlour. There Ramlal sold cloth, candles, pitch oil, twine, washing soap, knives, seed corn and almost every article you could think of that might be of use in the village. He also stocked sweets and marbles for the children. But his main concern was selling rum. It seemed that at any hour of the day and half way through the night, a man could walk into Ramlal's Parlour and get a rum. Two whole shelves were lined with bottles of the regular brands, like Vat 19 or Cockatoo Head, but it was said that the best rum came from under the counter, liquor which Ramlal himself distilled from the thick black molasses of the cane. He served the tots of rum in small blue glasses that looked like discarded eye-lotion cups. Men were always complaining that Ramlal's glasses were too dam' small. 'A humming-bird beak wouldn't hol' one of dose rums Ramlal does give we.' Ramlal was adamant however and he refused to accept the bigger glasses other men brought for him to use.

The only other liquor he served was cassava gin; the speciality of his wife. She had originally come from Venezuela, as had members of three or four other families in the village, and had brought from there the special ancient way of making this drink. First she put some large green banana leaves on the ground next to her hut. On these leaves she then spread cassava, grated, and mixed with water, and on the top of this a fine sage-green coloured powder prepared from the leaves of a plant which she called Yaraquero. The whole she then covered with more green

63

banana leaves and left to ferment for four or five days. You had to be careful because red ants especially loved the Yaraquero powder and came in droves for it. Sometimes you found hundreds of them dead between the banana leaves, killed by the fumes as the damp cassava fermented. The powerful liquor resulting from the fermentation could be mixed with water and canejuice, to tone it down, but it was clear that Ramlal considered a faint-heart any man who did this. He himself, and his wife, drank nothing else but this cassava liquor. With others it was not so popular. Rum, after all, was the staple.

I had been into Ramlal's Parlour occasionally. Alice did some of her shopping for the house there and I would go along with her sometimes to buy sweets or one of the small red wooden tops that spun on two inch nails of which Ramlal kept a few in his stock. I thought the people who were always there exciting and I delighted to listen to them talk or to hear stories about them from others in the village. Kaiser for one never tired of telling stories concerning what they were and what they did. I could tell he was proud of their achievements and their peculiarities.

There was Jess. He talked about her a lot. She was a fat negress of great age who one day had arrived in the village leading a donkey and had never left. She was a cantankerous old soul and cursed freely; everyone in the village, even Old Boss, was frightened of her tongue. But she was much respected for two curious talents she possessed. She was, first of all, what some of the villagers called a bird-butcher. She could hoot exactly like a small owl called the Jumby bird. And when she sat under a tree during the day and hooted in that remarkable way humming-birds and doves and other daylight birds, intent on mobbing a marauder who did so much mischief at night, and thinking him helpless in the sun, would collect from all over, and so be caught by the bird-catchers waiting around Jess. She rarely displayed this talent, and so was more respected for it. Jess said on occasion that she would like to kill the men and not the birds. She couldn't eat the birds anyway because she didn't have any teeth. Mostly she offered her services as a bird-butcher when she wanted some rum and couldn't get it any other way.

Jess's other talent was famous further than the village. She was

well known for it quite a distance around. She could stop a baby
coming when it wasn't wanted. Jess said that she was born in St
Kitts and there had picked up the science. She had a song she
used often to chant concerning it. Once in the rumshop I heard
her at it in an old hoarse voice. She said the song was made by
a blind musician in St Kitts called the Gingerland Gem:

'Ahoy, come to me, come to me,
  Let me teach you bush to boil tea.
Ahoy, come to me, come to me,
  The bush to kill the baby.

White pine board, mahalodo bush,
  Congolala and the black sage,
Mahogany bark, Cattle-tongue leaf,
  The bush to kill the baby.

Old-Lady-Body, Pumpkin belly,
  Mosquito wing, crapaud gill,
Blue fly belly, Policeman shoes,
  The bush to kill the baby.

When she pick up that mixture,
  Then she go to the dance,
Soon she give two little spin roun',
  They sing out that she mischance.

Ahoy, come to me, come to me,
  Let me teach you bush to boil tea.
Ahoy, come to me, come to me,
  The bush to kill the baby.'

She might or might not have employed the recipe she sang of,
but at any rate her skill that way was celebrated. Kaiser used to
call her the abortion woman: 'Here come the abortion woman
now,' he would say. I gathered that no one liked her very much.
  That Saturday I was in the village with Kaiser she was in
Ramlal's Parlour, sitting in one corner on a bamboo stool and

sucking at a dirty corncob pipe. Kaiser said she smoked nothing but Red Rose brand tea leaves.

I bought two pieces of candy at the counter and gave one to Kaiser. He ordered a half-tot of rum for himself.

'You too young to drink so,' Ramlal said.

'Min' you' business. I'se a customer, ent I?' Kaiser snapped. 'I'se paying good money.' In the corner old Jess grunted sourly:

'Gawd, but young people rude rude dese days,' she said. 'But I know what it is, you trying to play big man in front of the white boy. I see enough o' that sucking-up befo'.' She chuckled. Kaiser said nothing. 'It no dam' use at all, boy. What you got to be is you' ownself.' And she relapsed into silence, sucking her greasy corncob emphatically.

'You hear what she say?' Ramlal took up the tale. 'Little boy, don' play man befo' you is one.'

'Go to hell, eh. If I wan' a rum I going drink a rum, so what you talking.'

'All right, baby boy,' Ramlal scoffed. Kaiser took the blue glass and finished the rum in one gulp.

At this moment three or four men came in to the Parlour. They all ordered rums and one of the men asked for a top.

'Gi'me a balata' wood. Me son birthday tomorrow, an' he say that the best kin', it don't biscuit so easy.'

One of them was a great man of the village, Freeman the Knifeman. I had heard the story often. He was famous in the village for his four knives. He was an ordinary cane-cutter but these knives raised him above that station in life. The first knife that he was famous for was the knife that he fought with. One night another man had insulted his wife, and in the knife-duel that came out of that, Freeman had cut this man in the belly dangerously. The fight was already a celebrated event in the short history of the village. This knife Freeman had used in the fight had a handle of red-veined bone. Kaiser told me that it had been shaped by Freeman with chisel and steel file from the hoof of a fierce black she-ass; this gave it power. The handle of Freeman's second famous knife was just as wonderful. Made of hard lime wood seasoned yellow with vinegar it looked like a fat stick of old ivory and around it three thin bands of green leather were

66

fastened. This was Freeman's throwing knife. The exquisite balance of it lay deep in his fingers, and Kaiser told me that once he had seen him split with it the wagging tail of a stray dog from twenty yards. 'An' he was well drunk too besides.' The third knife I had seen myself most often, and thought it incredibly beautiful. This was his craftsman's tool. He kept it at his side in a sheath of white furred leather and sometimes he used it to carve boy's whistles and crucifixes for the Church, for no money. He used it also to make wooden dolls, in dancing postures, for a tourists' agency in Port of Spain. The handle of this knife was of bloodstone and had small dragons engraved in it. Everyone admired these dragons; laid in their eye-sockets with infinite artistry were golden pebbles of wood. This knife's blade was slightly curved, thin as leaf, and silvery as the moon. It must have been very valuable; Kaiser told me that once a collector had come up to the village and offered Freeman one hundred dollars for the knife, but Freeman, who was a proud cane-cutter, refused to sell. His reputation after that stood higher than ever.

But it was to his fourth famous knife that Freeman really owed his important status in the village. It was a big, sharp, straight knife, and its handle of tortoiseshell, glowing in certain lights with a whole treasury of sea colours, was palm-worn with years and years of use. This knife was a symbol in the village, for both Negroes and Indians alike. In it an old defiant gesture had grown large. The story went that at the time when slaves were freed an old man had snatched the knife from the saddle-sheath of his overseer and run to the saving hills. It was in his mind that the idea of the knife's special consecration had begun and when he died he gave it to a son from whom the famous knife had come through generations to Freeman, still the cane-cutter. It was told me that Freeman now hung the knife like a holy cross above his bed at night. In the day he used it for only one purpose. He used it only in the fields, used it only to cut the emerald ancestral cane. Old Boss of the village said:

'A slave have to be defiant, but a man mus' be humble.' Both defiance and humility were dignified in the meaning of the knife. If the village had needed a crest it for sure would have been Free-man's fourth famous knife on a ground of emerald cane, and the motto would have come ready-made in the words of Old Boss of the village.

Tossing back the first rums quickly the four men at the counter ordered further measures and took these to a rough, round-topped table made of crapaud wood painted blue as the sky. On this table, of all strange things, were four drink mats of worn green baize, bygone evidence of respectability. The men carefully set their glasses on these mats and sat down. One of those hard armless chairs they sat on was unevenly balanced and rocked from side to side with any shift of weight at all.

One of the men put a hand on his stomach and belched.

'My belly feel sour,' he said.

Freeman sipped his rum. He said:

'The cane grow dam' well this year anyhow. You remember las' year when no work fo' nobody to do because the crop so dam' bad. Boy, we was bawling.'

'It a good thing the crop big this year I telling you,' one of the men replied. 'Meriem say she going have a nex' chile an' I need money bad, boy.'

The others muttered in sympathy and rubbed their faces. For a while there was silence. Behind the counter Ramlal was washing his small blue glasses.

'All you comin' to the big fête tomorrow?' Freeman asked. There was a quiet chorus of assent. Skinny old Ramlal looked pleased with himself. I asked Kaiser what big fête they were talking about. Kaiser was playing with two dice he had cut from guava wood; when he answered me he stopped fidgeting with them on the table where we were sitting.

'It not so big, boy. They only talking holiday tomorrow so people coming to Old Boss yard to watch cockfight an' drink rum. They say it really to celebrate how the cane grow so good this year. People full o' money so they throwing fête wild.'

Kaiser threw two sixes with the guava wood dice and smiled at me. I admired his deft fingers.

'Can I come to see the cockfight tomorrow then?' I asked.

'If you wan' to come, boy, come. Who say you' Mam goin' let you, eh?'

'I won't tell her where I'm going. I'll just come.'

'Okay, man. Red Feather fightin' Serpent in the big fight. Fight for so, I telling you. Money flying wild over who going win.' He suddenly looked at me straight, playfully, grim.

'You know if police find we, we all going jail. So tek care if you coming or you not coming, sof' boy.'

I was touched with fear at this but the smart of the jeer made me say and determine that I would still come.

'Wait here. I going get the catapult to show you.' He left the dice. I sat at the table alone and threw them timidly. In fifty throws the highest score I had was a six and a four. At the other table the four men in their khaki cane-cutter's dress were talking about the next day's cockfight. Small bets were exchanged. Serpent was the favourite.

Overhead in one corner of the room I noticed a silver-grey web. In it two dead Jack Spaniards hung. I wondered where the spider was.

Kaiser came back with the new catapult he had made. It was fashioned from lemon wood. Three small notches in the handle told me that he had already used it successfully. We went outside to test it. As we passed her, Jess, sucking quietly in her corner, mumbled at us.

'Dam' good thing bird don' have slingshot too. Gawd, they should pepper you' arse up wid hard stone.'

Under the trees we shot at difficult targets. Kaiser picked off a solitary breadfruit leaf high up and that was the best shot. But from quite far I hit a rusty tin can twice and that also earned praise.

'It really shoots straight,' I said.

'Yes, boy, three bird already with it, a kiskidee, an ol' crow, an' a big dove. Oh Lord, if you see how I pick that dove! Sweet, sweet so!'

We shot for some time. Once a bluebird, the colour of evening between hills, settled on a jacaranda twig not far away. As Kaiser shot I closed my eyes; he missed it and I was pleased in secret.

Two young Indians came up to us from the village. They were the friends Kaiser was going to play dice with in the rumshop. He greeted them with a series of good-natured oaths. At once he began to seem a strange person to me. Our relationship was always transformed by the presence of each other's friends.

Kaiser asked me if I wanted to watch them play, but I excused myself, saying that it was time that I was getting home again. I saw Kaiser was relieved at this.

As I walked home the sky opposite the sun, now going down behind tree-coated mountains, was getting green-rose in colour. Milken gold was spreading further up the once blue helmet. And just above the mountains were hanging fat rubies and crowns of fire. Bats were already flying over the land as I walked on the road between the canefields.

The only thing I passed on the road was an ox-cart laden with pots of corn. The ox-bull's huge testicles swayed between the legs as it tugged the cart along. The man in loincloth driving the ox beat it regularly with a long whip, but the ox shambled on no faster for all that. It must have seemed a useless occupation even to the driver for he whipped with no temper, full of lethargy, by habit almost. A few black flies on the face of the ox were not disturbed by the whipping. Threads of gluey saliva hung from the ox's slimy black lips which, torn by countless fierce arrests, were ragged, ragged. Its eyes, filled at the corners with dirty gum, looked dangerous. The ox was taking the corn to a temple of Hosein, lover of men and oxen, near the village. I felt pity and fear and hatred and love as I hurried past home, and I didn't know which I really felt. The people of the village confused me.

2

The following day, after Church, I told my mother I was going over to play with Lee and Tanner Evans. We were going to play cowboys, I said. Instead, I walked up to the village fast to watch the cockfight.

I met Kaiser and Jaillin outside Ramlal's rumshop. They were arm in arm watching a game of marbles there. I watched too. In a circle drawn in the dust were scattered white, blue, and red buttons. Anybody knocking a button out of the ring with his marble could keep that button. For the village boys buttons were as precious as coins. Some even ripped off their fly-buttons to stay in a game. The boys Kaiser and Jaillin were watching played well. As I came up I saw a small fellow hit a mother-of-pearl button, worth five 'Khakis', out of the ring from over a yard away. He was using a keow. One of his opponents was using a shiny steel ball-bearing and the other a white crystal taken from an old soda-water bottle. All three were fiercely in earnest. The best object in the game was to hit an opponent's marble because then all the buttons left in the ring came to that marksman. It required good tactics to get close to the ring yet avoid coming too near to an enemy's marble. The three played warily, judging angles and distances. They all had their eye on a gilt button lying right in the centre, half-covered by dust. Kaiser told me it was worth at least a dozen 'Khakis'.

Jaillin was looking down at her feet and drawing patterns with her toes in the dust. I noticed her toenails were painted red.

'Why are your toes red, Jaillin?' I asked. 'I never saw them like that before.'

'She fin' a bottle of you' Mam manicure t'row 'way in the dustbin,' Kaiser answered for her. 'I help she paint them. Boy, Pap vex fo' so. He ask she if she think she is a whore or what. She ha' to pelt out out the hut or he would have lick she down. She 'fraid now but she don' want to tek off the colour. I tell she already she too dam' foolish.'

'I feel grow-up when me toe paint,' Jaillin said.

'Don' min' that, chile. You want to get beat or what!'

I laughed. Jaillin looked at me sad. Her black hair was untidy, unplaited, uncombed, but still beautiful. No tortoiseshell comb held it off her face and a strand of it strayed with the wind across her eyes, making her blink suddenly and toss the black hair off.

'Don't mind, Jaillin. When you are big I'll give you a whole manicure set!'

She went on making patterns in the dust with her toes.

Kaiser grinned slightly.

'Boy, by dat time you going expec' something back for any present you give she. An' she not going give you so easy. She bring up well, boy. I'm just telling you.'

I didn't understand this. I knew that Kaiser had taken my

71

words the wrong way though. I turned away to watch the marbles again and we were all silent.

Just as I turned back the game was over. The little fellow, kneeling in the dust, his rump high in the air, his eyes screwed up intently, pitched his mottled keow and hit the steel-bearing plumb, half-hidden though it was behind a root of grass. He yelled with excitement, and quickly pocketed the buttons in the ring, especially kissing the gilt one in triumph. His opponents were utterly downcast.

'It's danger to play that little boy, I'm telling you,' Kaiser commented. 'He shoot marble bes' in the whole dam' village. Once I lose three crystal, three keow, all Pap's pyjama button in one morning alone. Never again, boy.'

Now we walked away from the rumshop. I asked Kaiser about the cockfight fête.

'It not for 'nother half-hour. You know it going be over by Old Boss yard. They drinking rum there already. Come le' we go over.'

Old Boss's hut was set apart from the rest of the village. An acre, half bush, half corn, separated it from the other huts. I suppose in a way he was a philosopher and liked to be alone some of his time, liked not to be involved always in the incessant communal life of the village, the bare, unending, unsophisticated fight for living space, food, a little dignity against outsiders, the future of children, and in between the distraction of small passionate enjoyments. The villagers said Old Boss talked to the gods. He, in that stilted, pontifical way, a way for all that terribly sincere, derived from who knows what Bible or Talmud, in that way he used when delivering advice, a moral, one judgement or the other, he himself would say: 'At times, keep lonely with your mind.'

I knew some of Old Boss's sayings quite well. He repeated them often, and they were preserved by the villagers. Kaiser, his grandson, repeated them as the wisest words in the world. I knew by heart Old Boss's saying about the coward, 'He dare only swim in wave that roar in conch shell'; and also the strange boast, which in Kaiser's mouth seemed to me a whole speech of defiance: 'Only if it hurricane a wind can pluck out my beard; 'fraid no ordinary man.' The first time I heard Kaiser say this I laughed.

'That's funny. You haven't got a beard at all.'

He flushed angrily.

'You too blasted stupid, man.'

But he looked puzzled too. He had not seen the words literally before. For him, as for many others in the village, the meanings of what Old Boss said lay mainly beyond the words. The magic of their high sound invested the sayings with a quaint, unquestioned authority. For instance, the thundering season of rain was always prefaced by the old man's sad warning, which in that dangerous time seemed to thrust men under the mercy even of insects: 'The little grasshopper scrape he leg and man mus' run tek care of his crop.'

Some of his sayings were mysterious, capable of being interpreted many ways. The village held him in all the more awe for these. Now as Kaiser, Jaillin and I made our way in the direction of his hut on the other side of the bush and corn Kaiser came out with one of Old Boss's conundrums:

'Las' night we eating dove and callalloo wid he. Boy, suddenly after that he say: "When green twig lash it hurt mo' than old stick!" Wha' the hell you think he mean, eh?'

'Well, you know, it's true; a green tamarind switch stings like blast,' I replied.

'No, man. When he say something like that he have in he mind a bigger thing. He always so. Eh, Jaillin?'

'He have too many big word in he head.'

'What you saying, chile! You want me slap you here today. You don' know big word is education itself. Big word do dam' big things in this worl' here today. You don' know 'bout all the lawyer in Port of Spain using big word like mad. An' what they wearing, eh? What they wearing? Nice suit or what? An' they eating in Kimling and Tavern on the Green 'till they bus'ing with white people food. What you think I myself going start up learn to read nex' month so, eh? For peanuts or what?'

Kaiser subsided. Jaillin was hanging her head. They were both far away from me. But Kaiser gave me access to their world again quite soon.

'What I think it is about is how Pap tell he I so rude to Ramlal in the rumshop yesterday. You know when Jess go an' tell Pap he wan' beat me fo' that. An' now he tell Old Boss I have no dam' respec', an' Old Boss say he vex an' sad both the same time.' He shook his head.

'Anyhow, why they want me to respec' Ramlal at all. He only a dam' rum-seller. When I big what I going to do with rum-seller. I going drink rum an' soda in nice restaurant. No dirty man like Ramlal going serve me, dress-up waiter only, I'm telling you, boy.'

He was talking to himself. Jaillin and I were hardly there for him. I hadn't seen him in a mood like this before.

'What's the matter, Kaiser?' I asked. 'You sound angry.'

'What? Yes I vex. I vex wit' the whole dam' worl'. Lord, boy, when I get big I going piss on the whole worl'. A man was in Ramlal shop yesterday evening an' he telling how we Indians the mos' clever people in the worl' an' look whe' we is still, in the gutter, eh. Sweating our arses fo' a few cent in a canefield. Pap an' Ol' Boss say he no dam' good, he only a saga boy from Port o' Spain, an' it true he flashy fo' so, but Lord, boy, he speak some good good sense, eh. I remember Ol' Boss say one time he love we village so dam' much. Well, I fin' out 'bout that, eh. If you love to be poor live how we live, that what the man say. He right, yes.'

But Kaiser's mood was passing quickly. In a moment he was grinning.

'Boy, he was real flashy, chupid flashy. Hat stick up on he head wit' ribbon tie all over, two-tone shoe, sharkskin pants father, hot tie. He really dress to kill. An' you shoulda see some picture he show roun' so. Naked white woman. Boy, I bawl.'

I blushed. I got angry.

'Why are you so rude all the time?'

'How you mean rude, sof' boy? You never see woman undress befo' o' what?'

'No! And it isn't something anyone with any manners or anything talks about. If my mother knew she'd sack you.'

'Eh, eh, you vex! You vex for true.' He seemed surprised. I appealed to Jaillin.

'Jaillin, don't you think he's too rude?'

She did not answer me. She did not hear. She was holding on to Kaiser's arm with both hands. To keep up with his quick strides she gave little skips, her feet dancing in the dust. Sometimes she gave a big jump forward and then the silver bracelets on her ankles tinkled together. Her head was bowed all the time as if she was carefully watching what her pretty feet did. It looked as if she was enraptured in a private game. She seemed so young then. She did not seem to notice the sudden silence. As she gracefully played, Kaiser's eyes and mine met and we gradually smiled together. She did not notice. Kaiser winked at me over her head, and I smiled even more broadly. She did not at all suspect we had noticed her pretty game, and she skipped along delightfully still. But suddenly Kaiser began to imitate her, skipping as she did and giving a jump when she did. Then she stopped at once and looked up at him surprised. We all stopped, and Kaiser laughed loudly. I laughed more gently at her. She was dismayed and then got angry. I never saw her so angry. She turned on Kaiser and began to beat at him with clenched fists. He fended her off as he slowly retreated, still laughing at her. She began to cry with temper. Then suddenly she stopped hitting at Kaiser and instead ran across at me in a fury. I didn't laugh at her any more; I was frightened. She flew at me like a teased cat. She kicked and boxed at me wildly. The bangles on her wrists hurt me more than anything. Her little, white teeth showed sharp between her lips as she tried hard to scratch my face. Appalled, I resisted weakly for a time, then turned tail and fled. At once the tantrum was over. Tears of rage gave place to real tears then. Jaillin knelt down in the dust and sobbed with her face between the palms of her hands.

Slowly Kaiser and I came back to her shamefaced. Kaiser squatted down beside her and tried to look into her face. I put my hand very lightly on her scattered dark hair.

'What happen, Jaillin, child?' Kaiser asked gently. 'Why you crying so for?'

Silent, I dared to stroke her hair.

'We sorry too bad, Jaillin,' Kaiser said.

'I'm really sorry, Jaillin, we didn't mean to make you cry,' I said.

'Come go fo' sweet coconut water by Ol' Boss, eh?' Kaiser said. 'An' plenty roas' cassava cake, Jaillin. Come go, eh?'

75

Jaillin continued to sob quietly. Kaiser changed his tone with her.

'Lord, I done sweet-talking you. You a dam' foolish little girl. You can't tease or what? You think you is a big madam we can't fun you or what? Come, boy, le' we go watch cockfight.'

I stopped patting her hair. She looked up at Kaiser quickly, hurt. She had stopped crying. She wiped her face with the backs of her hands.

'What all you want to tease me for?' she asked sulkily.

'Eh, eh, chile, we was only joking,' Kaiser replied, smiling widely. 'Don' min' us the next time.'

She stood up. I helped her a little.

'Boy, look what you do,' Kaiser said pleasantly. 'You bruise up me han' like fire. An' look at Master Alan, eh! You like a wil' cat, chile!' There was a long scratch down my right forearm. A little blood had smudged on the skin. Jaillin almost smiled at me.

'I should have bite you,' she said playfully. 'My teeth sharp as hell, eh, Master Alan?' She was a woman again. I suddenly realized that while she had sobbed on her knees like a child, even while she had raged, I had felt closer to her than I did now.

'As fo' you boy, Kaiser. I should tell Pap you tease you' sister like she is a monkey or something. He going lick you.'

Kaiser was on accustomed ground now.

'Oh, ho! Boy, if you tell tale I going beat you' little backside fo' you like it was a donkey I beating!'

We began to walk along again. I sucked the scratch on my arm and spat in the dust. Jaillin no longer walked with her hands on Kaiser's arm. Nor did she skip along like a gay child any more. I felt how glad I was that I had seen her that once dancing like a child, unaware quite what the grown-up world meant.

We walked skirting the acre of bush and corn. The sun was very hot in perfect porcelain blue sky. No breath of wind relieved the stifling radiance. A few yards before coming upon a shady casuarina tree which grew out of the underbrush, I caught the smell of a dead animal. I sniffed.

'What's that stink?' I asked.

Kaiser and Jaillin had not noticed anything.

At the root of the casuarina tree, half-hidden by stinging nettles,

76

lay a dead dog. It had not died very long ago but in the heat it was already smelling high of corruption. It was a mangy brown stray dog which, like so many of its kind, had probably while it lived roamed the village ceaselessly for scraps of food. In death its stomach was horribly bloated, though really its body was so emaciated by constant hunger that its diseased skin hardly seemed more than tissue paper over its bones. Its lips were curled back in a snarl which showed yellow teeth. A few bluebottle flies were buzzing around it.

The dog had been stoned to death: its hind legs were broken, its neck was cut and just above the right eye its head was crushed in. I was almost sick. As we passed I didn't look at it again. It was too cruel a reminder of ugliness.

'That mangy son of a bitch, we chase he down this morning. Gawd, he was boderation in the village: steal food fo' so. One day it steal all Ramlal saltfish! Ramlal give us all sweet to pelt he dead wit' stone.' Kaiser turned to his sister. 'Jaillin, you know it bite Ram Ali direc' in he arse. Shave ice, you shoulda hear he bawl! When I tell you we laugh!'

'It good fo' him. He always playing brave boy,' Jaillin said. Kaiser nodded agreement.

Slowly we walked along at the edge of the tall green corn on that side of the acre. We could now hear sounds of loud talk and laughter coming from Old Boss's yard. A young woman shrieked with amusement. I was now very nervous about joining the fête.

'You know, Kaiser, I think I'm going to be out of place,' I said. There was a pause. 'I don't think I'll come on with you.'

'Don' min' that, boy. They drinking rum, they ent going to min' you, boy.'

'Don't 'fraid, Master Alan,' Jaillin gently said. 'We proud to have you at we fête, eh Kaiser?'

'You speak the trut', chile.'

Embarrassed, I looked up at the sky.

'Look! Look!' I cried in excitement and for something to say, 'Flamingoes!' I pointed up to where six red birds were flying, like barbs of blood in the sky.

They looked up too.

77

'Scarlet ibis, you mean,' Kaiser said. 'They resting down in Caroni swamp. They government-protected bird now, boy, if you try an' catch them down there, or rob their egg, you bad luck. They going jail you in one!'

'They pretty bird fo' true,' Jaillin said.

I kept watching them as they winged quickly down to the Caroni swamps. Their colour was really brilliant against that plumbago sky. There was a story in the island that these scarlet herons were drab grey originally along the banks of Indian rivers and that holy men, sad for the world, painted them that marvellous red and sent them as a warning to men everywhere. Certainly these birds only arrived in Trinidad some years to nest and fly about beautifully in the sky. Then old men made scared prophecies, and all bad luck was prefigured in their carnival arrival. At that moment they were rather sudden pretty mourners for the stinking dog dead under the casuarina tree. They pointed so typical a contrast in the land. Eyes revolted by scraggy-necked cobos rising off a refuse heap on a beach, greeted in the next minute the pure green flags of early morning over the sea. Beggars might walk in rags from door to door of the rich gothic houses in St Clair. Hate was just round the corner from respect and love; goodness and sin were in the same men hugely contrasted; in seconds despair might change to merriment. The sun cast hard shadows straight against bright savannas in that land; there were no grey declensions in tone. Knowing Kaiser and Jaillin, I lived the contrasts more intensely than others of my high-class world.

When the birds had almost disappeared Kaiser said, flourishing his hand in their direction:

'One time I see one of them scarlet ibis in Rio Claro. It was stuff in a taximan window. But it funny, it had big blue eye, an' I never see a bird wid blue eye befo' like that one.'

'A taximan's?' I asked.

'It what they call the shop, boy. A taximan. I don' know why fo' true. If you see bird that was stuff there! Humming-bird, jumby owl, paraqueet, bluebird, every sort, boy! An' not only that, eh. Monkey an' green 'guana an' I don' know what else too besides. They selling all them fo' millions of dollars, I'm telling you.'

Kaiser waved his hands about splendidly. I saw in my mind's eye the romantic shop in Rio Claro and envied him. Jaillin on her part watched her brother with enchantment in her eyes. As we walked slowly along listening to Kaiser's wonderful words her silver bracelets and her vivid toenails caught my eye again.

Old Boss's yard was full of people; together there they made a hubbub of gaiety. And the noise every minute was growing. Between two kegs of rum Ramlal stood measuring out the liquor into glasses from a wooden ladle. The glasses were big tumblers, three times the size of the blue cups he used in his rumshop.

'Lord, boy, I never see rum like this befo',' Kaiser said.

A group of men were on their knees in the dust throwing dice. They lifted up a great shout every time a play was made. All around faces were flushed with laughter and shouting and the rum. In the middle of a group a young man was showing how he could stand on his hands. The gay shirt he wore fell over his face, and his audience roared with laughter. Very soon he tumbled over on his back and then everyone doubled up in uncontrollable spasms of laughter which left them groaning with exhaustion and crying with the simple delight of it all. Everywhere everyone was drinking at great speed, as if they had all come late to the party and were now keen to make up for that.

The few women there wore their best clothes. One was dressed in a clean white sari. It swept around her body in pure turbans of muslin cloth and stretched up over her head gracefully. It left her right shoulder smoothly bare. The customary silver bangle at her wrist was in her case a serpent swallowing its own tail. She wore slippers of rose colour. Jaillin pointed her out to me.

'You see that woman by there? She call Haideen. You see those kin' of shoe she wearing? Well, she husban' give she them mo' than t'ree weeks gone now, an' every day so she only wearing them, wearing them all the time. Jus' because they from one big Port o' Spain store. She too proud.'

Another woman was wearing a new cotton frock and black, high-heeled shoes. She was a negress with remarkably delicate features. Her lips were always smiling. Her hair was ironed out as much as possible straight behind her and tied with a huge purple kerchief. This time it was Kaiser who focused my attention.

'She call Black Dove in the village. She kind to everyone. The only thing is she have no fix husban', an' the other women say she too dam' kind to their own men. One time I hear Mam call she a whore an' Pap vex: "What you want to bad talk the woman for?" he say. So you see already where she stan'.'

The older boys of the village, like Kaiser, were allowed in the party, though Ramlal refused to serve them with much rum. The small children, I saw, had climbed into the calabash and guava trees that grew around Old Boss's yard and ecstatically were looking on from there, chattering like monkeys running for nuts. Every now and then one slipped down his tree and ran to where a pile of green coconuts lay stacked. Then he cut off its top with a cutlass and ran back to share the sweet, cool water with his friends in the tree. For his pains they poured some of it on his head as he climbed up.

Boys in the guava trees were firing the squashy fruit at those boys who had no defences in the calabash trees.

We watched for some time, standing on the edge of the party. Kaiser fetched a green coconut for us to drink from. When we had drained it he cut it in half and we ate the sweet white jelly inside. Good drink, good food. The villagers said a coconut tree could keep you alive for ever.

'Le' we go an' see what happen to the cassava cake,' Kaiser said.

We followed him to Old Boss's hut, adjoining which at the back was a small wooden shanty roofed with rusty galvanized iron. This was the kitchen. The door was wide open. Inside, the floor was just hard beaten dirt which even no mat adorned. Six coalpots on six wooden rum-bottle cases marked 'Cannings and Co.' stood in a semicircle there. On each, vast iron frying-pans held many blobs of cassava paste sizzling in oil. Kaiser's mother and two other women were standing over these turning the cakes over and over. As we came up they were just filling two wooden trays with the hot, browned delicacies.

'Kaiser, tek this tray out fo' me, boy,' his mother asked him. 'An' bring a basket full wid bread same time.'

Kaiser took one tray, I took the other; Jaillin carried the big

basket of hot penny loaves. As we went out like waiters I felt
dreadfully embarrassed. I wondered what on earth my parents,
and especially Tanner Evans, would think of me if they happened
to see me like this, fetching and carrying in a coolie village.

When we had put down the food on long bamboo benches in
the yard we hurried back to the smoky kitchen. Bringing the
tray out one or two of the men stopped drinking and steadied
their eyes on me in surprise. But there was no hush in the party
to see a white boy serving them. Perhaps it was the rum which
took away their attention but I don't think so. My childhood
assured them with the courage and naturalness of equality. It was
not always so with the young Indians.

When we got back Kaiser's mother, squatted on the small patch
of dirt yard between the hut and the kitchen, was making more
cassava flour for cakes.

'Look these people eating out all my cassava,' she said. 'Boss
say they going want t'ree hundred cake mo'! They eating like
chupidness. Kaiser, look, tek out mo' tray there fo' me, eh?'

Kaiser's mother was rubbing the peeled cassava roots up and
down over a flap of tin, which had been perforated by hammering
nails through, and now made a perfect grater. From this rough
face the grated cassava ran down into the collecting basin, the
shell of a water tortoise. The bitter juice in this pulpy flour was
then squeezed and pounded out in a long wicker-work cylinder,
leaving the cassava dry and fine to make into the brown-crusted
purple-grey cakes, the aroma of which now hung in the hot,
smoky kitchen, indescribable quite, but as memorable as the
scent of a fire in which bay leaves burned all day.

In the kitchen we ate some of the sizzling, oily cakes, tossing
them about in the hands to cool. After, Kaiser rubbed the grease
off his fingers on his short pants. But Jaillin and I used a big
calabash of water which stood just outside the door of the kitchen.
The water was warm from the sun. It could not wash off the
grease and little oily pearls collected on our palms when we took
our hands up into the air again. Dipping into the water I
touched Jaillin's fingers without meaning to. The touch trembled
through me, as if a cold wind had blown. Our meeting fingers
stayed together. The two free hands played about in the water as

though innocent of everything. We did not look at each other. I softly pressed down on her fingers in the warm calabash pool. I knew I was blushing. She slightly lifted her fingers against mine —the cold came again in my chest—then swiftly withdrew them. She dried her hands in her frayed rose skirt. For a while I went on washing my hands in the calabash, to cover up. Jaillin went into the kitchen to carry out to the men another basket of bread. I followed her secretly with my eyes. She tossed her hair half over her face, then brushed it back with her hand. And suddenly with a pang that brought back everything at once I noticed her painted nails flashing like garnets in the dust as she almost tiptoed by; then rushed into memory again the dog and the ibis, the path by the cane, the casuarina tree rustling in a hot breeze, the gilt button, Kaiser's wonderful taximan's shop, how Jaillin had been a little child cuffing me, skipping beside Kaiser, and how she had become once more a frightening woman who knew everything better than I did. And my mind grew confused with love, I suppose, and hurt and desire for some beauty I couldn't focus and with all the puzzlement of my small life.

Inside the kitchen a cake fell from one of the frying pans and sizzled on the dirt floor.

'You' mammy's cunt!' one of the women cursed. I jerked myself then out of reverie and went to join the others in the yard. A few tears I think were burning my eyes.

Outside, the party continued as zestful as ever, the men crowding around the trays of cassava cakes. Burnley Hing I saw stuff a whole cake in his mouth and follow it straight with another one. Then he eased them down his throat with rum and coconut water. And wiped his thin lips with the back of his hand.

Two men in red sleeves brought out goat-skinned drums from Old Boss's hut. They were oldish, solemn men, and their eyes had watched the stars, finding there continually a statement of man's insignificance. They were lonely, religious men. They didn't live in the village but visited there to talk with Old Boss. Kaiser said they had once talked for three days and three nights on end; then the two men had disappeared and Old Boss had come into Ramlal's rumshop and got drunker than anyone had ever seen him, murmuring over and over again a puzzle no one could understand: 'Deaf Frenchman, God never going answer you' question.'

Their batons were two ball-headed blackwood sticks worn smooth and shiny with use. On the stretched goatskin of the drums were painted emblems, a pelican, a golden buddha, a peacock, a woman with a full belly. The men themselves wore those red-sleeved jackets, and strings of red beads' around their necks.

When they began to beat, thrumming, thrumming, rapid and mysteriously low, the crowd quietened. The beat spread out and captured silence. Then it got louder and louder to a climax of unbelievably strong, rapid strokes. In a moment that stunned, it stopped. There was a long sigh. Then the low hurrying beat began again. And this time half-way up that climbing beat their voices joined the fierce tremble of the drums. At first it hardly seemed to reach you it was so fine. But soon that soft peculiar wail searching for sadness of the religious chant of the old Indians completely filled the gold air in the yard. It rose and fell as if the changing wind in that place played upon a flute, telling of suffering and love and despair of love. So it seems to me now. Then, the first time I heard the Indian drum, the Indian chant so close, I just suddenly felt sad about the whole world. And I felt vastly afraid: like those nights when I dreamt of the terrible, exact moment of my death. I felt that the whole party around me was chilled by sadness and fear. The feeling was not exactly identifiable, but it was profound and had something to do with the littleness of life under the mass of stars.

Old Boss must have noticed something because he gave a signal brief as a wink and the two shadowy old men cut their chanting off so quickly that it still seemed to hang in the air for seconds afterwards, as if surprised at its recall. The old men tapped their drums twice for some reason. Then they hurried back into the hut, their red sleeves flapping in the wind. I never saw them again.

The old men had come and gone so quickly and had impressed something so strange, either too evil or too beautiful to grasp firmly, that their visit seemed exactly like a dream. This impression was deepened by the fact that no one talked about them after they had gone. It was as if their display, what it meant, would crack like glass hit by a stone if it was discussed. I had this feeling myself because I never even asked Kaiser about them, until some days afterwards. Then all he told me about their performance was that the old men were the best beaters the villagers knew and used to play for them on all great occasions, marriages, funerals, fêtes.

The party revived quickly. The noise of it began to rise again. But it was time for the cockfight now, so Old Boss lifted his hands high and called for silence.

'I hope all you having good fête here today,' he said. 'I know you working hard in the field an' you deserve it. The village doing well this year. It good. Everyone have work. We rice an' corn growing like if heaven touch it. You see that big field o' green corn there, you remember what I tell you when some o' we come here first, I tell you, "Give me three grain o' corn an' it going make a field o' bread for you," eh, you remember that? Well, all you work hard an' everything turn out like if heaven touch it. Belly fill all 'roun'. Money to spend all 'roun'. Ramlal exten'ing he parlour. We planting new rice fields. So today we have big cockfight fête.'

Old Boss paused. There was a confusion of applause at once. There were shouts of, 'You say true, Old Boss!' One man said affectionately: 'Old Boss well like to talk, eh!' One of the older men said: 'It true now, yes, but . . . well, I not saying not'ing . . . I see men behave happy befo' an' dey *dead* de nex' day!' In the midst of the noise like a practised orator Old Boss raised his hand again.

'It time fo' the cockfight self now. Fin' place for you' self where you able. You know how it is, six contes' an' the las' one is between Red Feather an' Serpent. All right then.'

In the middle of the yard was a shallow cockpit and now around this everybody began to look for a place. Everywhere last minute bets were exchanged. Most of the men took glasses filled to the brim where they sat. Kaiser looked uncertainly about, then said:

'It better we go in a calabash tree. We not going get good place to see 'roun' the pit.'

'An' the ol' people don' like to see we young people so close by anyhow when cock fighting,' Jaillin added. 'You remember las' time?'

'Uh huh. Le' we go over by that tree dey.'

It was a large tree with a few green gourds hanging on it. It stood nearest the pit and was filled with small excited boys. Kaiser helped Jaillin up to the lowest branch, after that she was agile as a cat in the branches. Kaiser had to give me a hand up too. The leather shoes I wore slipped badly at the footholds cut up the trunk.

'Man, why you don' tek off you' nice shoe, eh?' Kaiser asked. But I had been warned about leaving anything like that lying around, so I said I had a bandaged cut on my foot and had to keep on the shoes. Telling that lie withdrew me from them for a while.

On the best branch four or five little boys had crowded. Kaiser chased them off. He cuffed one or two to make them go. They clambered over to other perches scowling. When they had got far enough away they started shouting.

'Who you think you is, Kaiser? You think you grow up o' what?'

'What you bring dat dirty white man pushing here fo' at all?'

'What he got to do wid we fête, eh?'

'He you' fren or something? He loving Jaillin o' what?'

'Ha! Ha! Look, he going break he arse befo' you know what! He mus' a never clim' tree in he life.'

I had almost slipped off the thick, slippery branch. I felt their eyes on my clumsiness. I was hot and sweaty with embarrassment. Luckily the incident made them laugh, and they forgot their grievance, so that the emphasis of bitterness went out of their shrill voices.

'I never see dat! He coul'n't clim' a cocoa tree even,' the taunt came with laughter.

'Why all you don' shut you' mout', eh?' Kaiser said without malice. 'You know what, Master Alan don' bodder heself wid all dis small-time clim'ing, eh boy. You don' know he clim' up in air-plane higher dan you ever going clim'. You don' know dat, eh? Well, I telling you, he fly over Mount Tucuche so many dam' time he really sick o' flying up dere so.'

They were quiet.

'Dat is true?' one of them asked.

85

'Yes,' I replied, untruthfully.

'You ever see de devil man whe' he hide heself 'pon the cloud on top? You ever see dat?'

'Yes,' I said, daring everything. 'Twice. He had horns. And he tried to lash us down with his tail. Truly, you know.' I said it intensely, feeling I was getting back a little of my pride, feeling that perhaps Jaillin would be impressed.

'Oh, Gawd, man! You saying true?'

'Yes, I am.'

'It true what he say,' Kaiser said. 'You know what Old Boss heself say, "It nice to clim' up mountain but at the top o' El Tucuche you only going fin' the devil." You know it is he who boil up de t'understorm an' mek fire fo' lightning up dat cloud 'pon top.'

I had found a safe place on the branch next to Jaillin. I was leaning back so that I looked up at her from the side. She never looked at me. Sometimes she tossed her hair half in front of her face, then brushed it back with her hand. A few feet away Kaiser soon found a seat in a crook of the branch. He looked at me and grinned.

'Why you don' snuggle up 'gainst she, boy?'

'You think you're funny, Kaiser!' I said angrily.

Jaillin moved away a little. Kaiser laughed.

'Well, I never see dat!' he said.

I had the sudden desperate feeling that I hated them both.

3

Cockfighting is a forbidden sport in Trinidad so the villagers had to be careful. Over most of the island it had lost its popularity, but in a village here and there, like this one, it persisted, a special hobby of some of the older men. They remembered the great days. They still talked of Witch Hunter, the almost legendary cock, who won two hundred fights. When he died he was buried with an ornate cross like any ordinary soul. They gave him a wake afterwards too. If a cock was very good they called him 'another Witch Hunter'. Old Boss had one of Witch Hunter's spurs in a green, silver-buttoned pouch in his room, and when things were going wrong, say the corn crop was failing or the fowls dying of pox, he took it out and rubbed it like a relic.

It was getting towards the end of the cockfighting season when the fight between Red Feather and Serpent took place.

Between June and December the birds are in a moulting stage and their feathers too soft and full of blood to allow them to fight for very long or very keenly.

In December training for the best birds is begun. First each is clipped and spruced up, a dandy among fowls. Then each is given a bath in strong rum to get rid of ticks and lice in the feathers. This makes them drunk and the village children have a holiday of laughter. 'You never see a drunk cock? Talk 'bout Charlie Chaplin fo' funniness! Oh, Gawd, boy, I bus' me cheek wid laughing,' Kaiser said about this.

Sparring matches are then arranged. In these practice fights spurs are carefully guarded with cork so that no wound can be given. These matches give some idea of the condition and strength of each cock, and indicate what his technique is. He might be a brave straightforward slogger, he might be a subtle strategist. This happened to be the interesting contrast between Red Feather and Serpent. Red Feather was tough, quite old, scarred and experienced, a sturdy, magnificent mauler who had won fights from the brink of death even by his courage. Serpent was fairly new to the pit. Even so his record was devastating. His sleek, ingenious movements, his quickness and cunning, his artistry of thrust and counter-thrust, seemed to put him in a different class to any of his challengers. The betting that day made him favourite over powerful Red Feather.

Every morning during training just at dawn each cock is bathed in cold water and then tied to pegs in the sun for an hour or two. Then he is exercised, with another cock held by the legs and moved slowly in front of him as bait for his spurs. This cruel method had been introduced by the Indians from Venezuela in the village, and was not always used by others. Serpent had been trained by one of the Venezuelans.

The preliminary fights were not lively. All were between ordinary farmyard cocks starved a little and deprived of hens. A pair of Plymouth Rocks refused to fight, and their embarrassed

87

owners were hooted at, and pelted with guavas. Another cock just chased his opponent squawking around the pit, not meeting any opposition at all. At last the coward bird made a frantic effort to fly over the heads of the men squatting in a circle around the pit. That bird didn't get far; he was pulled down by quick hands and his neck wrung fast; then the body was flung to the feet of the owner. Matter-of-factly the executioner said:

'If you' cock 'fraid fighting, eat he. Dat one was dam' 'fraid, eh!' There was a murmur of agreement and the owner of the dead cock had to accept the situation. It was the fate of all coward cocks.

From that big calabash tree where we sat through the leaves moving very gently in the wind we could see over the corn to the thatched huts of the village. The sun beat on their whitewashed walls like on silver mirrors. Those walls were mirrors of all the beauty in the sky. Fiery sunsets painted them rose, moonlight touched them pale and stark as bone, the dusty gold light of approaching storms made them walls of brass which would ring if you knocked a thumb on them.

Further in the distance the white dome of the temple rose up out of a grove of pomerack trees, the red tassels of whose flowers bobbed on every green branch. At night the white dome reflected the stars like a pool of water in a garden.

Very close to me Jaillin was rubbing herself gently against my side. I could feel the cotton cloth of her dress moving on my arm. I felt as if all the eyes in the village were looking at us. I thought perhaps suddenly my father would come walking around the corner of Old Boss's hut and see us. I moved a little away from her. She stiffened and her eyes got a little wider. She didn't say anything. A leaf made a shadow like a heart on her face, moving in the wind from cheek to lips, from cheek to lips. That one leaf on a twig, patching her face here and there with its dark little heart, irritated me. I wanted to brush it off with my hand as if it was a stain from smoke. I was so fixed by the thought that I almost rubbed her cheek to take it off. At last I stretched up above her head and picked the leaf off between my thumbnail and fore-finger. I dropped it and it floated to the baked dirt floor lying there like a green heartshaped poisonous jewel in my mind.

88

'Look, Red Feather an' Serpent coming out soon!' Kaiser said, pointing down to the pit.

Two men with white cotton bags in their hands stood on opposite sides of the pit. In the bags were the two cocks. The men stood waiting for a signal from Old Boss. There was complete silence now among the men: the eternal cicadas deepened that silence, focusing every man's attention on the fact of it. I whispered a question:

'Which one's going to win?'

'Serpent, the one wid the yellow feather 'roun' he neck, he going win. I see that devil fight befo' an' he quicker than hell. No cock could match him,' Kaiser whispered back.

But Jaillin said then:

'Red Feather going win. He brave mo' than dat other saga boy one.'

'All right, chile, you going see,' Kaiser replied. 'You t'ink Serpent is coward cock o' what?'

With all the flair of an actor Old Boss let the tension draw itself tight up to a pitch where it might have been broken by the tiniest shuffle, then he gave the signal, letting his hand drop with a blue kerchief, like signalling trains.

A shout went up from the men. The two men in the pit loosed the cocks out of the cotton bags. Silence came again.

Serpent came out warily into the centre of the pit, his sleek wings shining in the sun like miniature ebony shields and the yellow feathers at his neck ruffling slightly in the wind. He seemed to walk solemnly, thinking of victory.

'He getting he eye used to the sun glare,' Kaiser whispered.

Red Feather when he was let out of the cotton bag flapped his wings and crowed. The wings were hot bronze. I thought if anyone touched them he would burn his fingers. He saw his challenger and rushed up to him to see if he would run away at once as young cocks normally did. Serpent put his beak half down to the fighting posture to show the older cock he was defiant, but at the same time edged away from actual battle, summing up his opponent, feeling the pit out.

'You see he coward,' Jaillin said.

'Chupidness!'

Advancing in the true fighting position Red Feather made the first attack. He leaped high, his spurs aimed to kill any cock foolish enough to raise his head in the panic of the moment. Many young cocks did this and died at once. Serpent just slipped well under the flying feet and turning behind him quick as a flash flew at the head with his own spurs. Red Feather ducked away as soon as he knew he had missed but the blow got him low in the neck and took away feathers and made a little blood come. And Serpent had him quickly by the comb with his beak, trying to thrust his spurs with sharp kicks into the body at his mercy. Red Feather had been quickly overwhelmed in this manoeuvre and might easily have been killed at once, but he too could fight and though bewildered more than ever before managed to parry the most dangerous thrusts with his two wings. The upper part of his leg was seriously cut through and bled a lot. Then with a surge of power he wrenched away from the hold. The cocks turned to each other again. Blood was dropping slowly from Red Feather's neck and the soft copper-coloured feathers on his upper leg were matted where a wound was.

The crowd murmured a little.

'You see, eh! What I tell you!' Kaiser said.

In the next exchange their feet met in the air and the strength of Red Feather sent the black cock falling back. He slipped away to the side, avoiding Red Feather's follow-up. Again the same thing happened. Red Feather's strength bowled Serpent back but he was not adroit enough to take advantage of it. The next time they sprang at each other Serpent must have struck differently because this time he did not fall back; instead Red Feather staggered, spurred in the comb. Serpent's striking was famous in the village and there was a loud 'Ah!' of half agony, half thrill.

'Who going win, eh?' Kaiser jeered. My hand was clenched white-knuckled on a branch. I heard a man below say: 'Serpent the devil's cock heself!'

In the next three exchanges Red Feather was spurred twice more; from the last of these a glancing cut over the eye half blinded him for a second with the blood dropping down from it. But for all that he flew up again at his rival and by that reckless-ness surprised Serpent, not expecting so soon a renewed assault after his success. He got in a good strike, inching a piece of red comb off so that the ragged end bled.

'Serpent think he could win too easy,' Kaiser said. 'But he not going let that same t'ing happen twice.'

'Red Feather meking a come-back,' Jaillin said, but her eyes told that she did not believe it.

The fight went on like that. Serpent was too quick and clever for Red Feather, yet was unsettled by the strength and determination of that brave cock's attack; his most deadly strikes were falling wide. Yet Serpent was wounding Red Feather all the time so that soon he was terribly torn; he dripped with blood from a dozen strikes. And still Red Feather seemed to be doing the fiercest attacking, driving the black cock back often, jarring him almost to sprawl in the dust, making him take small running retreats to safe positions, occasionally sending a few feathers flying by the strength of a blow. Once also Red Feather scratched him just above the beak and sent blood streaming. But for all that it seemed Serpent must win in the end. Red Feather surely would weaken and his strike grow more and more ragged, letting in Serpent for the kill. Only his unsettling strength was protecting him now.

The pace of the fight was desperately fast. There was no stalling, no pecking in the dirt in wait, in wait for the rival's move. Exchange followed exchange straight. Serpent's feathers were strangely out of place in a few seconds. In five minutes Red Feather was slashed as a practice bird. Afterwards men said that they had never seen a more breakneck, cruel fight. In less than fifteen minutes it was all over.

Suddenly, Serpent struck a vital blow. He hung back a little on his strike as Red Feather leaped again. That split second more he had to judge distance and find an opening was enough. Though spurred himself in the exchange Serpent got in the strike. His spur hit Red Feather in the eye and went deep into the head. That cock staggered on with his momentum a few feet, then fell on to his left wing, dragging it in the dust a little way. Red Feather was dying then.

The ring of men gasped hoarsely in sadness and triumph.

Yet the fight was not over. Serpent came in again to finish off his rival, quickly, angrily, incautiously. Red Feather lay on his wing quiet with his good eye looking at his killer. With the peculiar cunning of a dying animal or bird he was hiding his last surge of bravery and strength. As Serpent raced in and struck at his head again, he ducked it under his wing quickly. Serpent stumbled with the missed strike and in a flash Red Feather got up and rushed in at him. Serpent was only half ready when the dying cock hit him square and sharp with his spurs. One cut through his left eye, blinding him that side though not going into the head; the other pierced his breast under the right wing. Those strikes would have won any other fight for Red Feather. He turned again to kill his last rival, his power staggering. But Serpent, desperately wounded, by instinct and all his remembered skill dodged away from the rush and getting up close to Red Feather put his head under one of those battered, dusty, bronze wings into safety. While he was there Red Feather could do nothing; he no longer had the strength to break away from the position. The two cocks flapped around the pit, Serpent staying close all the time, his head under the wing. Red Feather was dying fast. He weakened and weakened in the struggles to get rid of his rival. Then suddenly he fell down. At once Serpent was away from him, and came in to kill. His spurs struck home, jarring Red Feather, but probably that cock was dead even before they hit.

The ring of men sighed with a sort of wonder. I was almost tearful with the tension and fierce cruelty. That ten minutes battered me. I felt I had seen men killed. Kaiser shouted:

'He win! He win!'

'Who win?' Jaillin said bitterly.

Serpent staggered about the pit a little, his black wings trailing. From under the right wing blood was coming quite quickly, mixing with the dust. His left eye was only a gash. Then so slowly it seemed as though he would never get them up he raised his wings and flapped them. A few black feathers came out. And lifting his neck so that the yellow feathers ruffled out a little from it, Serpent crowed faintly, metallically, hoarse with blood in his throat. The fight was over then.

'He win! He win!' Kaiser shouted again.

Serpent's handler ran out into the pit and took the bird up in his arms. He held him gently to look at how badly he was wounded. Blood ran down his hands. I saw him shake his head.

The villagers milled into the cockpit, kicking up clouds of dust. Talk was excited about the fight: shouts came of 'Fight fader, eh!' 'Fight Daddy-O!' 'Fight fo' so, eh, boy! What you say?' 'It was a Witch Hunter fight we see here today, boy!' Loud whistles for fun split the air. Gradually the crowd began to make direction for the village huts. Before long Ramlal's Parlour would be packed. Two small boys threw a young calabash between themselves as they ran along the path leading to the huts; tossed from hand to hand the gourd shone a fiery green in the sun. Everybody was happy with the cockfight fête. A thing like that gave days of content in a village.

'I see too much sour face in the village today; I going give a fête!'—that's what Old Boss used to say.

Two strokes came from the temple drum. It was some special holy hour. You could imagine the celebrants bowing along the white and blue corridors. 'Give me your strongest love or I will die,' words that my mother had read me once rose in my mind. I think they came from a story in *The Arabian Nights*. She had stopped and repeated the line softly, almost to herself, 'Give me your strongest love or I will die.' I was small and impatient and told her to go on with the story, but the line remained tenaciously with me, 'Give me your strongest love or I will die.' And often when all empty after absorbing emotion that line rose in me in the beat of bells or drums. 'Give me your strongest love or I will die.' Again two strokes came from the temple drum. The celebrants were walking in the blue corridors, bowing and bowing.

We got down from the calabash tree after nearly everyone had left. It was really hot as we crossed the pit. We were all sweating. Jaillin raised her skirt and mopped her face with it. The white pants she wore underneath had slipped down a little and I saw her navel in the smooth brown belly. I felt upset and empty as if I hadn't had food for a long time. Kaiser chuckled at her.

'Eh, Jaillin, you like to show off you' body to he, eh!'

Jaillin dropped her skirt abruptly.

'What you mean, eh? Who you think you talking to? You think you talking to Black Dove o' who at all?'

'You don' see he too nice? He don' like to see you belly expose so. He 'custom to white girl an' you ever see a white girl lif' up she dress an' expose she belly yet? Even when they marry they don' do that kin' o' thing. You don' see he looking like he smell a bad fish!'

'As if I ask he to look at me belly at all. What you saying eh? He own me dress o' what?'

'I didn't say a thing, Jaillin,' I protested.

'I well know what you want to say tho'. You think I don' hear what you' 'custom saying all the time? They not nice to play wid. They vulgar. That is the word. They vulgar. Everything we do that is the word: all we vulgar. I bet you think cockfight vulgar, I bet you think Ramlal Parlour vulgar, I bet you think all we is vulgar. That is the word, eh! Why you come 'roun' here at all if you see everything vulgar?'

I didn't say anything.

4

❧ The Sea Madonna

I

About three weeks after the day of the cockfight I had holidays from school. This time of the year my father always took a week or two off from his work and we would pack up and go to Mayaro on the sea, a quiet fishermen's village with a line of holiday houses near it in among the coconut trees. It was always a good time. The two relaxing sounds never absent—the surge and gentle roar of waves sprawling up the sand and shells, the noise of wind in the green rapier-leaved coconut branches—slowly cleared the mind and made the soul fit. A body got browned and handsome in the sun. A body got freshened and healthy in the salt wind, blue at morning, blue at evening, gold and hot otherwise, coming off the sea. Eyes got to be green jewels or blue or grey jewels in the sparkle off a white beach. There was a hundred per cent more laughing to be done there. Life reached its easiest, sweetest.

This year my parents decided to bring Alice, Kaiser and Jaillin to help with all the chores of a holiday. And my father was planning to make an estate foreman of Kaiser so he wished to show him around the Mayaro land under his survey as part of the training. My father always thought Kaiser reliable. He put a trust in him for hard work and faithfulness. Kaiser's future career seemed assured. Not many young men like him could hope for jobs comparable to estate foreman.

The day we went he appeared early, bright and eager to help, wearing tennis shoes cleaned with chalk, a new polo shirt, and khaki shorts patched with black thread in the rear, his black hair greased to a shine, carrying a few things tied up in a red cloth.

He ran around searching for work to do; it looked as if he wanted to whistle and shout all the time. Later Jaillin came, more subdued. She wore a strange little straw hat perched on her head. It had artificial berries stuck on the brim and it made her look old-fashioned. She was barefoot. A new dress fitted her better than usual. Always her eyes decorated the world. She played with her silver bracelets restlessly, pushing them high up on the arm, letting them slip down again.

'I get excite as hell,' Kaiser said to me as we were about to go off. 'You know what, I never see sea befo'. Yes, I see it one time down by the wharf in Port-o'-Spain. But I never see real true sea wid beach an' shell an' coconut tree an' everything. I swim in enough river water but it is the trut' I never bathe in sea water all me dam' life.'

'Oh, sea water is much better than river. The waves are more fun.'

'It is true you fin' sea horse an' pearl, Master Alan?' Jaillin wanted to know.

'I think so. And last year I got a pink starfish and a crab skin and millions of shells. . . . And a man gave me two lobster claws.'

I found it so easy to love them when I held the stage.

Alice at first refused to get in the estate jeep, which had come down for Kaiser, Jaillin and herself, and the extra luggage we wanted. Alice said she would walk wherever she had to go. I don't think in her whole life she had moved three miles from where she was born. In the old days that was often the case in Trinidad; now movement was less sluggish because of the search for work and for new houses, especially in the towns. And getting about was easier. People of Alice's generation had walked everywhere or gone in donkey carts. Their grandchildren had new buses and the trains to play with, and taxis penetrated even to the remotest villages quite cheaply.

'I 'fraid moto' car,' Alice moaned. 'I don' know how many people get kill like a lion by them.'

At last she was coaxed into getting in the jeep. 'Oh, Gawd! Oh, Gawd!' she murmured as it started off ever so gently for her. Later Kaiser laughed till his guts hurt, he said, because poor Alice got carsick and kept saying devils had come in her belly from the dam' moto' car.

All the drive over I thought how I would enjoy the holiday. Since the cockfight I had felt more uncomfortable with Kaiser and Jaillin than ever before, even when on a few occasions I was quite alone with them. I felt I had grown apart from them since that day. I remember for days afterwards the clothes they wore, dirty and ill-fitting, repelled me, something that had never happened before. I sneered at Kaiser's khaki pants with one leg longer than the other, and at Jaillin's shabby rose dress. What Jaillin had said stayed in my mind. Sometimes I did not bear to look at her lest she did something ugly, like picking her nose or spitting on the ground. Vulgar, my mind kept taunting me, vulgar. The thing that hurt me was that in her lively beauty I was now looking for meanness. In Kaiser also I searched to despise him. I was confused at why I did this. I felt myself a traitor against my will to love them more than any friend. I suppose I was beginning to feel acutely the contest between opinion and feeling: growing up, opinion ruled more and more. Now I felt in this holiday things suddenly would be easier, the power of opinion would fade to nothing, I could live near to the essentials I shared with them.

On the way my mother mentioned Kaiser and Jaillin.

'They have looked so much smarter lately. Jaillin has stopped wearing the worst of those horrible cut-down dresses. Kaiser has shoes on the whole time. And they both look *clean*. I wonder why.' My mother, turning the car-mirror to her, combed her bronze hair carefully.

'Of course,' my father said, 'their grandfather is a cultured man in his own right. Anyway, everybody seems to take his word for gospel. I know I heard him speak before a committee investigating a strike in the cane fields about two years ago and I thought him intelligent. Probably Kaiser and Jaillin have the luck . . . he probably has a lot to do with bringing them up.'

'Their father drinks too much, doesn't he?'

'Not really much more than anybody else, I expect. Kaiser says he doesn't have a tender hand with his wife or with cows. I expect the children get buffeted about a good bit too.'

'You know I saw him spearing frogs in a gutter the other day with a long sharp stick. He had six of them on a string . . . ugh, it made me sick . . . the villagers do these strange awful things . . . I don't understand. . . .'

'Must have been for food, dear . . . frogs can be a delicacy. . . .' For me the conversation petered out. I waited for a gap in it.

'Mum, why are Kaiser and Jaillin so vulgar? You know I saw Kaiser do number one behind a tree even when Jaillin was there once.'

'Alan, you know I have warned you about going around with Kaiser and Jaillin. I've told you time and time again that I don't want you to be with them so much. Dear, you'll have to speak to him about this. I don't mind you playing with them sometimes . . . I know Kaiser is a clever boy in many things . . . but you mustn't treat them as everyday friends. Do you ever see Alice or the washerwoman playing cards with us, son?'

I was silent. Then she remembered my question.

'Kaiser and Jaillin can't help how they behave, dear, they haven't been brought up properly, so they don't know what is nice and what isn't nice. Do you see?'

'But Kaiser knows about the rarest butterflies and all the birds and a lot of magic . . . and Jaillin . . . she . . . she . . . Well, they can learn about the nice things somewhere, can't they?'

'Remember they are different from you.'

The miles went by quickly. Just beyond Arima we had to put up the windows against a downpour of rain. Suddenly I could smell the leather cushions inside. Just before going Kaiser had polished them all and made them shine. The new polish scent reminded me of his arms going strongly backwards and forwards over the leather. He had seemed eager for the work. 'Gawd, I like moto' car, boy,' he said, kissing the shining leather ecstatically three times like a priest who bows to the altar.

We arrived at the green wooden house, called 'Wavereach Sunbonnet', by a road strewn with shells running in a myriad of turns between black-mossed coconut palms. As soon as we had helped carry the luggage in, Kaiser, Jaillin and I sped to the white beach fifty yards away. Kaiser and Jaillin stood for minutes considering the sea. The sea was calm. Waves came in small, spread-

ing lines of white bubbly foam only a little way up the bank of
sand. There in the bows and arcs of foam a few rainbows lit like
peacock's eyes for a second. Then that foam melted in the sun,
blew away in the wind, lost itself forever in the gold air, in the gold
sand. The waves went on rolling peacock's eyes up the beach.

'Mammy-oh! I never see a thing like dis! It true dat water
stretch itself all 'roun' the worl' so? It true it meet up wid Englan'
an' America an' mother India. An' whales running in it like
fire, eh? Jeeze n' ages, boy, I could be a sailorman every dam'
time I see the sea!'

Jaillin picked up a small pink shell and rubbed it with her
finger. Then she put it in a pocket of her dress.

'Dis whole week I going collec' shell an' mek a necklace fo'
Mam.'

We took off our shoes and went down the beach to where the
sand was wet. Kaiser made footprints just to watch the small
waves come and wipe them out. I showed him how a ball of sand
taken from that near the sea got soppy when I patted it many
times. He tried the trick himself time and time again.

'Well I never see mo',' he said. 'Jaillin, chile, come here an'
look at dis myst'ry.' And for her he patted another sandball wet.

Jaillin daintily lifted up her skirt a little and went into the sea.
She went gingerly as far as where waves splashed to her knees,
then she stood there uncertainly holding her rose skirt.

'Min' out fo' shark!' Kaiser shouted to frighten her. She glanced
at him quickly then went further in to show her defiance.

'Careful! Careful!' Kaiser mocked. Then he scooped water at
her with his hands laughing and laughing.

Jaillin shrieked. She let her skirt fall to touch the water, then
she waded in to splash at him furiously. In a moment they were
both laughing to tears, splashing the water anywhere so that it
showered in brilliants against the sky. They stumbled in the waves
and got wet right through. And they could not stop laughing.

I looked at them, amazed and envious. A red-sailed skiff bobbed
further out on the wind-chopped sea and I focused my eyes on
that, pretending to ignore those silly children.

The next thing I knew they had come closer, and shrieking with
laughter they splashed water over me fast. I felt the prickles of wet

99

through my thin shirt. I ran up the beach out of range, tears itching in my eyes, so angry at their fun. On the sand up there were scattered a few hard seeds, whitened in the sun, big potatoes that mysteriously came in with the waves from none knew what tree of Neptune. I took these up one after the other and without a word threw them as hard as I could at Kaiser and Jaillin, aiming to hit Kaiser at least.

He skipped about in the waves dodging the white seeds. He tried to catch one and the smart of it made him wring his fingers. All his antics he exaggerated and slowly I began to feel fits of laughter spreading up in me.

'What happen?' he shouted, and he pretended to fall flat in the waves. 'What happen?' he shouted, skipping about like a clown. And he made his voice a squeak so that I burst with laughing. 'What happen, big boy? What you bombarding we so for like we Germans? Boy, dese things as hard as donkey balls!' He caught one and threw it at a log of grey driftwood on the beach. He hit the log squarely. 'Sweet t'row, eh?' he shouted.

Jaillin stood in the shallow waves, quiet and still. Two of the seeds had gone near her.

I stopped throwing. In the pause Kaiser suddenly with a shout of laughter plunged at her. She squealed and tried to get away but he tackled her down into the waves. They came up spluttering and groping at the sun. The red-sailed boat rocked above them far out to sea. Gulls pursued it, creaking very faintly that distance away.

Then I burst out laughing with the fun of it all. I pranced quick down the beach laughing and laughing. Kaiser and Jaillin, wrestling in the waves, were laughing too. 'Look out! I'm tackling!' I shouted as I raced into the waves and dived near them. I came up gasping in the middle of them. Kaiser tried to duck me but I pulled him down too. Jaillin jumped on our backs and hammered us as we floundered. We sprayed each other splendidly in a three-cornered water-fight which jewelled the air with a maze of rainbows. My eyes stung with salt. I had the idea the water was becoming rose-coloured and hot. The noise of a whole ocean stretching around the world was drowned in the splashing and laughter.

We got tired and waded in to strand ourselves on the beach like strange, limbed fish pulled out of the sea by the beauty of sun and the ordinary wind. We were soaked quite to the skin. Jaillin's hair draggled watershining half way down her back; it had unravelled from the customary plaits and the silver ribbons that tied it that day were lost somewhere in the waves. The rose colour in her skirt was running a little; it sent trickles of pink down her brown thighs. Kaiser lay back on the white sand, his hands behind his head, and squinted into the sun.

'Boy, one thing I like is hot sun.'

'It true. Shadow only mek fo' spider,' said Jaillin.

'Ol' Boss say sun is de marrow of an Indian's bones.'

They were silent. Just offshore a pelican dropped like a bag of stones into the sea. It came bobbing up with a silvery fish in the tip of its bill.

'What snow is like, Master Alan?' Jaillin asked suddenly.

'Oh, I don't know at all. I've never seen snow. I've never been anywhere where snow is, you know.'

'But what is that at all. I thought all white people know what snow an' English thing like dat is.'

'But how d'you mean? I've always lived in Trinidad, nowhere else. How d'you expect me to know about snow?'

'You mean you is coolie jus' like we?' Kaiser asked.

'Coolie! I'm not a coolie!'

'You mus' be a coolie, boy. Which you eat, eh, apple or mango? Unless you is a force-ripe Englishman dress up in white flannel an' cork hat an' I don' know what else. No boy, you is a white coolie.'

'Well, I don't know . . . I don't know what you mean, Kaiser. I've never heard that before. White coolie. . . . Anyway, I do eat apples. Boats bring them from England and most of the time we keep some in the fridge.'

'Boy, you don' pick mango from a fridge tho'. You well pick it from a tree, birdstain an' all even. You ever see a apple wid birdstain, eh? You ever see a apple dat a bird *shit* on? Well, I bet you here dat is de bes' kin' of apple, de real sweetes' kin' of apple. An' you not going get dat kin' here 'cause apple don' *grow* here. Nice, nice, clean, force-ripe apple, dat is all, boy.'

'Well, I don't see what you mean. Apples taste lovely.'

'Even mango keskidee shit on better dan force-ripe apple.'

'You don't eat the nastiness, do you? What's that got to do with it?'

'Dat's what Ol' Boss say, boy. I expec' he have something big in he min'. You know how it is wid he. If he see a horse shit on the road he draw a conclusion. Anyhow, as you stan' here today, boy, I think you is a white coolie.'

I felt he was teasing me, knowing that I didn't like to be called a coolie. Jaillin was giggling.

'You're stupid. You're wrong. When I grow up I'm going to live in England. What about that, Mister Kaiser?'

'You only talking, boy. You ever eat cascadura? Eh . . . well you going come back den . . . you can' stop away for ever then. Anyhow, you not shame not to live where you born an' bring up big so? You know, boy, a humming-bird could pick out you' eye for dat. Dey revengeful fo' so wid people who gone 'way from lovely Trinidad easy like dat. One going pick out you' eye, boy, even if you is in Moscow. Look out, eh.'

'I don't believe that, you can't frighten me. Who ever heard of a humming-bird in Moscow, anyway!'

But I was a little nervous because he was very serious.

'Okay, boy, go on so. See what going happen one day. Mount Tucuche going fall on you' head. A Five Islan' sunset goin' burn you' eye out.'

'You know, Kaiser,' I said, 'you're another Old Boss. That's the thing.'

The red-sailed boat was still in sight. I pointed it out to Kaiser and Jaillin. 'Dey mus' be rich to have pretty sail so,' Kaiser said. Jaillin said the boat looked like a red water cockroach.

We got up from the beach. I felt my skin sticky with the salt from the sea that had dried there. We moved along the white bay-shore casually. Jaillin looked for shells all the time, finding here a glazed mother-of-pearl, there a pink slipper shell, and quaint hat shells which are easy to thread into necklaces because each has a hole at the tip of its richly-coloured, ridged cones; small Japanese hats they are. She called us to look when she got a very pretty one. Every time she called I went to see; Kaiser seldom went. Kaiser was hunting small sand-crabs with a stick. But they always got to their holes safely and dived down them in a little splutter of sand.

'Dey quick as a dam eye-wink,' Kaiser said. In exasperation he filled up their holes with sand. But at night they would easily dig their way out again and creep down to the waves under the moon, leaving those criss-cross tracks up and down the beach which every morning made it seem that strange birds had walked about all night. For some reason I used to think golden bees sucked at the core of the earth when it was dark out there on the sand, and left those signs.

When we had gone a few hundred yards I called out to them. We were coming to a small clearing off the beach where the Sea Madonna stood. It was famous in these parts.

'Kaiser! Jaillin! D'you know what we're coming to now?'

'Eh, man, what?'

'They call it the Sea Madonna. It's what they call a shrine. People put up candles for it and pray to keep the fishermen safe. It's Catholic.'

I told them about it.

The clearing was a hundred yards from the fishing village where boats called *Annie* and *Evening Lily* were drawn up under salty nets. At this place a rivulet trickled into the sea, on rainy days staining it brown with mud in a small arc. The good statue stood near the rivulet. In the fine season when the water was running clear the women of the village came down to wash their clothes and gossip, chatting about new cotton dresses from town and Nicholas, the village saga boy, built for bed. Afterwards they said a word of prayer at the statue of the Sea Madonna and put a coin for favour in the stone hollow at her feet.

The villagers told of how years before a red-bearded priest from Ireland had carved the statue from a thick branch of mahogany. He had worked at it for a year to make it perfect. He had worked so hard at it, they said, that he had even missed Masses on Sunday, so at last the bishop had dismissed him from the parish. But he had finished his statue. He cut the name 'Madonna of the Cruel Waves' in its brown-stone pedestal. Then he had blessed it and gone away. They said the thing was he had lost a girl to the sea once.

The lady has no lady-laced shoes. On the stone her bare feet stand strongly, kissed smooth by pilgrims who have come to pray there, asking for big mackerel in their catch or safety in evil weather. Her shawl is carved to fall about her shoulders like true cloth; it crumples into folds there, then falls straight to a belt of black cord, as if she fixed it in a hurried moment. The shawl is as white as bleached coral fan. The lady's carved black hair curls very lifelike from under the shawl. Her left cheek, dusky rose, is scarred by a thin wood knot. For her eyes, the priest inlaid river stones polished into jewel-ovals, smooth as the skin of melons. A mantle blue as the sea falls just to her ankles. Strung between two carved pockets on it is the priest's masterpiece, a rosary of wooden beads on a bright tin thread: the small gold beads are for the *Aves* and the scarlet beads, big as grapes, are for the *Paters*. At the end is a crucifix in jade cut by that priest from who knows what treasured private plaque. It has been so deftly done: take it between the fingers and you can see Christ has seven white teeth in His smile of agony, and you may feel each stone thorn of His crown.

Kaiser walked up to the statue slowly. He whistled, a gesture of admiration.

'Ey, boy! I never see mo'! Freeman could have carve dis.'

'Yes, it's even better than our drawing-room pillars.'

'She eyes looking straight at me, like dey really real,' Jaillin said from her distance.

'They say if you pray to her and put up a candle she really answers you.'

'How dat is? She have a power o' what?'

'I think so. She's Catholic, you know, and that's the real true religion. Last year I came once after dark and asked her to let me find a real red starfish with none of its legs missing because I'd only got two wounded ones. I put up a candle from the house. And, boy, the next morning I did find one. I spent hours searching and I did find one. And it was red all right. When it died it got grey and smelly but at first it was red all right.'

'She mus' have a power fo' true,' Kaiser said. He was always ready to believe in a magic thing.

I was holding the stage again and felt easy and happy. I was sure the Madonna was proud of me.

'But, hear me, Master Alan,' Jaillin said who had been looking in the Madonna's eyes all the time, 'you is Cat'olic, eh?'

'Yes.'

'Dat statue is Cat'olic too, eh? Well, I wonder if she would answer prayer from people who is not Cat'olic?'

I paused, not at all sure of the answer. Jaillin came up closer to the statue and touched its bare feet. Kaiser gave me a lead.

'If she have a power she have a power,' he said.

'Yes, I expect anyone can ask her for things and she might answer because she's so good. But it's better to be a Catholic.' I clung to my privilege. I had an inspiration. 'Probably when you're asking her you are a Catholic anyway.'

'Why we are not Cat'olics?' Jaillin asked Kaiser.

'What you asking me, chile? What we have to do wid Cat'olics? We have we own temple, we have we own prayer. What you want mo', eh?'

'But he say Cat'olic is the bes' sort o' thing to be.'

'He only saying. How he going know fo' true?'

'But it was the first,' I said. 'God told us we were the first and only ones.'

'You only saying, boy. Long, long time ago in mother India we had we God. Why you' God better? We is holy people, oui!'

I was puzzled and annoyed at the opposition. I knew I was right with a certainty engrained for many years but I felt helpless to convince Kaiser and Jaillin. I felt sure Kaiser was just spiting me by talking like this. They never seemed with me in anything I finally had to believe in. I looked for words.

'But . . . but that's pagan, I mean, heathen. That's not even as good as Anglican.'

'Boy, dat's you' sort o' word, oui. You know what you call by a whole lot o' people in the worl' . . . infidel, dat is what!'

'You'll go to hell!' I shouted furiously.

Kaiser lifted his hand. He was tight-lipped. Jaillin was peeping at us from behind the statue.

'Min' what you say! You think you is Mussolini! I might kick you up you' arse.' The anger had gone out of him though.

I calmed quickly this time.

'Well, I'm sorry.'

'All right. Boy, jus' because you white don' try force things down me t'roat, eh. We have we own way to live.' He was serious. He was defiant. 'Christ, man, you white people think you mus' be better everyhow, it not so you know.'

'All right, Kaiser, all right. Don't go on and on. I'm not saying we're better than you. Why do you always think that? I'm your friend, aren't I?'

'O.K. man. Yes, we is friend.'

Jaillin came out from behind the statue. She didn't look happy. She was smoothing her dress nervously.

Kaiser pulled her hair. She tossed away from him irritably. 'Whe' you was hiding, girl?'

'Behin' dere. You done quarrel?' Her face brightened. 'I stop me ears up so I didn't hear what all you was saying.'

'It wasn't anything anyway,' I said.

She was as eager to drop the matter as I was. She showed us a smudge of blue paint on a finger.

'It mus' have jus' paint. A piece behin' still wet.'

'Then they shoulda put up a notice . . . a notice wid "Beware Wet Paint", like I see one time on the Government Farm gate.'

'Don't be foolish, Kaiser. Who ever heard of putting up a notice like that on a holy statue!'

I saw a danger and went on quickly. I was glad to keep on external things.

'Joseph from the fishing village must have painted it. He paints it every year about this time. They say no one can do it so well as he can.'

'Joseph was a gruff fellow. People said he had been old and cross for as long as they knew him. You often saw him along the shore beachcombing. I wondered what things he found. Sometimes he helped to pull the seine but he never went out with the boats. He forecast the weather for the village. When he saw a soursop tree turn all its leaves on the silver side he warned about storms: it was one of the signs he used.

As a rule Joseph was not religious but the week in the year he repainted the statue of the Madonna, he saved his soul. At least I was sure of that. Every year he made beautiful something dedicated to the Mother of God and so to God Himself, therefore he would be saved. Just like the church-builders everywhere. I wanted to be sure in my own mind about this, because I meant to build a church or make a wonderful painting of Christ on the Cross when I was older and so go to heaven. I thought gruff Joseph a test case. I told Kaiser and Jaillin I thought he'd go to heaven for doing that painting job.

'Maybe so, boy,' Kaiser said. 'I don' know 'bout dat kin' o' thing . . . but yes, if she have a power she going reward he some way, dat is true.'

'Well, that's not exactly . . . well, I suppose so . . .'

'Anyhow, why you want to talk so much religion today, at all, boy? You is in church down here o' what?' He was poking fun at me; he wasn't annoyed.

Jaillin shook her head.

'You have to talk 'bout dat kin' o' thing sometime, he right. Ent Ol' Boss religious fo' so? He always in de temple; he always speaking wid de priests.'

'Religion fo' ol' people. What I concern? I going die soon or what? Anyhow, we religion is diff'rent so it no use talking.'

'It shouldn' . . . Oh, Gawd, every dam' thing different, eh!'

She clutched her hands hard, hard suddenly when she said that. We were silent. Kaiser looked at her darkly. I felt a surge of hurt, not definable. Jaillin's face relaxed. She opened her hands slowly. She looked down at them. Surprise gathered in her face. The nails of her middle fingers had pierced each palm and made them both bleed. She held her spread hands slightly towards us. We looked wonderingly at the blood coming out of the crescent marks. She looked down herself, half proud.

'Why de hell you do dat fo', chile!'

'I don' know. It happen.' She still looked at her hands, half surprised, half proud.

I was impressed by this thing, and wondered at it. I felt tender and loving towards Jaillin. I felt she had taken my part against Kaiser; perhaps I sensed she had made even a blood sacrifice for our friendship.

Jaillin took away her hands. She sucked the open palms, spat the blood on the ground.

Kaiser and I stood still and embarrassed. She had done some-

107

thing visibly powerful; a puzzle to know what it meant though. For a minute or two I concentrated on the sound the waves made and the palm wind. It came to me that the roar and whisper was not just the eternal background. It had a purpose of its own. It was going on in a straight line to some end. It had a gigantic task and it was getting on with it. Its task might be to wear away the whole island, or it might be something vaster, perhaps annihilate the universe itself, but whatever it was its concern was mighty and had no regard at all for our lives. Only Jaillin's gesture seemed to challenge its overwhelming victory.

The silence between us lengthened.

To get over the embarrassment, which was making me sweat, I spoke some more about the statue.

'You know, he painted it with a parrot's feather.'

'Why he do that at all? He mus' be chupid. He can' get fine-hair brush in shop, o' what?'

'Oh, it isn't that. He uses a brush to paint the fishpots. It's just that the priest who made the statue used a feather like that when he painted it, and now Joseph won't use anything else. Of course it takes him much longer.'

'I still say he chupid, boy. Anyhow, how he get a parrot feather at all?'

'Well . . . well how do you expect me to know?' Kaiser was irritating me on purpose I was sure. 'He could have just found it. Don't we just find bluebird feathers sometimes? You even found a dead humming-bird once in the hibiscus hedge, remember, with all its feathers. You said it died of old age. Perhaps Joseph found a dead parrot.' I was pleased with myself. I felt I had foiled Kaiser.

He looked up. A glint came in his eye which should have warned me.

'Parrot don' die, boy. Dey jus' live an' live till dey is a t'ousan' year old den dey . . . dey,' he paused only a fraction of a second, 'dey turn into mango bush.'

'Oh, blast, Kaiser, you know you're just being foolish . . . Parrots die, everything dies.'

'Why, boy,' he said, still keeping his serious face, 'you ever see a parrot dead? How you know?'

I was furious for the third time in an hour. I was helpless. It was unfair.

Suddenly, however, he let me off the hook. He said he was teasing. He showed plainly how his good humour had returned.

'O.K., boy, you is right all the way!' And he swept his hand around in a gesture which rubbed out our differences.

To get back to the house we walked inshore to the road, skirting the fisherman's village on the way. As we passed one of the huts there, three dingy potted zinias standing out of place on the window ledge, a shirtless man gutting a swordfish in the yard called out to me:

'Hi! Hi! Master Alan. You back dis year, den. How Mister Holmes an' Madam doing?'

'How d'you do. They are all right.' I said it hard. I remembered the man's face from the year before but I couldn't remember his name. I was sure he wasn't anybody special. To me he seemed too forward. I thought he didn't have the right to be so gay with me.

'You coming to fish fo' lobster tomorrow night, boy? You remember how you give we luck fo' so las' time, eh? You better come. You better dan de statue even!' And he laughed, stretching his worn neck towards us, showing his teeth. All the time his fingers automatically scooped in the swordfish.

So that's where I saw him, I remembered. Every Sunday night during the season they fished for lobsters by flambeau torchlight. It was just as much a holiday outing for the folk as it was business. I remembered the excitement last year: the dark water which here and there the smoky orange torches lit up in splashes of fire, the snapping red lobsters, the spear sticks, the laughter at the simplest things, so rare and important to people like that.

'I expect I will come again!' I wanted to show I was proud, that I did not approve of his manner.

'You bet, boy. You give we luck.' He grinned to himself. He threw some guts to a stray dog. I caught one of the swordfish's glassy eyes. It gazed somewhere beyond me and I was so foolish I nearly turned my head to see what it was looking at.

When we got away from the hut I let my excitement out.

'Yes, must go tomorrow night. It's really fun.' I told them about it. 'Mum and Dad'll let us go.'

'O.K., boy. What you say.'

'What do *you* say, Jaillin?'

'I don' know, you know. I never swim in water at night befo' . . . I think I might 'fraid.'

I was pleased. It gave me the feeling of protecting Jaillin.

'Oh, we'll look after you, Jaillin, don't you bother. You'll see, you'll really enjoy yourself.'

'I don' know.'

'She'll come, boy. She not so coward as dat.' Kaiser looked at her with a smile.

Jaillin didn't say anything more.

So that was settled. I was glad. It would be something I could share with them in which for once I would be the one who knew, the leader. I could take charge of things, I could point out highlights. Here was a chance to hold the stage, show them that I knew things about life which they did not know about, prove that I was superior at last out of my own resources and not because of what I represented. It would bring me nearer to them. Earlier, telling them about the Sea Madonna, bringing them into share what I knew already, I had felt the faint stirrings of that impression in my mind.

As if to give evidence at once to the thought, I suddenly found, turning a corner of the road, the chance to shine before them again.

What set me off now was the bridge which came into sight as we rounded the corner. It was nothing special itself, planks of pitch pine clamped down on iron girders, no handrails even, but I knew what we would be able to see up river when we got there and stood on it: a glassy stretch of river, then the eye would focus on another, more impressive, bridge. This bridge had long ago stood ruined, its fat white pillars sticking up out of the river slimed with green, its broken shafts of parapet, still decorated by two evil-faced gargoyles, resting on the pillars but not joined to either bank. This bridge must once have leaped across the river as beautiful as a white stallion. Now it was a poor greenish skeleton. The year before I had got the whole story from my father.

'Oh, I'll show you something when we get to that bridge,' I said. When we got there I pointed out the ruined bridge.

'See. There's a ruined palace in the trees there.' I was happy to see the impression I made. Kaiser and Jaillin looked eagerly where my finger pointed. 'I've been there,' I said proudly.

It wasn't a palace that had once stood there, only a large rambling building made of white stone and grotesquely decorated. But it must have seemed like a palace to those who had once lived near it in that out of the way corner of the island. Even now hereabouts there was nothing a quarter so grand as it must have been in its own time. In those days men must have conjectured, I could see, a hundred legends from its white, imposing beauty. Even nowadays its ruins, isolated in the trees, gave the impression of a broken shrine where perhaps ghosts prophesying still walked.

'A prince, or something, from Italy used to live there. You should see it. It has pretty floors, butterflies and birds and things in stone, but nut grass has grown right up over it, and lots of bush too. It hasn't got a roof any more. He used to have a roof to keep out the *stars* that fell, not the rain, that's what Dad said. That's funny as blast, isn't it? He was afraid of *stars* falling down on him!'

'It's a danger, boy. I hear 'bout a man one time who get hit by a star. It split he straight down in half!' Kaiser said, and cut his hand down through the air.

'Well, anyway, he wouldn't go out anywhere at night. Boy, you should see it. It must be marble or something. It's all hollow inside, you know. I went there once at night, you know . . . thousands and thousands of fireflies . . . blast, boy, it looked ghostly, I can tell you!' I'd never been there at night at all, but I was pleased my fancy had soared up to this height. It made an extra good story.

It wasn't all my fancy though. Some Italian had lived there more than a hundred years ago. Why he had built in that lonely place, why he had come at all, wasn't known. Perhaps he had been an exile. He had just come, lived there alone a number of years, and gone away. When he went away he had had the house and the bridge broken up. Of course legend had taken hold of him. Dozens of stories about him were kept in the village and round about. 'Boy, dat man used to walk tiger 'bout plain so, my gran'mam done tell me.' It had probably been a large dog. You heard how at night he talked to devils in a huge musical voice. One of the stories I heard really appealed to me.

'And you know what? Well, I'll tell you. Once he went and walked all along the beach throwing out *mermaid's* teeth from a bag. Mermaid's teeth are magic, you know. Joseph once found one. He said it's pretty as hell but you hear a magic sort of song night and day, night and day, until you throw it back in the sea. It might even have driven him mad, he said. Anyway, mermaid's teeth are very rare. They're hardly found at all.' I, the King of Fancy's Son, told them.

'Boy, dat is thing fo' true,' Kaiser said. 'I wonder whe' he get de mermaid teet'!' I could see Kaiser was interested. It was the sort of thing he really believed in. His face was serious.

'Oh, in Italy, I suppose, from mermaids. He probably caught them in a net like fish.' I was dignified and explanatory.

'Boy, if I could fin' one! I bet I wouldn't t'row it 'way so chupid!'

'If I could get one fo' Mam necklace, dat would be a thing in t'rut'!' Jaillin said.

'But they're bad magic,' I said. 'They might make you go mad.'

'I don't know, boy. I could give dem a kin' o' spell. Anyhow I going watch out, eh.'

'All right. We'll all look for them, shall we?'

We went back to the beach. I led the way. I had triumphed. All the way home we searched for mermaid's teeth.

I was flushed with success. As we came near the house I looked for a way to press my advantage in, making up another claim.

'You know, I have Italian blood in me. I think Mum's grandmother came from Italy. Perhaps she knew the prince even!' Why, I was a genius! The King of Fancy's Son.

Things fell apart.

'Maybe you have Indian blood running in you too besides!' Kaiser said.

The suggestion stunned me for a second. I never thought at all before I spoke. I never thought at all before I spoke. It cracked out from my reddened face.

'What! Don't be mad! I'm white, don't you see that? Well . . .'

'Why you would be so shame to have Indian blood mix in you?' Jaillin pounced on the terrible prejudice. 'Why you would be so shame at all? What wrong wit' Indian, say that?' Her eyes gleamed at me with tears—I thought of the red crescents in her palms. 'How many white man . . . Indian woman befo', say that? Dey *like* Indian den, eh?'

I squirmed and sweated. Kaiser thought it was too much.

'All right, girl. Tek it easy, tek it easy. He don' feel so much like that. It jus' surprise out from he. Eh, boy?'

'That's true, Jaillin, that's right. It just came out.' I hurried on with it. 'Perhaps . . . perhaps . . . I don't know, perhaps I do have Indian blood a little in me.'

She looked away from me. Suddenly she looked like a child.

'I don' know what . . . some place in India you know dey have Indian nearly white.' She blushed.

It was true that it had just come out. I hadn't meant to hurt them, but I could see now that it must have been cruel. The blood rose in my face. If anybody showed such disgust at the mention of white blood in them! All of a sudden I saw our position more clearly than I had ever seen it. The force called prejudice had spilled out in front of my eyes. What was I to think? It had come out of me naturally as a sneeze so I knew that it was not something I could easily get control of by conscious thought. A proper opinion about certain things I had engrained in me like religion. I felt now a little of the power that was wrenching our friendship apart. I would have to keep that automatic feeling hidden until I could conquer it. Yet that would be practising deception; and if I did succeed in the end then I would anger so many people, my mother, my father, so many people. I was growing up. Society was closing around me with its masks, distinctions, special instincts and cunning.

I walked behind them to the house. I clenched my hands and tried to make my palms bleed. But my nails were not long enough.

2

Sunday morning. The bells began to ring early. There were big iron ones in the church at Crossroads village more than a mile away, and these came, faint, sonorous, at steady long intervals; they were beating Matins. But those most insistent on the ears were the little brass bells of the chapel just up the beach. They were cat-on-hot-bricks bells, ringing sharp and quick, up-up and down, up-up and down, come on to church, come on. They were brisk and clear and full of music. Faintly I associated them with the word Virgin. When they rang they insisted that men should be good. Once I was up in the belfry to look at them: they were painted red and this shocked me because I expected that they would be white. I thought then, I don't know why, 'red is the colour of the heart, red is the colour of the heart.' From that moment the colour they rang was red, not white any more, just as the Crossroads bells rang elephant-grey and the cathedral bells in Port of Spain rang gold as the sun.

I was up early to go to six o'clock Mass. My mother and father would get up later and go at ten o'clock. To tell the truth, with so many exciting things to do, I wanted to get it over with. I didn't even think of skipping it because I had a deep sense of my soul in danger, but I wanted to have the duty of Mass finished quickly, early, so that I could have the whole day to myself. I thought, with no feeling of uneasiness or comedy, that after Mass God and I could safely go our own ways.

I met Kaiser and Jaillin on the beach. They had come out even earlier and bathed in the sea.

'Blast, boy, it must've been cold!' I said. 'It's really too early to bathe, you know.'

'It wasn't so col'. Anyhow we jump up fo' so, so we get warm. Dis sea business good, boy. The wind sweet like honey too besides.'

'You reach down here early you'self, Master Alan. Whe' you going dress up so nice so?'

'I'm going to Mass. You know, church. It's up there. Hear the bells?'

'I hear dem, Master Alan. I could go wid you?'

'Y . . . yes, Jaillin, if you want. Have you been before ever?'

'One time I went, yes, it was the Cat'olic Church by Tunapuna. Dat was long time tho'. Jess bring me, an' I remember white candle an' flower fo' so. Boy, I was frighten, there was so much white people in dat place. But Jess tell me, "Chile, dis is God's place, eh, you don' have to 'fraid white people here." You is the same as dem, girl, dat's what Jess tell me dat time.'

'Don' worry wid dat, girl,' Kaiser said. 'You can' be same as white people any place. Anyhow, what happen to you wid all dis church business? I going see by the village now. They going out fish soon soon. You coming?'

'Don' harass me, nuh!'

'All right, chile, don' fret if something happen.'

'What could happen, eh?'

'All right, chile, I not saying not'ing at all!'

Kaiser walked off down the beach in the direction of the fishing village. He kicked at the sand as if to say he didn't care a damn. Once or twice he bent down and searched with his fingers under stones and seaweed. Perhaps he was looking for mermaid's teeth.

I turned to face Jaillin. She pretended to be looking out over the sea where the sun was just rising out of the bank of green cloud at the horizon. The sun brought with it rose and gold. I saw a cloud that I thought looked like a fat man putting on his trousers.

'The sky pretty, eh?' Jaillin said, pointing.

'It is, isn't it? Dawn is always like Technicolor or something down here. You know, that's one thing grown-ups miss: they get up so late.'

'I don' know. Mam an' Pap up early every day.'

'Oh, yes, that's true.' I paused. I was puzzled at how it was difficult to get even small things on to a common level.

Jaillin was still looking out to the sea. The waves rolling in were stained with the blood of sharks fighting and huge goldfish skipped along the waves. But her eyes controlled that beauty; if they turned away the colour would get dull: Nature would cease taking pains to enchant.

'Hi, Jaillin, look!' I pointed up at the cloud. 'Don't you think it's funny?'

She looked up. Really now it was more as if he was pushing a wheelbarrow. Looking along my finger, Jaillin was puzzled and silent. Then she looked at me and laughed. I was glad.

'Yes, I see, boy! Crab walkin' funny, eh. You could see funny thing in the sky fo' true. One time I see Ramlal exac' image an' I nearly bawl wid laughing.'

I flushed. It is strange how hurt I was at this misunderstanding. After all, things like that happen every day, everywhere.

'No, Jaillin, that's . . . oh, don't worry . . . Look, we'll have to hurry. Church begins in a few minutes.'

We walked apart from each other, embarrassed. I had the feeling in me that a tension was growing fast between us which must soon reach a pitch and break. Everything had finally become so taut between us. The tension was not derived from the continual irritation of misunderstanding and difference. It was not the tension of growing distrust, though I think now that must have come in. It was the tension after all of growing together, not growing apart. Tension grows between two duellists as they come near to fight, tension grows between lovers as they come near to love; I think the tension between us was something like that, but not clear cut, a mixture rather of fear, wonder, annoyance, and a growing passion. As I walked with her I sensed that in the last day some new, intenser impulse had been generated. I remembered the crescent marks in her palms bleeding. With Kaiser not there it was even stronger. I think he knew more about what was going on than either of us.

Suddenly I noticed how drab and coarse Jaillin's clothes were. Oh, they weren't good enough to go to church in! It wasn't respectable. As we came up to the chapel, set like a white box among the palm trees twenty yards from the beach, I was frantically thinking of a way to get over this difficulty.

There were two entrances to the chapel, the large main entrance at the side and a small door at the back facing the sea. I thanked God for the back entrance. I took Jaillin around to the door and slipped in quickly. She was looking scared. I didn't even take time to dip my fingers in the holy water stoup. We sat in the last pew of all, at the end where the altar was half-hidden from us by a post on which was nailed a slotted black box marked 'Money for The Poor'. The chapel was crowded, but suddenly I realized that it was not Jaillin who was out of place, it was I. Nearly all there were fishermen and their wives who knew of no such thing as Sunday Best. Some of the young men were bare-chested. The women wore brightly coloured scarves on their head: those were their gloves, their lace, their jewellery. I suddenly noticed Jaillin had no head-covering. I took out my handkerchief and touched her on the arm, whispered:

'Hey, Jaillin, put this on your head. You're supposed to have something on when you come into Church.'

She looked scared. Without a word she tied the white handkerchief under her chin so that it bonneted her dark hair. I could smell the eau-de-cologne on the handkerchief.

We had come in late. At the altar the priest was sombrely, resonantly reciting the *Gloria in excelsis Deo*. He was a tall, thin, bony man with eyes like the Indian musicians—they saw beyond the kettle or the lily or the woman they happened to be watching at one moment or the other. He had been there the year before and had showed me the belfry. He had a long scar at the side of his throat which I made up all sorts of fantasies about. I had no doubt someone once had tried to cut his throat. He was a German.

'*Gloria in excelsis Deo, et in terra pax hominibus bonae voluntatis.*'

I leaned over to Jaillin again.

'Just follow what I do. And say whatever prayers you want to yourself.' I knew she couldn't read to follow the Mass in the missal I had with me.

Jaillin nodded. She followed me faithfully, kneeling, standing, genuflecting when I did. I was amused to see how awkwardly she made the sign of the Cross. I felt a million years older than the little girl. When the collection came around I put in three pennies for her, three pennies for myself.

'*Munda cor meum ac labia mea, omnipotens deus . . .*' Mass went on, but I couldn't concentrate. Jaillin did that better. She followed every movement of the priest with eyes intent on the beauty of his white and gold vestments, fixed to the sacred gestures of his hands, and his lips murmuring wonders she could not understand. When her eyes did leave him they turned raptly to watch the oil flaming in the ruby glass above the nave, the plaster stations of the cross lined along the walls. She craned to see one of those out of her sight.

'Don't fidget, Jaillin,' I said.

She watched an old woman in front of us who was whispering over her rosary, gnarled fingers caressing the huge wooden beads. I could see she wanted to ask a question about it, but she didn't dare speak. I touched her on the arm.

'That's a rosary, Jaillin, see it? Like the one on the statue. Each bead is a prayer.'

She nodded.

'If you say the rosary every day of your life you get to heaven,' I whispered.

I had lost the place. Before I could find it I saw it was time for the sermon. I think the one thing Father Adrian hated was making sermons. He grunted them out quickly and was done with it. He said things vividly though. I still remembered from three years ago a question he had asked: 'Why does God come to us in bread and not in a mango or a breadfruit?' I didn't remember the answer.

Father Adrian spoke briefly on the subject of theft. He said there had been an outbreak of petty stealing in the neighbourhood; even the chapel had suffered. 'What is the sense of going to hell for a few pence, a dishcloth, a silver knife and fork!' He was angry. I could see it in his stark face, his charred eyes. 'But that is what will happen to those who steal. They begin with small things, but small things twist the soul away from God in the end as well as big things. Yesterday someone stole a bag of lemons from Thomas' shop. His or her soul in that act twists away from God, my children. Look into your consciences, and if you are safe in your *own* consciences take care if it is necessary to look into the consciences of your friends in God who may not be in His house today. Warn them.'

The congregation shifted about uneasily while the short sermon was going on. A few men looked aggrieved, as if they were being accused personally. But the old woman in front paid no attention. She whispered over the rosary.

Jaillin had listened tensely to every word he said.

Father Adrian had a famous saying. Every Sunday after the sermon, before he said the Amen and went back to the altar, he glowered at his congregation, bowed low, and said:

'My children, we are all brothers and sisters in this world. Do

118

not be bitter. Love your brothers and sisters in God. Go in peace.'
And he bowed again.

It made me sit up quickly. I didn't remember from the years
before the strange, unvaried, pronouncement he became famous
for. But it struck me now. The hurt and uncertainty of true
action which groped deeper and deeper in my mind since I knew
Jaillin and Kaiser seemed to demand these words of authority.
They directed me to love her, not suspect difficulties nor believe in
the force of opinion I lived more and more in fear of. I looked
secretly at Jaillin. She was peeping at me too. I could see how long
her lashes were. We both jerked our heads straight in embarrassment. I felt the blood creeping up my neck. Oh, I didn't really
love her! I *could* if I wanted though: that's what the priest said.
I stuck my head deep in the missal.

'*Deus, qui humanae substantiae dignitatem mirabiliter condi-
disti . . .*' My body began to glow. I decided to show Jaillin how
the words went. I touched her.

'I'll read the words low to you. Listen: 'God, who in creating
human nature hast wonderfully dignified it . . .' She followed
my finger on the page intently. I felt as I never did feel again
except once, that we were safe and blessed, in that corner of the
chapel behind the poor box post. In the altar space two acolytes
robed in scarlet and white padded here and there on bare feet.
A clack-clack of the brass censer prepared me for the sweet, heavy
scent in the air. The blue puffs rose and soon the incense came
down to us. Jaillin made little sniffs at the air. She smiled ever so
slightly and spoke the only words she dared that morning in
chapel:

'That nice,' she whispered.

'Yes, it is.'

'*Accedat in nobis Dominus ignem sui amoris et flammam
aeternae caritatis,*' Father Adrian growled.

I giggled.

'He sounds cross, doesn't he?'

Jaillin was only prepared to be serious. She pointed her finger
in the missal. I went on reading again.

When the Communion bells rang I closed the book and got up.
Jaillin started to follow me.

'No.'

She looked at me, her eyes fled into darkness. I shook happiness off.

'You can't come if you're not a Catholic, Jaillin. You can't come.'

She crouched back in the pew. The old woman never stopped whispering over the rosary. It irritated me measurelessly.

The wafer of bread was sticking on the roof of my mouth when I came back. I made an unexpected sucking noise with my tongue getting it off. The heat began to creep up my neck again. How could I be proud? How could this be God that I was taking? Then I believed with terror that, thinking that, I was doomed in mortal sin. I almost spat out the bread, but I thought of the disgrace. In anguish I swallowed the Host in a small wet lump.

My eyes smarted. Oh, God, what had happened? I deeply felt that Jaillin was mixed up in this humiliation. She sat quiet, hands in lap, crouched in the corner of the pew. Was God in heaven vexed that I loved her, that I had brought her to His chapel? His priest had said I might love her. Why had I been made unhappy, like a sign? Jaillin looked so sad too. She wasn't taking an interest any more, sat almost huddled in her corner. I determined to defy God if necessary. I bent towards her.

'Jaillin, don't worry. I love you.'

She knelt down with me. We were so close we touched. I pointed out the words to her again. But the confiding moment of happiness had gone for good. Father Adrian was growling the Mass to a close.

I read for her.

'Pour forth upon us, O Lord, the spirit of Thy love, that by Thy mercy, Thou mayest make those of one mind whom Thou hast fed with one celestial food.'

God, let her share! But of all those people crammed in the chapel she was the one from whom I was furthest apart. I mocked the priest's words in my heart. I heard Tanner Evans, say 'Quite right, you know . . . dungcooker!'

Outside Jaillin handed me back the white handkerchief I had

lent her. The charged atmosphere in the chapel was almost blown away out here in the wind. A boy carrying fish passed on the beach; he whistled; he splashed his feet in the waves. The sun was up and beginning to burn the sand white, find glints of colour in each green throb of the sea. I drew a long breath. I had the impression that it had become unbearably stuffy in the chapel; outside I could breathe sweet air instead. I put on a blithe front in the hope that hurt had been cancelled.

'Well, Jaillin, how did you like. . . ?'

'Why, you didn' . . . ?'

'But Jaillin, it isn't allowed! I can't help it. You mustn't think it's me.'

'All right. What it is then?'

'Well, I don't know. I suppose the Pope or something. You aren't a Catholic . . . oh, I can't explain.'

'All right.'

'You liked the incense, didn't you? The powder's blue. I once got some on my little finger and it smelled sweet for days.'

'Yes, I like that. I like how you read as well as that. How you read so well so, Master Alan? You so young even.'

'Well, I just learned. Mum taught me, only the cat bit the dog, you know. Then I went to school. Well, I got ninety for English last exam. Did you like how I read, Jaillin?'

'Yes. One day I going learn like that.'

'Father Adrian reads well too. Of course he reads in Latin.'

'One day I going learn read that as well then.'

'Ha! Ha! What would Kaiser say if you talked to him in Latin! Frater Caesar! Frater Caesar! . . . I wonder where he is?'

'Master Alan, I now remember, you too modes'. You should have gone in the front place an' not hide you'self so. You not better than all those coolie fishermen people o' what? What you have nice clothes fo'?'

'Well . . . I didn't mind. That seat was the nearest, you know. Oh! I forgot to put anything in the poor box. I just remembered. Mum tells me always to, but I forgot.'

'Anyhow, I like it better than we temple. It not so tall an' big, but . . .'

'Oh, we have big ones too. You should see the cathedral in town! Pillars as tall as samaan trees, huge candlesticks on the altar. You should see it!'

'Anyhow, I saying it suit how I feel better, that is what. Gawd, don' tell Kaiser tho'! He would vex. I respec' we babus you know, I not saying no.'

'All right, Jaillin . . . Hey! Look! They're starting to pull the seine by there. We'll go and look, shall we? Boy, you should see the fishes they get sometimes. . . !'

'All right, Master Alan . . . Race you then!' And she was off.

I followed half-heartedly. She got there first, turned back towards me.

'You slow, eh.'

'I wasn't trying.'

'You too proud.'

The men were in two groups some way apart on the beach holding the long ropes. Far out the heavy seine net was being cast from two rowing-boats. Small squares of lead pinned the whole length of it under the waves while black corks kept it buoyant on the surface. When the net had all been paid out in the sea, a giant trap for fish, the men on shore began to drag it in. A low African chant like an interrupted groan accompanied the slow, slow tugs. A little jumping man gave the sad beat on a drum, yellow-skinned as evening sand, which hung on his bare stomach by straps of leather around his neck. His capering was in ridiculous contrast to the melancholy shout and his taut, serious face. The bobbing, cheerful black corks far out seemed to defy the sadness too. I wondered why these tough black men, clad in trousers of sailcloth, some wearing handkerchief hats against the sun and sweat, were so sad. Were they sorry for the fish they were going to catch? I knew it couldn't be that: their faces flashed with delight when they had a good catch. I remembered the gay songs I heard on the radio all the time—some of the old waltzes were sad, and 'Loch Lomond' and John McCormack singing 'She went to the Fair', but the radio didn't have these often. Why didn't they hum those tunes at their job? I could show them how: 'Baby with the Red Red Hair', that was a good one. Instead the slow chant dug in the stomach. In the village yard listening to the Indian wail rise above the emblemed drums I felt the same. I would not listen to it for choice (I'd switch on the radio and get the bright playful tunes), nobody would surely. It rasped, it made you imagine a particular day, 12 May 1962, when a bayonet would run into your stomach in some war. But there was something that made me glad I heard it, an ancestral gladness which had a vision of crucifixions, an elephant with a stake through its heart on a green hill in Africa, the dirt-grey Ganges drowning a bony, screaming man, flesh whipped into patterns on the backs of a thousand generations, pyramids falling into ruin, sadness, inescapable cruelty, the power of time—yet still maintained the sense of joy that men loved to be alive in the world. It was music which had stopped but never ended. The last, blood-filled note of a cornbird with a cut throat. I certainly could not explain or define the gladness to myself as I stood watching the negro fishermen haul on the salt, wet ropes, up to their knees in the waves, chanting low and sad on and on. I told Jaillin: 'It's silly, isn't it? They just go on and on the same. It makes me hurt in my stomach.'

Kaiser was pulling at one of the ropes. He didn't notice us at first. He was sweaty, hair was in his eyes, he looked happy as he pulled and groaned with the men.

'Look at Kaiser!'

'He always playing the fool like that!'

'What's wrong with it?'

'He lowering heself!'

'But, Jaillin, I've helped them pull too sometimes.'

'You all right. They know it would be a game wid you.'

Kaiser saw us. He laid off the rope, waved to us, came over. A man shouted at him: 'Whe' you going, boy?' 'I tired pull,' Kaiser called over his shoulder. 'You fo'get the money, boy!' 'Don' min' that. I done pulling.' He turned to us. The man rejoined the chant.

'So you finish wid church then. All you feeling like saint now o' what!' He laughed and whipped sweat off his forehead with a thumb.

'You better have respec', eh,' Jaillin said. 'You should have hear what the white pries' stan' up an' say. If you t'ief you gone to

123

hell, eh. An' you know how much mango you t'ief already from Mister Godfrey tree. An' that time you run 'way wid a top from Ramlal parlour. You better watch out, boy.'

'Don' talk chupidness, chile. Anyhow, what he know? He talking white man hell an' thing.'

'Oh, don't argue so much. Let's have fun. Look! The fish are beginning to jump already. That's mackerel, I bet.'

The net was coming in close now. The men were pulling faster and the chanting quickened in accordance. The little, tireless jumping man was dancing in a frenzy, working his drumbeat up to a tattoo. His features did not move in wonder or fun or joy. From the closing urn of broken water fish were jumping in the sun. They were frightened of the mask which drove them in, the water getting shallower and shallower. Again and again the sea unsheathed its silver swords. The pace of effort reached a climax. The ritual of the operation was forgotten. Each man pulled as hard and fast as he could and the drummer joined in. They remembered just the money they had to earn from the sea. Men were now waist-deep in the water seeing to it that the line of lead weights dragged along the bottom. Each heave of a big wave brought shouts of dismay: 'Oh, Gawd, if you see good fish gettin' way here!' 'You fuckers can' pull fas'er o' what!' 'You ignorant black people!' 'Pull the net! Dollar passing here!' 'Pull that rope!'

A man appeared beside us. He grinned.

'I bet the whole net full o' shark.' It was the man who the day before had spoken to me near the beach.

I looked at him sternly.

'You should be helping.'

He smiled ingratiatingly.

'All right, Master Alan, I going. How Mister Holmes today, eh?'

I didn't answer him. He went down to the water and took a rope.

The women who had come with their men were getting baskets ready. The children with them scampered about their legs getting more and more excited. We too were getting excited to see the treasure. The men and women rushed about grim-faced and flustered. After so many years they were concerned with what the fish would bring in the market and nothing else. One child got in the way and he was knocked down; no one paid attention to the little boy crying.

The separate groups of men came together. The net was dragging through a foot of water only and you could see the white bellies of fish writhing in a fury. Then in a last effort all the men rushed the net up dry on the beach. A blue handkerchief from one of the men's heads came off and floated away. He didn't notice it. Everyone was sweaty, chattering, happy. 'We pull like giant! We deserve a catch, man!'

Kaiser, Jaillin and I went down close to see. 'You should see the things they get!' I said.

It was a good catch. At least a score of mackerel flopped in the net; these alone made the catch worthwhile. There were some kingfish too, their small scales scurfing off like soap flakes in the struggle for life. But these common fish didn't interest us: you could see them any day cold and dead on slabs of wood in the market stalls. Only the dangerous, the spectacular, the weird were attractive. So we crowded around the three small hammerhead sharks that were caught. They seemed soft and safe creatures. Their long, curved mouths looked pathetic. When Grannie's false teeth come out it looks like that, I thought. Their hammer-shaped heads made them look clumsy. I was sorry for them at once. No one else was. A man right away came where they jerked every now and then, and clubbed them to death with a mallet of wood. 'Oh, don't do that! You don't want them. Throw them back!' The man laughed. 'They done dead! What happen? You want to get you' leg tek off in one when you bathing!' The sharks lay sandy and pathetic on the beach, blood staining their deformed heads. The man threw them in a basket; some poor people would pay a small price for shark flesh.

A whole basket was filled with peacock fish; the net must have picked up a school of them. Small, flat, coloured bright yellow, red, blue, they splashed the tarry net with beauty when it first came in. Now they still kicked in the basket. One jumped over the brim and lay on the sand like a jockey's cap. A woman speared it with a sharp stick and flipped it in again. I thought how it all seemed monstrously inhuman, as if they were just packing grape-fruit. Even fish should be treated gently.

A centre of interest for the children was the large tangled number of cutlass fish, long, thin, silver whips whose edges cut like knives if they caught you with a flick. Mothers shouted warnings continually: 'Min' out! How many time I done tell you min' whe' you stepping wid cutlass fish?' 'You hear me! Don' touch! It going cut you' han' open!' 'You think I bothering wid you any more, you harden' little chile! Move 'way!' If they had the time, these were the only fish the fishermen threw back. Even for bait they were useless. Today a man just scooped them into a basket, took it down to the sea, where he emptied the fish back into the waves. Most of them were dead and sank to the bottom like long curls of silver paper.

All the fish were soon cleared from the net into baskets. A few servants from the holiday houses had already come down to haggle for fish. I noticed the men took no part in this; their women did the job. The children found something to do with what remained in the net. All this consisted of was a mass of white huge jellyfish which had been swept in with the net. They had merged into one another until they looked like one colourless, icy mess of jelly, dotted with mauve seeds which once had been their separate vital centres. The children took the jelly up in handfuls, threw it at each other, shouting with laughter.

I held up one of the sharks by its tail.

'It's all such a filthy mess!' I said.

'I never see mo' in trut'. Look those little children like they throwing cotton ball 'bout only!'

'One time that was really 'live?' Jaillin whispered.

'Yes. But that kind doesn't sting, you know.'

'I feeling sick.'

'But, Jaillin, you don't feel sick when you see Kaiser chop off a fowl's neck . . . I do . . . but I don't feel sick at dead jellyfish. They're nothing.'

'I not 'custom see thing like that. I feeling sick.'

'All right, we'll go away.' I took her arm protectively.

'Len' me you' kerchief again, Master Alan. The smell mek me feel good.'

'All right. You can even keep it for good. Wear it when you say Catholic prayers or when you go to a Catholic church again.' I was quite serious, but I laughed.

'All you fo'getting me o' what?' Kaiser came in. 'I is a piece o' stick here! You only talking talking all the time wid each other.'

'You're jealous, Kaiser, that's what,' I joked, feeling powerful.

'Oh, ho, boy! You' think that? Boy, all you better look out, eh. You too young. You skin not colour the same way.' He turned away, and walked off.

'I don't know what he means, Jaillin. Don't bother with him.'

Jaillin said nothing. She gave little sniffs at the handkerchief.

The man who had said the net would be full of sharks, smiling, smiling, came up to us.

'What I tell you, Master Alan! You bring we luck, eh. Today catch wort' forty, fifty dollar. You better come tonight, Master Alan. An' too besides I going gi' you a lobster to tek bring you' Mam.'

'I may be there if I feel like it,' I said proudly.

Jaillin was silent, looking out to sea, a hot blue now.

'Race you back to the house!' I said.

3

'But why isn't Jaillin coming?'

'Well, boy, she say she 'fraid the sea when it dark. She hear fish breathing in it, she say. Don' bother, eh. I not so sorry she not coming.'

'Why? I'm sorry, and you're her brother, eh. I'm *very* sorry. She said she was coming.'

'You too concern wid she, Master Alan.' He was very serious, for he hardly ever called me that. 'I not good 'nough fo' you, boy, o' what?' His tone changed. He teased.

'Of course you are, Kaiser. I'm glad you've come. But it's always more fun if Jaillin's with us too, don't you think? The three of us. I just think it would be more fun, that's all. It doesn't really matter.'

'We could tell her all 'bout it after, eh. She will satisfy wid that.'

'Perhaps we could see her right afterwards and tell her?'

'She might a went to bed already. Enough time in the mornin', eh?'

'Yes, you're right I expect.'

We walked along the beach quickly. The night was so clear that it made me feel naked. For a change it was still as death. The three stars in Orion's belt sparkled so brightly that they seemed to ring like bells. Betelgeuse, my favourite star, burned red as the eye of a swamp crocodile. Beside us, out of deep black, waves rose up like luminous walls for a long, threatening second then curled over slowly to crash in a smother of white. There was a big swell coming in; probably a storm far out of sight caused that. The foam kicked up by the rollers stretched like a glowing white carpet on the edge of the black sea.

'It's rough tonight, isn't it?'

'Rough as hell, boy! I not swimming fo' nobody.'

'Well, Mum and Dad told me I mustn't go in on any account. They said just to watch.'

'They right, boy.'

'It's a pity though. Last year I caught a lobster myself. They showed me, but I got it myself all the same. It's quite easy with a spear stick. I could've shown you how. I wanted to show you and Jaillin.'

I was feeling depressed. This night had, since the day before, accumulated such a promise of glamour that the disasters which suddenly developed dampened my spirits completely. First of all my father just before had spoken to me so seriously that I was shaken and a little frightened by it. He told me that he would have to forbid me to play with Kaiser and Jaillin so much. This was the first time he had talked to me on the subject. My mother was silent now.

'But, Dad, there's no one to play with down here.'

'A Mr and Mrs Simpson are coming down tomorrow and they have two sons. Anyway, it was the same the last few years, wasn't it, son?'

I turned my head. My father continued.

'Alan, I hear you and Jaillin were in church together this morning. Now that is the sort of thing I mean. Son, you must have more respect for yourself. I'm not going to say anything more now but I will expect you to have less to do with them from now on.'

'But, Dad . . .'

'All right, son, that's all. It's not a serious matter really. I like Kaiser a lot, you know. But you'll understand when you get older. Now run along to your lobsters! But don't be late.'

And my mother had told me I must on no account swim, it was too rough. And now Jaillin had not come. Excitement dissolved away. Perhaps they had even spoken to Jaillin, told her not to come! I flushed with shame. No, they couldn't have done that. If they had . . . I'd be furious with them! I'd rebel! I hadn't really taken to heart what my father told me. I saw vaguely that it was an ultimatum in a sense that none of my mother's warnings had been. If my father spoke that was it, I knew. But I didn't picture myself taking direct and immediate action on his words. I couldn't suddenly imagine my friendship with Kaiser and Jaillin in a sense different from that I knew already. My mind refused even to think about such a changed tomorrow. I would go on acting as I had done before, and probably nothing would happen, just as nothing had happened when my mother warned me in the past. Something would turn up. When we got back home I would take steps. Anyway I had begun to feel too uncomfortable with them when I was at home, I thought, too insecure, so I probably would have acted differently even if my father hadn't spoken to me like that. But out here it was a different world. No one would stop me being their friend. In any case I was too excited by the new feeling I sensed had grown between Jaillin and myself to care much. That was the bitterest thing, that she had not come.

'Do Mum and Dad know you're coming, Kaiser?'

'What? No, I don' expec' so. I jus' come out from we room an' come.'

'Did Mum or Dad have a talk with you or Jaillin at all today?'

'How you mean, man? They tell me what work we have to do.'

'Oh, never mind. You don't understand.'

Down the beach about two hundred yards a line of rock speared out into the sea. There a score of flambeaux torches of pitch pine were burning a wild orange, pocks of flame in the dark. Some were steady, some moved excitedly here and there over the rock. So the lobster hunt had not been called off. It was rough enough for it to have been called off. Waves broke against the rock angrily, hissing, sent spurts of water flying like white dragons' tongues in the air. Every now and then spray would half put out one of the flambeaux. As we ran up to the rock I could hear the splutter as water hit the lighted torches: it sounded devilish, like hidden snakes which warned, subsided, warned, their poison ready. I began to be frightened. The suck and groan of the waves around the rock sounded like dying men.

'So you come, Master Alan!' It was the smiling man. He held a torch which now and then dropped pinkish sparks about him. The flame lighted his face on one side so that one half of his un-ending smile was lost in shadow. To me it seemed sinister: per-haps on that side of his face the smile suddenly twisted into a look of hatred which I could not see. Like most of the men there he had a big curved gutting knife stuck in his belt on one side and on the other a sharp-pointed stick. He had been into the water up to his chest and his body dripped with gold-brown pearls.

'Yes. I decided to come after all. It isn't a very good night for it though, is it?' I was meek.

'It rough, but don' min' that, Master Alan. You bring we luck now, I sure. Sometime rough night is the bes' for lobster.'

'Well, you mustn't blame me, you know, if . . . I brought Kaiser, perhaps *he* is bad luck.'

His smile got wider.

'You' luck mo' strong than he own, eh, Master Alan. You going see we going catch good tonight. But, eh, eh, I fo'getting! You want go down fo' one you'self? Come go.'

'No, no! You see, Mum told me I mustn't go in at all tonight. It's too rough. I'll just watch, thank you, though. Dad told me not to, too.'

'Well, don' min' that, Master Alan. I going catch one me own self fo' you.' And he went off towards the end of the rock where a number of torches had now collected in a bunch, a head of fire in the air.

I breathed slowly out with relief. I wasn't enjoying it at all. There was a tenseness in the air. Everybody was too excited. Men shouted to each other across the rock and flourished their torches. The element of danger spiced the whole party.

'Come by here, boy!' Kaiser shouted.

I went uneasily over to the head of the rock. Five women squatted down there holding torches high. The orange light squirmed below in the water like fiery sea horses. Every time a wave rolled in the horses butted against the black rock below and snorted with anger. The faces of the women were impassive, strained. One of the women mumbled a little, uneasily.

'I don't think I'll stay long, Kaiser. You can if you want to though, naturally.'

'Wha' happen, man? Look! Look whe' they going!'

The water below the head of rock was really quite shallow; it was low tide; only when one of the rollers heaved in did the depth get near the height of a man. A number of the men had climbed down the rock and were picking their way forward in the sea. They worked in pairs. One man held the torch over the water, and the other every so often, when no roller heaved in, ducked his head under, searched with his hands for a lobster in the hidden crevices of rock. In one hand he carried his spear stick ready. The torchlight was supposed to mystify the lobsters and lure them out of their hiding-places. The torchmen stood like dark statues grotesquely lit while their partners bent at their knees as if at sacrifice, and drowned themselves momentarily, it seemed, in some terrible rite. When the big waves rolled in the two men stood and braced themselves against the lifting water; the man with the torch held it up far over the dark surging back of water, let himself ride with the wave, found bottom again; his companion some-times, in fun or pride, struggled all he knew not to give an inch. I had the feeling that a deadly struggle was in progress. Grave-yard feelings crept in me. The torches became hectic flowers burning over a world of darkness, turbulence, and danger.

'They'll never catch anything,' I said despairingly. 'It's too rough.' Everything to me seemed doomed to failure.

'They catch already, boy. So what you saying? Look there, eh.'

I looked and saw that behind the five women a number of baskets stood, and in one of these five lobsters, perhaps more, lay tied in brown string. Only their long speckled feelers moved at all; it seemed to me that they waved not in hurt and surrender but in a hideous gloating triumph. I thought with a shock of horror of the lurking crabs up the river. The lobsters were not beaten; they would escape; finally they would tear the men and women to pieces, and me as well.

Kaiser's excitement was rising the whole time. The dark, the magic torches, the big dangerous waves, seemed to get his blood up.

'I going down too, boy! I going catch one!'

He began to climb down the rock, slipping a little in his bare feet. I didn't try to stop him. Let him go down, I wouldn't have a thing to do with it: I decided I wasn't in the mood after all. While he was in the sea I would take the chance to slip away and return to the house. The smiling man was also in the sea, so he wouldn't notice me go either. I didn't want anyone to think that I was a coward. I began to walk casually back along the rock. Spray had collected in small pools here and there; starlight jangled in the dark, tiny oval mirrors: I felt I could pick them up like a piece of glass or a shell; Jaillin would admire a rock-cup of water for her mother's necklace! I stopped and pretended to look with interest over the rock's side so that no one would suspect that I was frightened and going away for good. I shuddered to hear there only the groans of men dying.

There was a shout of agony from the sea back at the end of the rock. 'Oh, Gawd! Oh, Gawd! Oh, Gawd!' I heard a woman scream. It galvanized me. I no longer hesitated for reasons of pride. I took to my heels and sped for the beach. As I went I heard faintly the raised voice of a man:

'It all right, woman! It all right! It only Packo get bite by a dam' eel!'

It was a trap, I knew: the lobsters had got him; the lobsters would get all of them. I raced on till I got safely to the beach, then I slowed, breathing easier. My heart was pounding.

My depression was overcome by growing, superstitious fear for a while, but now it returned worse than ever. The whole world seemed lifeless as I walked very slowly back along the beach towards the house.

All of a sudden I noticed a glint of light off the beach between the trees. I stopped and was curious for a second what it was. In my state of mind I was ready to believe in soucayants; they sometimes appeared as balls of white fire. Then I remembered: it was the statue of the Sea Madonna, lit by candles. But why hadn't I seen it when coming up the beach? I went to see who might perhaps be praying there offering a candle. The idea took hold of me. I decided to say a prayer myself.

And it was Jaillin. I stood quiet as a stone. Warmth spread in me, whether of embarrassment or pleasure or excitement I do not know. Jaillin hadn't heard me coming and I did not call to her. She was kneeling in front of the Sea Madonna, her head deeply bowed. She had fastened the kerchief I gave her beneath her chin; it bonneted her dark hair which fell out under it in disorder. Her feet were bare, and she was wriggling her toes in an agony of concentration. Four long white candles stood in the iron notches on each side of the statue, burning straight and clear. Jaillin held her right hand on the chaplet strung across the Madonna's blue mantle; the candlelight gleamed on the tin thread. I watched her slip her fingers from a *Pater* bead, big as a grape, to an *Ave* bead. Each she rubbed in wonder between her fingers.

'But Jaillin, what are you doing?' I whispered. She did not hear.

I stepped very softly towards her. The impact of every moment hurt as if time had armed itself with the power to inflict actual physical pain. Everything had an intenser value: my feet crushed golden dust; all around stems of ebony curved upwards to a world of emerald fans; the cheeks of the Madonna glowed in the candlelight with the rose of human blood.

I touched Jaillin ever so gently on the shoulder. Her body stiffened upright as if all of it had suddenly become bone. Then she collapsed low on her knees. I thought she had fainted. 'Jaillin . . .' She twisted around and I saw her eyes full of hurt, fear and excitement.

'It you, then, Master Alan.' Her voice was calm, calm. It surprised me; I think I had expected a sort of passion.

'Yes. It's me, Jaillin. What are you doing?'

She ignored the question.

'I t'ought you gone fish fo' lobster. What happen?'

'I was afraid. But, Jaillin, what *are* you doing? You must tell me.'

'I was praying, you didn' see? Like you tell me, jus' that way so. Each bead is a prayer an' I say a prayer every time I hol' on a diff'rent one.'

'But you don't know how to say the rosary, Jaillin. You must have made up your own prayers.'

'Master Alan, you mus'n't say that at all.' Her voice went high to the edge of tears. 'I is not funny. Why you say I is funny at all?'

'Oh, Jaillin, I promise you, I promise, I didn't mean it like that. But why didn't you tell me; I would've come with you and helped.'

'I have my own prayer to say.'

'All right, Jaillin, but you must say the real ones first. I know. I'll show you right now, right this minute, shall I?'

'Master Alan . . . you' Mam . . .'

'But, Jaillin, where did you get the candles?'

She blushed.

'I borrow them from the house. I going put them back when I get back. They only would be a little bit burn.'

'Yes. I could say I borrowed them. We'll say the prayers now.'

I knelt beside her and guided her fingers on the chaplet. I told her to say the *Ave Maria* and the *Pater Noster* after me. I whispered them slowly and she followed.

'We'll only say a decade. The whole thing's too long. But if you learn the prayers by heart you can say it all whenever you like.'

'I like that.'

'Well, I'm glad, Jaillin. I'll teach you another prayer. You should always try and say this one when you're praying to the

Virgin. It's called the Litany. You can say it after me if you like.'

I had forgotten everything but the place and moment. At the foot of the candlelit statue the world stripped down to a few things—the Madonna, the power of God in it, Jaillin, and myself. A sort of exaltation seized me. My voice must have got louder and louder.

'. . . Mystical Rose, Pray for us,

'Tower of David, Pray for us,

'Tower of Ivory, Pray for us,

'House of Gold, Pray for us,

'Ark of the Covenant, Pray for us,

'Gate of Heaven, Pray for us,

'Morning Star, Pray for us . . .'

A twig cracked somewhere, like a dove's bone broken. I started.

'Oh! It was too loud. Were you saying it after me?'

'Yes, Master Alan, but sof'er.'

'It's beautiful, isn't it?'

'I don' understan' it too good.'

'Never mind. Now just say a quick prayer of your own and I'll say one of *my* own then I think we'd better go. They told me to come back quickly.'

'All right, then.'

We bowed forward to the Madonna and our brows touched. I was too confused to say a prayer so I just waited for a few moments then got up. Jaillin looked up at me and got more slowly to her feet.

'You say a quick prayer?'

'Well, yes. Weren't you finished yours?'

'I was jus' saying over what I prayed befo'.'

I took the candles from the notches and blew them out, then I put two of them in each trouser pocket. The Madonna was wrapped again in darkness, her arms stretched out pleading to the waves, blessing them invisibly.

'Well, let's go, Jaillin.'

'We better go back separate, Master Alan.'

'Why?'

'You' Mam goin' vex.'

135

'Well, she won't see us. We'll just creep back in like ghosts. I'll go in and say I was out on the rocks fishing for lobsters.'

'You' Mam . . .'

'Don't worry, Jaillin. It'll be all right, really.'

We walked out on to the beach. I breathed the sea-smell deeply, the smell of leather and tamarinds and the oyster man who came every week. Not a cloud in all the sky. It seemed the sky was more full of stars than I had ever seen it. I pointed out Betelgeuse, the red giant. I knew it would be dead, grey, in a million million years: the book said so. I would have liked to watch it all that time, gradually shining less red.

'Look! That's my favourite star.'

'True?' She hardly looked.

We walked along in a silence which strained at some big expression.

'Jaillin . . . Jaillin . . .'

'Yes? What it is, boy?'

'Jaillin . . . I want to hold your hand . . .'

She gave me her hand, let her hair fall, brushed it away.

'Does it hurt where you cut them.'

'Yes.' I held her hand more gently.

We went on more and more slowly. I heard the stirring of crabs along the sand. Somewhere or other we stopped completely. We looked at each other, quiet as at the centre of a stone. Jaillin turned her head towards the sea.

'Master Alan, le' we go in the sea an' bathe.'

'Yes. All right. I was . . . thinking of that . . . I think I was.'

'I felt so, boy.'

Jaillin took off her clothes quickly, without any show of embarrassment. When she was naked she stretched in the night as if she was proud of her body in front of me.

It was slender, brown, awkward as a young deer. I undressed with more hesitation, pretending to fold my shirt carefully, bending deliberately to untie my shoelaces. She waited for me patiently. In the end when I was ready, she laughed and put out her hand.

'Come go. Le' we run straight in one time.'

The carpet of foam glowed as if struck by moonlight. The sea wreathed and eddied around our feet very cold. The powers

136

of each wave were diminished here to a crest of bubbles, but as we went gingerly forward hand in hand the crests rose higher up our legs and the broken waves got gradually colder, deeper, more powerful.

'It's cold at night, cold as ice.'

'I don' feel so col' but I 'fraid the big wave little bit.'

'Oh, don't worry, Jaillin. We'll get through them all right and it's easy to swim when they haven't broken yet.'

'Hol' me good then.'

'All right. Don't worry. Look, I'm diving under now to get all wet.'

We both dived under. I realized how much whiteness there is in the dark when I looked up towards the surface; it glowed there like glass. I came up gasping with the shock of cold, smiling. I found Jaillin smiling too.

'You know something, Master Alan, I never went in water at night befo'. An' I think I hear fish breathing. But I not 'fraid now.'

'I've been in before at night quite often . . . But this seems different you know, Jaillin. It's exciting.'

I held her hand again. Her wet hair gleamed. It was darker than the night yet it was more full of brightness. I began to feel a complete peace coming into me. The only problem left in the world was to get beyond the breaking wave; everything would be confiding quiet happiness then.

Soon we had to brace ourselves against the strength of the water. I held Jaillin steady. Her skin felt warm in all that cold. She shivered just a little. The luminous walls looked menacing but I didn't feel any fear any longer.

'Jaillin, look, we'll just go on. When we see a wave going to break we'll duck deep under it and come out on the other side. I'll hold on to you so you'll be safe. The big ones don't come in very often so it'll be easy.'

She nodded.

Jaillin and I could swim well so it was easy. We swam deep under two big rollers, our stomachs scraping the sand. There was a slight wrench as each wave crashed down behind but that was all. Under water I felt pieces of seaweed drifting about in the currents. I felt Jaillin flinch as one piece eddied past her face. Before we came up I kissed her on the cheek.

Treading water, we floated in the sea beyond the line of breaking waves. As each roller heaved in from a thousand miles away we soared up on its back then settled gently down again. We stayed close together.

'It's lovely. It's like a roller coaster . . . Like a hammock.'

'It mek you feel you is a bird.'

'Yes, that's true. Like those scissor-tail swallows and how they *swoop* up, *swoop* down, over the rice fields. You know?'

'Jus' like that fo' true.'

In this place where the waves had ceased to burst into whiteness it became a hundred times darker than before. The sky was all at once a pure polished black in which the stars shone like pin-tops in a satin cushion. The sea slid by cold stained by a million octopus. No fear though. Above everything the sense almost of desolation, the world all gone away to die, leaving us alone, alone, secure, the only children in the world. I whispered and she whispered.

'Let's stay all night here.'

'We would get tired, boy.'

'We can float on our backs all the time right till morning.'

'We would get col', boy.'

'I could keep you warm.'

'How, boy, how?'

'I don't know, Jaillin.'

'When you grow up big . . .'

'When I am grown up . . .'

'What?'

'I don't know.'

'You skin feel smooth, boy.'

'So does yours, very smooth. I like touching your skin.'

'I barely see it is white at all, you could be a Indian.'

'No. We both could be anything we wanted. Let's pretend we're purple or green or blue. Let's pretend.'

'You really chupid, boy, you mek me laugh.'

'Jaillin . . . Jaillin . . .'

I was tired with emotion that was all spent and I wanted rest.

A roller big as a hill lifted us up. At first it shocked me to see how far away the carpet of whiteness was from us, then it pleased me.

'We're drifting further out, you know, Jaillin.'

'True? Master Alan, you think we could drown here?'

'I don't know. I wouldn't mind though, with you.'

'What you saying!'

'Jaillin, let's drown each other.'

'You mad in trut'. Don' talk so.'

'I'm tired.'

'Le' we go back, boy.'

'No . . . Jaillin . . . Jaillin, what did you pray for?'

'Don' min'.'

'You must tell me or I'll drown you.'

'You joking, boy.'

'Well, what were you praying for at the Madonna?'

'I really cold now. Le' we go in.'

'You must tell me, Jaillin, you must.'

'Well, boy . . . boy . . .'

Suddenly we stiffened into silence, listened towards the beach. A low shout was repeated two or three times.

'Oh, Gawd, Master Alan, who it is?'

'I think it's Kaiser. I'd forgotten him.'

The low shouts were repeated nearer. They came distinctly, 'Jaillin! Jaillin!'

'What is it, Kaiser? We hear you.'

There was a sudden quiet, then the splashes came fast in our direction. Kaiser called hoarsely.

'Oh, Gawd, chile, oh, Gawd, what you do!'

'Kaiser, what's the matter with you?' I said. Jaillin was crying suddenly, so that you could hear her.

'Oh, Gawd, Jaillin, chile! Mister Holmes an' Madam coming down. Look what you do! Oh, Gawd!' He was in an agony of fright and despair. He wasn't angry with Jaillin; despair never thinks of anger. She was crying and would not say a word.

'How do they know we're here? How did *you* know?' I asked.

'I fin' you clo'es. Oh, Gawd, Jaillin, it happen. You get us fire an' wha' Pap going say? What happen wid you?' A flash of anger.

'They won't find us,' I said. 'We'll keep quiet and they'll go past and we can go back secretly, you see.'

I felt relieved. Why were they so shattered with fear? At once I half despised them.

Now after all I was stronger, fearless, the better man.

A loud shout sounded from the beach: 'Alan!' It was my father.

'Oh, Gawd! Oh, Gawd!' Kaiser whispered.

My father shouted again.

'Alan! Come in now! I know you're there. Tell Kaiser and Jaillin to come out with you.'

We stayed quiet. Jaillin and Kaiser were close together and I had drifted apart from them. My heart and mind hardened against them. The indifference which gripped me more and more made them seem abject to me. They had done wrong; I was a victim; now I was free from them and it didn't matter any longer. In the terrible reaction I felt emptied of everything except a hard and thoughtless cold. A spasm had gutted me of every old emotion.

'Oh, do stop crying, Jaillin!'

'Alan! Come in!' My father called out again.

'Well,' I said to Kaiser and Jaillin, 'it's nothing much anyway. He'll scold us, that's about all. We'll say what fun it was swimming in the dark. Come on.' I began to swim in.

'Oh, Gawd, Master Alan, whe' you going?' Kaiser pleaded to me.

'We can't just stay and drown, Kaiser. Have sense. Anyway, they'll soon find us. He saw where you came in. I'm going in.'

Jaillin retched in the sea. It was so ugly. Then she said in a little voice that had nothing in it, fear or anything, and it touched me like a flame.

'An' I is naked . . . boy, I is naked, you know.'

'I'll explain to Dad. It'll be all right . . . Coming, Dad!'

I swam back in well ahead of Kaiser and Jaillin. My father was waiting up the beach.

'Go back to the house, Alan, and get dressed. I'll wait here for Kaiser and Jaillin. Go back and get dressed now.'

I picked up my clothes. Jaillin's dress lay in a small heap a few yards away, and I started, paled, to see it, as if she had died and this was a sudden memory of her. I ran away up the beach, glad not to have to listen to what he said to them.

5

🎠 Carnival

I

Kaiser and Jaillin, they were sacked for good. I endured at first the direct reproach of my parents' sad anger, afterwards their forgiveness of what they realized was an immature folly on my part. They allowed for that in a boy.

Kaiser and Jaillin were sent back the morning after that night. It was sudden and final. I was used to nice transitions of mood and action, the one more chance given before punishment, the immunity from unwarned hurt or any real disaster, so I saw the difference in this. From a window of the house I peeped at them as they got in the estate car and were driven off. Kaiser carried his red sack of belongings in complete dejection; it looked heavy as if it was full of stones and tears. He was abject and defeated to an extent I had never imagined he could come. His clothes were unkempt like a clown's. His whole body trailed like a wounded, weak animal. I found that I despised him. But Jaillin I saw was strangely proud. Her hair was perfectly combed into a fall of satin; that measured pride. She wore her silver earrings and that measured pride. And she flung the long hair about like a fierce woman I had seen in a film. She had made a bag of my handkerchief and carried it now full of the shells she had already collected for her mother's necklace, Japanese hat shells, slippers, bat-snouted shells, crowns and lyre shells, mauve, red and silver, and flushed with salmon colour. A bag of sand-trinkets soon to be ordered into a fashionable noose. I thought of her bad-tempered, withered mother wearing the bright necklace while she milked smelly, crow-perched cows, collected dung in a pail for the lettuce and sweet potato beds, took the pips off chicken's tongues, gouged calabashes into bowls for water, sifted the nests of wood ants for their speckles of pupae, hammered nails into a rice-box long and small as a coffin. In time Jaillin would wear the shells, for with them each gift was given down the generations, like a Wedgwood china set. And in time Jaillin would also grumble and grow old over her mother's undone occupations. That was their life; I had my different life to live; at last I made the distinction actual and sharp in my mind; it came out of the subconscious, like a bird, or a bat, out of a cave into evening. Sad at the window I remembered the hoot of owls in the village, and the white walls of the huts, the marble-players in the dust playing for that gilt button as for a perilous diamond, the temple pennons stuck up in red and blue and white triangles on a bamboo pole, peacocks painted in the blue corridors, a pot of corn spilled under the hooves of huge-testicled oxen, the flies on that dead dog under the casuarina tree and the barbs of scarlet ibises in a Madonna-gown sky. A child is as unsentimental as a cynic. Nostalgia for him is just the insistent mental demand for a previous pleasure, is not nostalgia at all, not the pleasure of memory, sweet or harsh, for memory's sake. But a child then grows into a sentimental and nostalgic attitude, some more, or more suddenly, than others. At the window I was overwhelmed by the hurt and beauty of the past just because it was the past and would not come again in that way. The green hutches to hide in that we made out of the cane fields, and the smell of rum at Ramlal's, the sari I had once seen Jaillin wear . . . The estate car started up with a bang of sound. For a long time it went along the bad road through the coconuts in bottom gear and I could hear the engine straining at that pitch; then the driver changed into second and the car went smoother and smoother out of hearing.

On the ground below the window two brown doves settled down from a loblolly tree. They were flirting with each other, chirruping noisily, scattering their wings. Continually the male was picking up and putting down a jumby bead shining like a little garnet. He was tempting the female with the most vivid grace. He turned little circles with the red seed in his beak, he dropped it, picked it up again, he seemed to half-offer it to his female, then he withdrew the prize again. She all the time made a tiny dance to him. All of a sudden, for one moment, his gaiety stopped. It was as if the little bird had abruptly remembered something important. His small, skittish body got still; in a brief, indistinct movement he deposited a spurt of excrement in the dust. Then he went back to the lovely game, putting the bead down, chirruping delightedly, picking the bead up again, making a tiny dance of it. Looking at them secretly I thought how funny, how strange, if humans played their games with a regard like that for the niceties of behaviour. I imagined there would be no obstacles to the enjoyment of life. I saw the dreadful capacity of people for being embarrassed, for attending to any aged opinion. A dove is not embarrassed, I thought, the joined marbleus are not embarrassed; I am always embarrassed. I was jealous of the birds. And I was slightly disgusted. Maliciously I waved my arms at them and they flew off, leaving their courting pearl forgotten on the ground. Good! I had spoilt their game.

Afterwards in that room my father spoke to me seriously. He told me all the things I expected to hear, dreaded to hear because now I more than half-believed them. He didn't mention the night before bathing naked with Jaillin; later I gathered from my mother that they had told Jaillin not to go out with us. He told me it was best that I shouldn't see Kaiser or Jaillin again, that I should not visit the village any more when I got back home.

'All right, Dad. I was getting not to like them anyway. They're too coarse, aren't they?'

'Now, don't think you're getting any sympathy. You're trying to put the blame on them. Don't do that, don't pretend. If you realize the position now, well and good. You acted stupidly when you should have known better. Now I'm sure you'll go on fine. But what you have you're lucky to have. Please remember that.

'All right.'

'By the way, those boys have arrived next door. You'll have someone to play with.'

But I made a sacrifice to the older friendship. I did not want to make the sacrifice. Kaiser and Jaillin had now officially been put beyond my further concern and I was easy, eager to have it so. No doubt the new friends would be a lot of fun, not make me nearly so uncomfortable. I wanted to find out. But I was prompted by a loyalty for the past which overcame the urge to have done with unpleasantness, go on to a near pleasure. It was a matter of will; I was rather proud of it and rather puzzled. I stayed in the house all the day, pointedly I did not go out, though the beach burned gloriously in the sun like a coat of gold and the sea roared a big welcome.

'You're sulking, Alan,' my mother said. 'What's the use?'

'No, I'm not. I'm just not feeling very well today. I think I might have got a cold. That's all.' Dignity mingled with irritation and bitterness.

I didn't see much of Kaiser and Jaillin for many years. Occasionally I passed one or other of them on the road; then I raised my hand in polite salute, murmured something indistinctly; and each would make a gesture of the hand too, try half a smile. At first these meetings had the intimacy at least of shared embarrassment: as we got near each other I could see Kaiser or Jaillin begin to fidget with shyness, begin to search for something with their eyes, a singing bird, a tree against the sky, a hedge flower, to look at, and so did I, so that each of us could avoid the greeting of eyes until that last moment of pretended surprise. And on those occasions my ears tingled, my neck glowed warmly, sweat broke out a little, and at the end I had to sigh with relief. But as time went on this changed. It no longer mattered one way or the other. Sometimes even I did not hesitate to walk by them on the road as if they were stones or unknown people.

Once or twice, though, it pained me as I passed her with a nod to see how Jaillin was growing into beauty more and more. One morning, about three years after we had gone apart, I met her under one of the plum trees by the railway line. There was no one about so I stopped. She stopped too and raised her hand to her hair in that familiar movement. She was dressed for some festival, probably a wedding in the village. She wore a sari of heavy silk squared in colours; the new cloth shone like a parrot in a cage. She had slippers of blue felt on; buckles like square gold coins clasped each at the instep; the heels flapped loose when she walked. She had on earrings different from the silver ones that were her mother's: these were clear mother-of-pearl drops on a pin-stick of silver and they hung like raindrops heavy but not quite falling on a twig. Blunt icicles of glass hung round her neck on a piece of cord, as if a small chandelier had been broken up to provide the pieces. This ornament looked tawdry compared with what else she wore and the lapse in taste comforted me against her beauty. Lines of dark colouring stretched the shape of her eyes and made a cleaner arc of her eyebrows. She had a blob of scarlet in the middle of her forehead, as if, I thought, a child had aimed well one of those play arrows with a tinted rubber cap. It was a religious emblem but I did not know this; I thought perhaps it was a kind of make-up, like lipstick, for decoration. She wasn't wearing any lipstick and her mouth looked paler than a man's.

'Well, you look nice today, Jaillin.'

'Yes, you think so?'

'Yes. What is it?'

'Something we is celebrating.'

'That's a new sari, isn't it?'

'Yes. Yes.'

'Well, you look nice in it.'

'That's something I learn. Mam teach me. No white woman could wear a sari, you know that?'

'No. Why can't they?'

'They can't, eh. They don' have the grace o' body. That is what.'

'You have it?'

'Yes, man.'

She had got prouder. A breeze was moving the sari against her legs and thighs and belly and I watched with desire. She saw me and turned away from the breeze. I kicked at the grass and pretended not to see that she had noticed.

'Jaillin, what's happened to the old earrings?'

'Which ol' earrings at all? Which you mean?'

'You know, the silver ones. I just wondered.'

'That is you' business?'

'Well, I just wondered.'

'Mam keeping those till I get marry, man.'

'Oh, I see.'

146

'You good see.'

'Well, goodbye, Jaillin.'

'Well, you say that, boy. Goodbye.'

'I have to go back. I'm sorry about things.'

'What you sorry fo'? Don' sorry now. Goodbye, boy.'

'Goodbye for now.'

That talk got close to me and hurt me. It hurt me certainly. But those were nearly all of a handful of words we exchanged in many years. Gradually even in her beauty the brown colour of it became a defect, as if she had hair on her cheeks or as if her eyes squinted a little bit. Soon I could pass them on the road, meet them in the market-place or Curepe bus station, and remain cool and easy, off-hand, natural.

'Hi, Kaiser, hi, Jaillin. How are things?' Perhaps there was too much heartiness after all.

'O.K.'

'Nice, Master Alan, nice,' she replied.

'Well, I hope so.'

So opinion changed me, and I changed friends. Life got much easier to live. The pressures building up before died down. It was as if I had had a worry in my mind like a difficult equation and that equation had been resolved by applying a mathematical rule so simple that I could laugh at my old despair that all my life the sum would go unsolved. It didn't occur to me that the formula so many people used to solve the problem might involve a deep corruption of principle.

I drew apart from the world of brown faces. I disengaged myself from the village and all to do with it. I entered the white colonial world which from birth I had belonged to but from which I had walked away for a time. Wanderings up the black-rocked valley stopped. I played tennis in the afternoons and drank cold lager afterwards in each clubhouse. I began to like dancing fairly well, went more and more to parties in private homes where petite gigglers with gold hair attracted my growing and definable boyish lust. Sometimes eating a red-belled pomerack I remembered an old view of the village, but that was very seldom. Kaiser and Jaillin from time to time emerged from the past, now as romantic figures, now as comic, but in any case as lost as the gnomish storybooks I used to read as a child. I told my new friends about them and laughed, or praised them too extravagantly as wild creatures, 'who knew how to *live*, Ann, Jane, Thomas, Alastair, unlike us.' Sometimes, too, an extra bright firefly or red Betelgeuse brought back a memory.

2

When I was eighteen I met Kaiser at a bazaar held for the Roman Catholic Church in Tunapuna. I had by then become a new person, had thoroughly undergone the subtle change which takes place in the growing boy living in a community where races are mixed. It is a matter of older opinion. I didn't get intolerant but the heart changed. An unthinking racial distaste had been grown in me out of sight. Knowing about it I hid that distaste and was too polite, too kind, to Indians or negroes I met one day or the next.

It was the annual bazaar held in the churchyard at this time, the Sunday before Carnival. It was to raise funds for parish work. Every year the priest at the church—sometimes an old, white-haired, stalwart man ripped from green Sligo at his time of life; sometimes a young, spare priest from the College, intent on the new asceticism—would beg for months beforehand for all the faithful to contribute. There was always so much to be done in the parish. There was a long-term plan to rehang the bells that now rang cracked for every Angelus. The wall near the road had to be replastered and whitewashed. They had to buy a statue of St Joseph for the small side altar. A leading parish family had asked for a new pew to be put in for them as theirs was really too shabby.

The priest in the parish that year was Father Scotland. He was a tall, straight, determined man with ironed-out grey hair. He had a gold tooth. His sermons were brisk and happy; 'and may all of us praise God in Heaven,' he used to end benevolently. Father Scotland made more out of the annual bazaar than any other priest. He was an indefatigable workman, going himself from door to door to compel contributions. And if you gave him only some glass beads on a string, even that made him genial. To add to funds he sold lilies from his own garden to a flower shop in Rupert Street. It gave him such pleasure to be able afterwards to announce his successes: 'the sugarcake stall, eleven dollars and thirty-three cents . . . the hat stall . . . the raffle.' And then he would with gusto and benign satisfaction launch into those schemes for his parish's good: the churchyard gates could now be painted the green of leaves, holy water basins supported by stone angels could now be set up at the church doors; traveller-tree palms could now be planted in a pure line for the coming generations. He was a good man. He was loved all right. A year later he was transferred to a forsaken village in an Indian rice district where no doubt he built indomitably and bent as ever very carefully down over his communicants to give them each with boundless gravity the white miraculous wafer.

In the end nearly everyone gave something or other for that bazaar. An old negress gave a cent enclosed in an envelope and sealed carefully. People gave their white elephants, discarded toys, books whose covers and leaves were eaten into crumbling mazes by the pretty insects called silver fish, faded shirts, cushions with designs of Victoria as Empress of India on their unravelling quilt, packets of dull needles, rasping Harry Lauder records, numberless old missals. Every gift was recorded with care and the complete list of benefactors read out in church the earliest Sunday possible after the bazaar: Mrs Robert Lupin, a small ornamental table, bringing three dollars and fifty cents; Miss Desirée Brown, a bead bag, bringing twenty-two cents, and so on. That Sunday the biggest congregation of the year, excepting Good Friday and Christmas Day, came to church to hear the names read out, for the bazaar list was an important registry of worth. After Mass the list was analysed. 'Well! Desirée Brown only brought in twenty-two cents. You remember her tea-cosies last year, five dollars at least!' And that was a weighty slur. The sensation of one year was the donation by Anonymous of a set of six silver coffee spoons, their stick-thin handles ending in ivory balls of pink and white, pink and white, pink and white. This treasure brought twenty-five dollars and parishioners speculated vexedly for many days about who the showy contributor might be.

The temporary wooden stalls were set up around the church-yard. Chains of coloured paper, Christmas leftovers, and green branches decorated them. As the afternoon went on the branches full with leaf drooped in the sun, faded from emerald to the grey of green colours under rain or relentless heat. Pots of tangled pink coralita stood on the counters of the stalls, fresh, most beautiful bouquets. I saw a child pick a bud of coralita and put it in his mouth. Perhaps he thought it would have the taste of a sweet. Then he spat it out again like a blob of pink saliva. I walked about the stalls looking for something to buy. I got a cameo brooch on a brass pin for forty cents: its black and green cats seemed to glow with a sort of Persian fire. I got a copy of one volume of Lloyd George's *War Memoirs*, riddled with silver fish, for ten cents. I felt I had done my duty by the bazaar and Father Scotland. I examined a set of four angels carved from pearwood, but they cost too much to buy.

The crowd circulated, dressed wonderfully well for the occasion. Ostrich-feathered hats kept the sun off in a modish way. The men of the parish were dragged there in suits with styled cravats; all afternoon they ran their fingers around hot collars. The children enjoyed themselves the most; fat Botticelli angels cooed in their prams under the shade of a dozen palms; older children ate and drank purposely like small pigs at the ice cream, roast corn, and coconut water stalls, and played their own unofficial games. Well-scrubbed little girls in best cotton dresses skipped intricate patterns with dyed ropes, going faster and faster as that game of experts went on: 'Sugar' was slow, and 'Salt', 'Vinegar', 'Pepper', were the more and more rapid tempos for those little frenzied dancers, shouting 'Red Pepper! Red Pepper!' and clapping their hands as one of them excelled in adroitness when the rope flashing its colour, whistled round faster and faster, snapping smartly at the ground with each quick turn.

The boys played marbles on the asphalt with agates and crystals and precious keows, mottled with all the colours of the rainbow and flecked with minute knots of brown stone, like ants' eggs. They were playing for 'knuckle-blows'. Whoever won got to give the others in the game for keeps four blows with the biggest marble he had; he pitched it from three inches against the knuckles of hands held fisted down on the ground. White bones could be fractured. Other urchins played hopscotch, taking off their shoes to balance better in the chalked squares. Most of them used pennies as the counter, but some used their own inventions, a piece of white pine wood carved to the shape of a triangle, a large brass curtain ring, ordinary grey slate-stones filed flat and smooth; some favoured the tops off soda water bottles. They were all happy and shouted a lot.

Walking about idly, having bought the brooch and the book, I came across Kaiser in a crowd by the knick-knacks stall. He was alone, fingering the small tokens. He was well-dressed, white shirt buttoned at the wrists, blue tie fastened with a scimitar pin, serge trousers, tan shoes. I noticed a cloth emblem tagged to the breast of his shirt: the words in scarlet thread on it spelled 'St Vincent de Paul Society.' I had not seen him at all for over two years, and he surprised me by looking so respectable. Something was subdued in him. When I saw him I turned away instinctively so that we wouldn't meet. But I thought again. Partly through curiosity, nostalgia perhaps, partly through a conscious tolerance, I went up to him and hit him on the shoulder.

'Hello, Kaiser. Well, very long time no see! What're you doing?'

'Well, hi, hi, Master Alan. I rec'nize you now. . . . What I doing? I searching to buy some sort o' ring thing . . .'

'No. I mean what're you doing, where're you living, where're you working? I haven't seen you around for so long I thought you must have left the village. You know.'

'Well, yes, that is what happen. I get sen' down to a school down by the south. I gone 'way fo' a long time altogether.'

'Really. That's a good thing. Did you like it? What'd you learn? Come tell me.'

We walked up the churchyard to a quiet place under a coco-nut tree. The tree had been carved on and a little gum ran down from the hearts and initials and a liner with three funnels called 'The Queen Mary'.

'I learn to write like a master, boy,' and he said that with a sign of the flourish I had known when we were boys. 'I learn to write big sentence like "Procrastination is the thief of time" an' "A thing of beauty is a joy forever." I learn spelling. I learn arithmetic. I well get educate.'

'Well, that's good. What're you doing now?'

'I keeping the books in Ramlal new shop in Tunapuna. An' I write he letters whatever time he ordering stock o' answering customer. I meking money, boy.'

'Your clothes are smart.'

'Yes. Well, that is it.'

'Aren't you living in the village any more?'

'Nuh, man. I done wid the village long time. That is foolishness there, boy. What I have to do wid cutting cane an' min'ing cow like a fool! I done wid that.'

He took spit on a finger and rubbed out a smear of mud on his shoe. I could see the way they shone was a matter of pride with him.

'But who paid for you to go to that school?'

'Ol' Boss. You remember he?'

'Yes. Yes, well. My father used to say he was a good man.'

'He was always talking an' talking 'bout getting the Indian man educate, so he pay fo' me to go an' learn down by south by Fyzabad. That was a school, boy! I had a desk all by me own self an' a million exercise book!'

'Is he still alive?'

'Ol' Boss? Murder, yes, man. He talking as much as ever. You know how he was. When a donkey shit in the road he ready to draw a conclusion fo' you right away.'

'Lord, yes, I remember that. "You can't put grain down and catch a mongoose." But didn't he want you to come back to the village?'

'I done wid that. It is so he used to talk, how everybody mus' have a loyalty. Big talk 'bout loyalty to the lan'. Well, I fin' out something in this life, boy. The only dam' loyalty is loyalty fo' you' own self. What I have to do wid cutting cane in the dam' mud all the time! You ever hear a big shot cutting cane like he is a axe o' what? No, boy, I done wid that.'

I smiled, wanting to tease him. But I stopped smiling when I saw how serious he looked, leaning a straight face towards me as

we rested our feet on the long, grey, ringed curve of the coconut tree. 'The sweet ben' of a palm tree explain the whole world'.'
I saw what was subdued in him: it was the gaiety of the land. I knew he had lost his pleasure without thought in the smell of a river and a view of humming-birds, in cursing a donkey in the fields, in roasting sweet potatoes with his sister. A shabby, clever brashness remained with him, the dregs of his vigour for life. He brushed away a few specks of dirt on his shirt, straightened the crease of his trousers where it was crooked at the knee, and talked again politely.

'Well, what about what you doing wid you'self, Master Alan? What you doing these days?'

'Well, nothing much. Really idling. Last December I passed H.C. and now I'm just waiting to go over to England in June. I'm going up to Cambridge University at the end of the year.'

'True? You know you lucky man. You have a chance there. You studying fo' a lawyer?'

'No. I'm going to study History.'

'Eh, boy, I never know that befo'. What is that fo', eh? You is going teach o' what? History is a hell of a thing. Ol' things like that, eh, man.'

'No. Not teaching for me. No. I'm just interested in History. I think it's important.'

'How's that, boy? Well, O.K. Let that one pass. One History book I read once. I remember it have a big picture of a army in red armour wid spear stick up in the sky like mad on it cover. I was expecting fights. Boy, all it have in it was about fiel's plough up in one way o' the other an' a million things 'bout England's Ol' Parliament an' woolsacks an' the people's abbots. I couldn't bother wid that, boy.' He grinned and snapped his fingers in one of his old ways.

'Well, Kaiser . . . I like it . . . Hey, what's that St Vincent badge on your shirt? You aren't Catholic.'

'I turn, man, I turn. I was advise so. You see how it is. Catholics have power to help a man, that is what. I get up far now, man; helping wid the altar fun' an' all.'

'But Jaillin . . . ?'

'Jaillin would never turn, man. You don' know she now.'

'But you remember she liked it?'

'That was a long time, man.'

'What's happened to her? Lord, I haven't seen her for a long time now!'

'It bes' so, boy. Ol' Boss had a word on that one. He say, "If you driving nail, knock he one time an' done".'

'But I'd like to see her again. What's happened to her?'

'A lot o' things happen to she.'

'What then?'

'A lot o' things, boy.'

'What?'

'She waving she belly fo' a dam' Syrian in Port o' Spain, that what happen.'

'How d'you mean? Well, how d'you mean?'

'I'm telling you, man. She doing dances two times a week down in Cobo Hut, flashing she belly bare like a mad woman.'

'Well, how did it happen?'

'Money, boy, money.'

'What?'

'The Syrian man paying she well, as it is a fac' that she does dance well an' attrac' customer, an' too besides he want to fuck she bad so he paying she like a millionaire. That is what happen. God, boy, he is a nasty man.'

'Well, I'd like to meet her again. I'd like to see her dance. You know, I've never been to Cobo Hut.'

'True, boy? I'll tell she.' There was some irony.

'Where does she live then?'

'Now wid Ol' Boss in the village. She wouldn' move from the village. An' Mam and Pap die so she does help out Ol' Boss, an' then flash she belly those two times a week.'

'Well, Kaiser, has she grown up pretty as ever?' I laughed, wanting to pass the question off as banter. But I was serious.

'People say that.'

There was silence between us. The bazaar went on noisily all around. The sun pitched counters of gold through trees high up on the church roof. A person shouted for beads from one stall to another. Children shouted for ice cream. Father Scotland was

154

standing up on a wooden bench and auctioning off missals, vases, cheese-graters, old boots. He smiled like a saint at each bidder.

I fidgeted, thinking of Jaillin. Suddenly Kaiser said a word coldly.

'She hate white man now.'

'What? Why, then?'

'She hate white men. Boy, you should hear what she say even 'bout that Syrian man! She say she could put honey on he cock fo' red ants to bite. She say she could bu'n out he two eye wid hot piss. Boy, Ol' Boss reprove she fo' those bad words she always saying 'bout people, but even Ol' Boss heself 'fraid she these days. Boy, she could spit right t'rough all you.'

'Lord, but why?'

'Not me, you know. What I going vex wid all you fo'. Not me, boy. I have a respec'.'

'Yes, but why Jaillin?'

'Yes, well that is something a million people couldn' say, I expec',' he said foolishly.

'Well, I'd like to see her.'

Kaiser didn't answer. We walked over to where Father Scotland was still auctioning beatifically. I put in a bid for a rose-embroidered tea-cosy, clearly full of moth holes, and it was accepted. I had a tea-cosy for sixpence.

'It look like a one side of a brassière,' Kaiser grinned. 'The tits would poke t'rough though.'

'I'd like to see Old Boss too. Perhaps I could visit them.'

'If you really want, I could tell them.'

'Yes, tell them. Couldn't you bring me?'

'Well, boy . . .'

'Of course you can, Kaiser. It's something I've wanted to do. I haven't seen the village for more than an age, you know. Bring me tomorrow night.'

'Why quick so sudden? You mek me laugh.'

'Couldn't you?'

'Tomorrow is Carnival. You not jumping?'

'Well, nothing definite.'

'I tell you what, boy. I jus' think something. Come jump-up wid

me in Tunapuna. We could go after to Ol' Boss an' see Jaillin an
have roti an' rum. What you saying?'

'Well, I don't know . . .'

'Don' worry you' head, boy. You could wear a mask an' brown
up you' han' wid coffee stain an' who going rec'nize you?'

'I'll come.'

'Well, this is a thing fo' true!'

'It should be fun. You'll tell Jaillin then?'

'I'll tell she, yes. Well, this is a thing fo' true! You really
coming?'

'Of course. I said so.'

We arranged where to meet the next day. Then I left the bazaar,
still noisily and busily going on, and biked home down the Main
Road. The sound of steel bands practising for the next two days
came from behind sweet shops and iron-smiths' shacks and a
coffin parlour along the way. The coffin parlour had a sign up
outside. 'Coffins Sold for Young and Old', and I shuddered and
smiled. I got a cold sweat, remembering some things Kaiser had
said, but I was confident I could brazen it through all right the
next day. After all I was grown up now and superior.

3

All night the green barrels of bamboo, primed with kerosene,
popped like guns. Bare blue fireworks went up. Loud drums came
from the villages. Carnival started at midnight and the steel bands
began to clash and hum like giant new night-insects. The noise
and the iron beat in the air would now be continuous for two days,
and the muffled feeling of crowd would shake along the skin.
What mattered most in life to Trinidad had started.

Carnival summed up what was authentic in the life of the land
—colour, rhythm, sensual thought, rum, calypsos, industrial
African tremor of music, the occasional rosy explosion of excitement. And the Indians joined in and made of it a mystery and a
holiday. And it was the time when the white people got into the
spirit of their adopted world best.

One year down a green street in St Clair I saw a band of high-class colonials and creoles, dressed in colours, tricked out as ghosts, huntsmen, queens, railwaymen, Varangian Guards, apple girls, moving and jumping and laughing. The costumes were tidy, well-cut, new. They had their own steel-band, glistening, serious lads dressed meticulously as admirals, beating and beating tirelessly on the iron. The dancing was precise as a polka, but had in it too the right sexual flavour for a hot Carnival day. Young girls, pink and sweet as blood dropped in snow, moved their hips slowly and pushed out their bellies a little as if offering to a man. In Spanish fashion they held their arms square and pointing, looked down each shoulder proudly to tempt a stare of desire. Every now and then one of the white boys pranced ahead, turning circles, flourishing two black chac-chacs on which open-eyed owls, the fabulous jumby-birds, were painted in white. 'Glory, Mama, glory!' they all shouted the road-march lilt again and again. 'Glory, Mama, glory!' Little negro boys, in tall white paper hats and red sashes as costumes, stood beside the road, shook their limbs and grinned. 'Glory, Mama, glory!' The band came on to Maraval Road and turned to go jumping around the Savannah. A Varangian Guard, lithe as Theseus, lifted his head and shouted a whoop of joy.

Then I saw another band was coming up in the opposite direction, turning the corner by Queen's Royal College. This was different. It was the Vanguard steelband and followers. They had come up marching and beating from Henry Street in downtown Port of Spain, the small shop and half-slum area. Negroes, hot black in the sun, Chinese saltfish retailers, holidaying, with eyes like bleeding olives, thin, straight-faced half-Indian, half-Portuguese cartmen, coloured boys and freckled poor-white girls, followed the vibrant kernel of tough negroes. Over them a scarlet-lettered banner flourished—'Vanguard!' A man in brass-coloured armour carried it, standing out like a nugget in a coal face. The followers straggled in the heat hundreds of yards all the way behind the band. They were not decorated, wore only hot shirts, pyjama pants, khaki, dirty singlets, canvas-patched trousers, cotton blouses and skirts dark with sweat. But the steel-band was extravagantly costumed. Some of the men wore leopard skins; necklaces of jaguar teeth rattled on their chests. Some were dressed as kings, and had yellow crowns and yards of false ermine. Some were bronze men, shining metallically, some were dark cardinals. All were overdressed, loading on necklaces, ribbons, feathers, and bangles wherever possible. They soaked with sweat. It was the second day of Carnival and they had probably been beating almost non-stop for thirty-six hours. (In bands like that to keep going was an honourable thing; a bandsman would open his pants and urinate as he marched rather than drop out.) Yet they stood straight as the royal palm, beating the scarlet-worded pans which hung heavily on their bellies. They groaned with pleasure. It was a wild, sweaty, dirty, straggling band altogether, jumping and spinning like drugged unruly ecstatics. The noise was terrific, hammering, unsponsored, cruel as a violin shrilling in a silver desert.

The two bands approached each other along the road in their different ways. The small white band showed no hesitating sign. They jumped on boldly and joyfully as ever. And the ragged band came up drumming fiercely, limbs playing sexually. One or two screamed like animals. I'm sure people thought there was going to be a clash; there was a sort of hush outside the noise. I thought a battle would take place, that men would even be killed. I was thrilled and frightened. I did not think the white band would lose, but I feared seeing the blood that would splash on the road. Five policemen rode up on bicycles, slowly, suspiciously, holding white batons.

When the two bands came together there was extra confusion for a while; movement was restricted to a milling standstill as the followers on both sides piled up on a thickly confused centre. But it was clear it was no matter of metal smashing against metal. There were no shouts of rage or bitterness or distaste. A few of the white girls came out of the crowd on to the pavement, wiping away sweat with great sheet-kerchiefs and smiling. They didn't go back. But they were the only ones that came away. Slowly the muddle sorted itself out. The bigger band won the fight for direction. The white band turned around and followed their admiral bandsmen, mingling in the huge, exulting Vanguard troupe. Colours merged and flowed again on the hot road around the Savannah. An apple girl took fruits from her basket and tossed them into the crowd behind her. 'Glory, Mama, glory!' the massed chant grew much louder than before. The huge jump-up pounded the smooth road rhythmically. It sounded like tremendous, measured laughter.

At first I was almost shocked that it had happened like that. I bit my knuckles in wonder. Then I was pleased. I found I felt warm and glad that men behaved well. I felt the same one day when I saw the Africans and Indians clap and shout applause for Jeff Stollmeyer at the Queen's Park Oval when he walked in from the wicket after scoring a century. 'That is cricketer father,' they said. 'That is strokes, eh!' White men were accepted. I felt safe and confident.

I was awake early and lay happily in the fretwork of gold that the sun worked through the white mosquito netting. The sheets were cool and unrumpled, and I knew I had slept well. I was excited and could feel excitement in the air. I heard shouts outside in the road and knew that it was some old masks out even that early going from house to house to ask for pennies. It was a ritual set down for Carnival Monday, just as on Tuesday the big band parades took place and the lorries filled with stamping troupes circled the Savannah slowly. 'Here is a ol' mask here, Madam! Give a penny fo' a ol' mask.' I got out of bed and looked through the window, grinning. Three boys in papier-mâché masks with long, long red noses had come up the drive. Their voices were muffled behind the great white lips and ample pink cheeks of the masks. 'Jour Ouver'! Jour Ouver'! Ol' mask day! Give a penny fo' a ol' mask!' Their gargoyle faces looked up at me. I grinned at them and waved a hand. 'Jour Ouver! Give a penny fo' a ol' mask, sir.' One of them had a Cow and Gate tin in his hand and he began to beat on it with a stone. The other two did small, ridiculous dances around him. The deadpan fantastic faces suddenly seemed much too big for the legs and arms underneath, big clown skulls on their midget bodies.

The cracked tinny banging brought out Alice quickly. She had been cooking breakfast and had on a white apron, spotted with egg and butter. She was sleepy and very vexed. She bawled at the boys.

'You dam' li'l 'rab boys! What you meking all that noise fo'!'

She waved her arms, as if she was chasing hens. 'Go on out o' here befo' I vex an' call a knife to all you' little bottoms!'

They scampered down the drive. It was odd to see how the bulbous straight-faced masks expressed no feelings; I imagined the looks of mischief and fright on their faces underneath and thought the masks should be showing that too.

'Wait, Alice,' I called down and laughed. 'Call them back for a little.' When they came back slowly I tossed them a shilling. They scrambled for it in the pebbles, then ran down the drive and out of the gate. Alice waved her arms behind them. 'Go on. Go out quick,' she threatened. I called out to her, 'Oh, Alice, let them have their fun.' She went back in to the kitchen grumbling. I smiled secretly and whispered, 'Carnival, Carnival. What a day!' I laughed at myself.

After breakfast I dressed up. It was like growing up quickly, in a day, overnight. The costume was a hodge-podge, garnered from Grandma's old press and the heavy costume box in the low room under the stairs where I always went for pirate cloth and Red Indian feathers when I was young. I remembered the smell of the box well: it was between musty and biting-fresh, and I imagined cloves in a jar full of old moth wings, and the sunny smell of dried khus-khus. The box held a new world. I put on green pantaloons that were tight and dainty on the calves, and a white shirt with a long red cord-tie at the collar flapping down the ruffled front. I put on black soft shoes; round the lace holes were little silver rings of metal; the laces were bright orange. I put on a gallant Napoleon hat, stitched with rose buttons round the brim at the back. I put on yellowing kid gloves; I remembered the old fingers that nestled there once upon a time and the oranges and seashells and eyelids they in their time touched.

I went on to the important part of disguising myself. I mixed a little water with ground coffee. Then I smeared it on my neck and up my throat, over my ears into the small hairs on the nape. I smeared it on my ankles and all down my arms too. I was careful to put it on carefully, like a paint, leaving no gaps of white skin. Then I put on a black velvet mask that fitted exactly over my white face. I was a mixture of executioner, Indian Prince, and Charlatan. When I was finished I looked in a mirror. I was pleased at the transformation I had made. I was sure no one could possibly recognize me. A difference had come on me like new eyes. Garbed and coloured, I felt a balm of confidence that all my actions would be anonymous. The pleasure of feeling safe from having to be careful and mannered in the sight of others all the time rose in me.

In my world one acted a polite and superior part every day in the presence of the lower crowd, controlling outbursts of any unseemliness. That is why when Norwegian sailors with beautiful blue eyes and hair blond as a cornfield came into harbour and got drunk in the rumshops along South Quay, bawled and fought and spat dirtily, their negro and Indian fellows, amazed and delighted at the downfall of a glazed idol, grinned and pointed, hugging each other's discovery that a white, mysterious skin really held no special stability and pride of blood; and *we* felt the precarious strongpoint we held, defended by suavity and conscious scorn, weaken a little, sink back a small way into the encroaching flooding river. When she read it in the court news in the papers my great-aunt Ida, rocking vexedly in her bedside chair and fluttering a petal- and bird-strewn fan in agitation, would say of them, 'Oh, what an example, what a terrible example! The foreign hooligans! What right have they! They help them to give us a black name without right.' She had belonged to a world invariably correct in its behaviour. Now we were slowly failing in our duty. The impression of fine, sober aloofness gave way, for instance, more and more at Carnival time: she recalled the days when Carnival meant stately costume balls at Government House and a secret visit or two in fancy dress by coach to visit close neighbours and friends of the family. And now these bad foreigners completely disgraced the island: very different from the polished crew in sword-belted uniforms who had visited before the great war from a German cruiser, a glittering ship whence the young girls in their delicious dresses, bouncing over full petticoats, were rowed and where they danced the night through between lines of chaperones and stiff officers the measured rhythms of polka, mazurka, and daring waltz. She told me all this between beads of her rosary, as she sat in her rocking chair. And a sad, helpless, race-remembered pity and nostalgia would rise in me like a physical ache as I saw the tears form in her eyes.

The tears would never fall. She would put down her rosary and take out the yellow ivory egg in her sewing basket to stitch up a hole in a sock, beautifully, with fine deft movements, so that she could be useful in her old age. And I would go away, determined to remember for ever the old ways and defend them perfectly.

The defence was a strain, and conflicted with my sense of a West Indies growing in a new world and way of life. It was the great paradox and difficulty of my thought and feeling that had been growing ever since I had been forced to reject Kaiser and Jaillin and enter into the inheritance I was born to. What Kaiser and Jaillin stood for, an emerging, different, mixed, mutual love, kept as a background to my changed opinions and what with sincerity I had become convinced of too, the exclusive love, descended through old families and many decorous years, of a solemn, happy, artificial, sweet life. In imagination I called up the village, and heard the new strenuous voices in the Legislatures around the islands. In imagination I called up great-aunt Ida doing up her hair and putting on her rings before church on Sundays. How could I hold the two images together so that I might lose neither the young attachment nor the antique respect? I grappled with the question all my life, one day swayed one way as I talked to Jaillin deeply in Old Boss's hut, one day swayed the other way when I listened to great-aunt Ida tell a tale from her rocking-chair with the big silvery cushion, as she said her rosary beads, big as grapes.

Meanwhile, I made no concessions normally. It would not be right to sacrifice the correctness of behaviour to the other emerging way; the correctness was something to contribute to its raw spirit. So I kept correct among the wharf and village folk. The responsibility weighed very heavily, and this morning it was a relief to take off the appearance of a defender of the faith and become one of the raw, breezy crowd. I could do that, you see, in a complete disguise. There was no need for pinchbeck metal to ring true. I would not be known as a representative. I lost the tense feeling and wary spirit of a protagonist.

I walked up the Long Circular Road, past big moaning casuarina trees, a dense governor plum bush cut into the shape of a squat green hat box, and pearly-leaved, peacock-barked eucalyptus giants, to where the way branched across the railway line into the Main Road running into Port of Spain. Just at the corner of the intersection stood Dufauld's cake shop where I was going to meet Kaiser. Dufauld sold the best coconut cakes in the whole of Trinidad, pink and frothy white, seasoned oddly with valernum and nutmeg. As well as selling cakes Dufauld had the job of closing the iron crossing gates when the trains came by on the line. Once he had been fired because, busy selling cakes to a passing boy, he had forgotten to close the gates and a train had rushed past dangerously over the unprotected road. However, no one was hurt, and Dufauld soon got back the job.

He was a gentle, coffee-coloured man and always had a kind good morning to say. He kept his shop bright with new paint and clean as a flame. Even the most desperate hardship couldn't make Dufauld sullen, nor any great happiness make him too joyful. He was one of those men who live and die unnoticed. But it is men like Dufauld who help to form that tough, angelic film on the mind which (as the thinnest embellishment of varnish keeps off water) protects the hardly held conviction that man in soul is good and keeps a grip on some essential truth. I greeted him good morning and he replied gently.

Kaiser came up dressed as a sailor. H.M.S. Navigator in blue ribbon was stitched on his cap and tunic. He held a little whistling pipe in his hand. He was sweaty as a workhorse.

'I really jump this morning, boy!'

'Already?'

'Since all las' night I jumping the blood heat up in me body like a fire. Oh, God, but Carnival is something in trut'!'

'How do I look? You recognized me right away.'

'I was expecting to see you. But you' costume is pretty, man. You dress up like a prize winner. You dress up like Sinbad.'

'Well, anyway, let's go.'

'Let's go, boy, let's go! Eh, Dufauld, there, le' me tek a sugar cake to borrow. I hungry fo' food.'

Dufauld gave him two cakes and marked him down for them in an exercise book.

'Eh, eh, Dufauld, man, come an' jump! I bet you could jump like a giant!'

163

'Come on, let's go out,' I said.

'Let's go, boy, let's go,' Kaiser said.

We went into the Main Road and began to walk up towards Tunapuna. Kaiser had clearly been drinking in the night. A fixed smile set a gay curve on his face. He hummed little Indian ditties under his breath and chuckled at them to himself; his voice broke amusingly on a couple of thin, high wails. I walked up the road beside him gladly, safe from the world in my rag-bag costume.

The crowd got thicker as we walked up nearer the market place in Tunapuna. There were not many complete flamboyant costumes, but everyone had a bit of something strange on to distinguish the occasion—a beret with a bouncing red knot of wool, a green sash, a lion-coloured kerchief round the forehead, a dagger of wood washed with silver paint hanging at the waist, chac-chacs or thumb-bells, something or other: as if they were all humming fragments of the same tune. Children in rags like the coloured tatters of a clown skirmished about; a favourite spot was the wide gutter running through the place: a small boy in purple apron held a white duck on a length of string and laughed and laughed at its quacks. Another boy wearing a wide-nosed white mask carried a basket full of paper ribbons and dipped his hand in often to scatter one or two like coloured rats' tails on the road. Four boys all dressed in white Arab silk with sapphire crescents woven in at the cuffs and gold tassels fringing all hems, had placed a pink leather drum on the ground and were very slowly dancing around it. They held thick white sticks in their hands and as they stepped slowly dancing around the drum each tapped it in turn with his white stick. It was a marvellous thing to see.

'Kaiser, what're we going to do?'

'What're we going . . . ? We going jump wid a ban'. Jump fo' so! See over dey?' He pointed unsteadily across the market-place.

Round the standpipe near the big Post Office building a band was forming up to go out jumping. We walked over there through the bright crowd. The standpipe was full on and people were bathing their heads under it one after the other. The steelband section that would give the music for the jump-up were sounding out their pans now, lightly beating on the seasoned iron. There were seven of them and their faces were straight and serious and weighted with the responsibility of making good steel music to jump to. The full beat on the pans was held back but every now and then one of the men would break out into hard, strong rhythm on his pan and the sound would tremble in the air as if trees of metal were shaking.

The band they were going to lead and behind which we would follow gathered around them. They were dressed as stickfighters of the old days. I knew about those men. The bataille bois was a great sport in the old days and still survived in remote bush villages. I'd heard the old men in the village speak of it sometimes. Lives form around facts and the greatest lives around the greatest facts, so the old men spoke of the bataille bois, their greatest fact. They talked about the great stickfighters, La Cour Harpe and Gros Adams, Tiepin and Chinese Patrick, Laptong, Blood and Muscovi. They talked of how the men wielded their yard long poui sticks, polished, balanced in a fine way, centred with charms, snake-teeth or bones from the Belmont graveyard. They had endless strong tales to tell of the blood pits of Sangre Grande, and complained how in the green hills around the villages now there was only the whine of hill women cutting grasses.

One day long before in the village I'd sat with Kaiser and Jaillin near to Old Boss and heard him tell the story of the fight between the two marvellous champions, Mangamouche and Placide. He'd shown us a big flat stone on which a picture of the fight had been roughly carved, to send it down to the future. Old Boss told us. It was in a fighting pit near Rio Claro. Mangamouche was a giant, big as a hill and tough as stone. Placide was a little man but defter than Ariel: they said he could beat away any stone flung at his body, however hard, from however close, with his baton in a quick turn of the wrist. Days and days before they met to fight the drum-men, honoured to be proclaimers, beat the news of a major bataille bois on their jointed tambour bamboos, goat-skinned and many-coloured. Men came from seventy villages, barefoot or in donkey carts, and their women carrying melons and coconuts to sell in the hot afternoon. Even three Englishmen, their skins newly burnt to the colour of freckles, came. They were dressed in white drill and wore cork hats.

Everything was quiet. It was afternoon and the sun was very hot. Mangamouche and Placide faced each other. They wore only khaki shorts held up by belts of dog's teeth. The wary beginning, the skilful work of the stick, sweet to the eyes of the old men. Then the heavier, direct blows with their weight of knotty black muscles. They fought all afternoon with hard, watchful eyes. All afternoon the hard poui sang whap whap; there was a tinge of iron in the wood. When night was coming like a great black pig they rested for one hour. At that time all the colours of the day came back to burn and praise them in the sky. In that interval women bathed their skin with cool water from the river and gave them drink and corn cakes to eat. Then followers set up flambeaux on iron drums in the circle, and Mangamouche and Placide fought again by the orange flames full of smoke in the rich, furious pit. Three stars flashed with silver tails in the black above them. Mangamouche had five broken fingers and all his finger nails were torn off; Placide had deep injuries in his belly and his face burnt with the sweat in all the poui cuts. But both had their eyes to judge and hit and parry, and they went on. The women began to moan. The men thought they would fight forever: and, indeed, as men will tell you, they fought for longer than forever. Then Mangamouche, with his strength of a giant, swung his red poui for a thousandth time and Placide had only bitter weakness: the blow swung from his shining arms, big as samaan boughs, burst six of Placide's white ribs. It was then the real pride began. A shout more of general pride than of single praise for either man sprung round the fighters; two small boys fell off a calabash tree in excitement; pouches of jumby beads and pennies were cast in the scarred pit. Afterwards they carved it on big river stones. And they sang of it: the sweet-harsh songs, songs of the stickmen, strong kalindas shouted by the red-sleeved jacket men, 'Je t'aime, Mangamouche, Je t'aime triste Placide, Je'vous aime, grands noirs hommes.' From the moon of a humming-bird's wing to the moon of a rich plum the legend sprung in the song, found roots as tough as the nut grass.

'D'you remember what Old Boss said about them?' I asked Kaiser, as I watched the band dressed as stickfighters form up in

position by the standpipe. Kaiser looked puzzled. I reminded him
of the story told us when we were boys.

'Now I remember what you saying. Dat is a ol' man, eh! He
tell a lot o' thing 'bout dat fight. I don' know if all o' dat is true.
He could mek up . . . he could mek up a piece o' shit so you
could eat it.' He shook his head. 'An' who in the hell wan' to
eat shit. But I don' know, boy. Le' we go jump.'

The steel-band at a sign of the tenor pan took up the full beat
and rhythm of the road march that year, 'Casey Wallah mek a
Bid.' They got going with the stickfighters behind them. Kaiser
and I came in behind and began to jump with the rest. We followed the music and the red-sleeved jacket men into the Main Road
and headed down to Curepe and further to San Juan and beyond.
The sun had got up pretty tall in a clear sky now and the air
burnt and glowed against the skin. Sweat poured and shone on
every body. The road was crowded; cars moved slowly through
the gay people on the road and blew their horns sharply. Kaiser
and I jumped down the road with our band. In that jubilant Carnival road my hips got looser and my toes bounced up and down
all the way. Kaiser's sailor hat jiggled on his head as he jumped
like a paper boat on a fountain, until he took it off and stuffed
it in his hip pocket.

I was soaked with sweat to the skin and dog-tired in three
hours of jumping with the Tunapuna band. In that time we had
got to San Juan, joined in there with a big parade of bands in the
Bus park, and gone on a little further towards Port of Spain and
then turned around. The band and its music never lacked followers all the way; 'piss-hot band,' they shouted, and waved to
others to come in. I was limping badly and my shoes felt as if they
were full of hot spit and prune stones. We were on our way back
to Tunapuna. I hopped along beside Kaiser as fast as I could get
along. He was fresh and jumped as if there was a permanent spasm
jerking his body about. He had a bottle of rum in his hand and
drank from it occasionally; the dark rum dripped down his chin
like tarry sweat. I had seen him drink a bottle of rum that morning
and sweat it out again. He offered me a mouthful of the rum but
I said no. The dust had begun to tower up over the road. The blue,
mirror-smooth sky pitched a glare in the eyes as solid as a block

of hot metal. The road seemed to stretch ahead as long as a year.
I turned to Kaiser and put my hand on his shoulder. He turned
bright eyes on me and smiled.

'Hey, look, Kaiser, I'm hellishly tired. I've got a stone in my
shoe or something. I'm going on home now. O.K.? I'm going to
have a bath and sleep. But I'll meet you again tonight to go to
Old Boss's. You go ahead.'

'You tired, boy? Nobody start to jump as yet!'

'I've finished. I'm going to be stiff as hell. Where shall I meet
you tonight?'

'I now beginning to jump. Fill you' mout' wid rum an' you
going feel like jumping. Feel dat beat, eh!'

'No. I've finished for now. Where shall we meet tonight?'

'O.K. den. I never hear o' sleeping in Carnival, boy. I going
meet you. You know whe' we start up from, by dat pipe in the
market? Dat is where. I going meet you by the pipe.'

'All right. I'll meet you there. About what time?'

'Any time, boy. I going be dere. A big crowd jumping dere
from seven, to Invaders coming up from Port o' Spain. They
coming up to beat.'

'All right. I'll meet you right by the pipe. I'll come up about
half-past.'

'Invaders going to be beating!' He bent his body and leaped
high with a shout, stretching his arms wide above his head. Drops
of sweat flung off his face and fell on me.

'Hey, Kaiser, you're sure Jaillin and Old Boss know I'm coming?'

'I tell you I tell dem, boy. I tell dem. Jaillin meking up a
curry.'

'All right. D'you think it'll be all right, Kaiser? What about
Jaillin, if you say she hates any white man or person now? What
d'you think about her? I can't think she'll be very welcoming.'

'Don' worry, boy. What you think she going do at all? Jook a
knife in you?'

'No. But it could be embarrassing. I'm not sure I should go after
all, you know. You see?'

'No, boy, don' bother wid dat. You promise to come a'ready
an' it going be a good thing. Why you worrying you' head?

I tell dem you coming a'ready. You not going let me down, eh?'

'All right. I'd like to see the village again. And Old Boss and Jaillin. You're sure it's all fixed?'

'Yes, boy.'

'Right. I'll see you.'

The band had come up to the way which turned off the Main Road and led to our house. I left the band and crossed the road between the slowly moving cars. The road leading home was quiet; the silence after the middle of the band was like ice on the skin. I passed Dufauld's cake shop. Dufauld was standing in front of the shop with his hands behind his back. As I passed I called out to him, 'It's hell out there, Dufauld!' He waved a hand and smiled; 'Take you' time, Mister Alan!' he said.

4

'Casey Wallah mek a bid!' Invaders were beating the tune in the market. They were a famous band and they lived up to it. Their boast was that they never stopped beating the full forty-eight hours of Carnival; when a bandsman tired, felt burning needles in his wrists, another took his place at once; the pans never stopped beating. Invaders pans were all coloured white and they caught the light like white iron tubs. The band was stationed in the middle of the market and jammed around it were a thousand revellers, jumping to the tune and shouting out the words of the road march. Two streetlights, standing like giant pruning hooks near the Post Office building, lit the glassy-eyed, fatigued bandsmen and a crowd struggling fiercely for pleasure. On the fringes of the crowd a few men pushed wooden carts carrying bottles of rum and sweetdrinks. Their carts had small flickering wick-lamps under glass which threw shadows of their fingers as big as long balloons as they served the drink. They were doing good trade; they put the coins in their pockets with relish as if each copper oval or worn threepenny piece held all the meaning of their lives. One man was selling slices of bread; on some slices he spread a little margarine and sold them for a cent more. The men and women took the bread away and finished a slice in two bites, with a swallow of rum or Coca-Cola or Ju-C. Then they went back to jump to Invaders' beat. 'Casey Wallah mek a bid!' The tune did not change.

I had cleaned right down and slept. When it came to go out to meet Kaiser I dressed in a hot shirt and khaki trousers to fit the mood again. Now I wandered about on the fringes of the crowd and listened to Invaders beating and looked at the men and women feeling the bite of Carnival in their bellies, furiously and strenuously packing a year's waiting into this intense, private, passionate, short time. I could see them sharpening their lives like they sharpened steel on a stone. A woman passed on the edge of the crowd, slowly moving her hips and tramping in time to the beat of the white pans. Her lips were a little apart and her eyes gleamed and rolled. She was carrying a child on one arm. The child's face was more serious than the face of the woman who carried him. Laughter was not near the face of the child; perhaps his eyes were strained on the verge of tears, because they looked out steady and solemn on the crowd. An impish, sensual Madonna and a boy intent only on the sadness of the world. The child bounced up and down on the woman's arm; as she shook to the beat it clutched on to her dress. 'Carnival!' one of the men selling drinks said. 'Why it can't be all the year, like the sun!'

I went over to the standpipe through the crowd. People looked at me and laughed. 'Jump up, boy!' they shouted. I was very pleased by their good nature. Kaiser was right by the pipe. He had lost his shirt and his chest gleamed with sweat in the streetlight. I remembered him in the canefields and up the river where he had always gone bare-chested. I remembered him like that, strong and bare-chested, masterful, but as I recalled these times it struck me like a splash of icy water in the stomach how the image of him in my mind had irrecoverably changed. He had become a little Indian commercial clerk. My eyes could not focus on the older image. Kaiser was a little Indian commercial clerk. He was shallow, poorly educated, and he liked his rum. I liked him with pity. He stood behind a counter and wrapped and sold plantain and flour and saltfish to barking women. I could not see the boy, strong

and bare-chested, important as a hero, who hunted the Blue Marbleus up the river and once strangled a mongoose caught in a
cage of ours with a noose made of tree vines. He stood by the pipe
bathing his feet in the flow of water. There was a green slime of
moss in the stone basin at the foot of the pipe and Kaiser slid his
toes along the moss leaving clean white marks.

For a moment we stood by the pipe near to each other looking
out into the crowd, keeping silent. An open truck, pasted along
its sides with bright tissue papers, turned into the market place
from the Main Road at speed. It came in fast, its horn sounding
sharply, and the crowd scattered gaily in front of it as it drew up
near Invaders with a noise of scraped tin. The people in the truck
cheered roughly and jumped out on the ground. They were all
hung with many strands of glass beads, and as each jumped on
the ground each clinked and jangled like a hundred flakes of
metal flung against a wall. It was the Bead People Gang. Their
sandals were worked in beads and their tall socks gleamed with
stiff lines of bright beads. Their black canvas trousers and girl's
slacks were stitched all over with a sea of beads. The men wore no
shirts but countless necklaces of beads hung to different lengths
on their chests; the girls wore brassieres made of red beads. The
men and girls jangled like bags of coins as they began to move to
the steel band rhythms right away. One fellow shouted from the
crowd, 'How's you' beads tonight?' and quick as the twitch of a
gold bee the answer came from one of the men, 'Swell up wid
screwing tonight, boy!' There was a ring of laughter around the
man, and he lifted his face to the sky and laughed loud for himself. Kaiser and I grinned at each other. We began to walk through
the tumult of the crowd. Where Kaiser had left the pipe on the
water continued to flow in a bright stream into the stone basin.

We crossed the railway line which ran near to the market place
and we left Tunapuna by the road on the other side. As we
stepped on the silvered lines I could feel the beat of a train coming up from Port of Spain, throbbing under my feet as if a strong
dog was bounding down a tunnel under the earth. The smell and
taste of smoke and oil lay along the line but only twenty feet away
the road went under tall green bamboo and the air got sweet with
river fern and cool as cold bracelets. A jumby bird hooted from

one of the plum trees along the path of the road. The road led out to the cane and rice fields in the middle of which the village had grown up in a pile of discoloured white boxes. Kaiser and I walked on our way very quietly. He was tired and sometimes his chin dropped almost on his chest.

I did not feel like talking. I looked up and the sky was glorious with stars. In the purple black bowl over the land the stars crackled like bees beating their wings. I breathed deeply and the cool bamboo scent reached deep in my lungs. I thought of the whole land I lived in, the mountains covered with trees, the burning mangrove swamps, the rivers tossing down white over rocks, the big town full of bright lights and lust and busy men, the sea coves at Mayaro strewn with shells and spotted red crab skins, the industrial oil fields smelling of dirty gas and clean paint, the wide acres of ripe cane tossing all their white arrows in sun, the sun and again the sun, a hot brass whip, beating down at noon, the sun in the evening bringing out its bright and glowing capes like a woman. I breathed in the whole land I lived in. I remembered the moon over the fields of citrus my father owned, a globe of ice. I thought of the whole land I lived in, all the land from Chaguanas to Toco and stretching further than that beyond Trinidad to the other islands held in the same strong grip of history and sun. For a moment suddenly I was filled with a rush of delight as if my blood itself was happy. I hadn't had that feeling of rising joy, sudden as a cut, for years.

When I was young with Kaiser and Jaillin the feeling had often been with me clear and sharp and sudden, spontaneous as a stallion tossing its head, leaping up like a burst of fire from brushwood, and I had not thought about it at all. It was a part of living, like the length of my arm and the colour of blue in my eyes. But now I realized that these last years it had faded down. More and more I had taken beautiful things for granted. And I knew I would never recapture the feeling for long or often, the sheer bite of un-analysed, overwhelming pleasure. I looked up at the bright bees covering the skies and grinned in despair. Later on, in the village, sitting with Jaillin and Old Boss, at a few words from the old craftsman, I remembered sharply how I felt now.

When we got there I saw the village had changed. The land had been cleared of bush in a wider area and there were more huts. But that was not the biggest change. Although the village had grown it had not prospered, and now the huts were shabbier and gave an impression of untidy, fitful poverty, poverty without that saving pride of careful work to make the best of things. I thought I smelt dilapidation in the air.

We walked between the huts. I stepped on an oyster shell and heard it crack beneath the leather. In some windows smoky kerosene lamplight danced; a bowed head in silhouette crossed one of these windows and the shadow moved in the dust outside in wavering ebony. The smell of cooking between the huts was not the sharp smell of that night's fresh cooking, but the accumulated cooking smell of years in the huts, sunk into the walls, sunk into the dry grey thatch, seeping every moment into the village air—the smell of curry and boiled rice and roti and oily sweet potatoes. It was a stagnant smell. It depressed me. I had the curious feeling that I was swimming in a long pool of tepid sink water floating with a scum of grease and potato peels. I wanted to dash cold, brilliant water all over myself and come out with a clean skin and clear eyes. I began to see only the tattiness in the village now. I forgot the green, smooth-leaved calabash trees and the hushed corridors of the temple further away. I saw in the fitful kerosene lamplight grey curls of plaster peeling away from nearly all the walls of the huts. And when a child, a thin little girl, darted out of a doorway I noticed her dress was torn into a thousand witch-claw shreds.

Old Boss's hut was still separate from the rest of the village, though the patch of corn and bush which lay between had been pared down to make room for a few more huts there. Jaillin was staying with him now. Kaiser and I walked through the corn in the night wind towards the hut. All the way I played with some coins in my pocket nervously. I felt nervousness spurt in my stomach and I almost retched. I spat on the ground to clear the throat of sour saliva that had got there through the nervousness.

The hut was cleaner than the others in the village. It was newly white-washed and the thatch on it was trim. There was clearly a pride about it that the other huts lacked. A young lime tree grew twenty feet from the door and the sweet crystal-sharp scent of white lime buds came to the nose. That smell mixed with the steamy smell coming off the manure and cut grass piled at the foot of the lime tree. After the smell of stale cooking in the village it was good to have that in the nose. It was a healthy smell, hopeful of good growth and good fruit. I looked up at the sky covered with stars like bees and I thought I had never known a night more beautiful.

We went in. A kerosene lamp hung from a rafter put in across the middle of the hut. The lamp flared and sputtered and threw grotesque shadows sprawling all over the packed earth floor. The floor was swept dustless. Just inside the doorway a plaited rope mat lay, tacked into the earth by long nails. A cross of red surrounded by four white fish was woven into the plait of the mat. Kaiser wiped his feet on the mat and I took care to wipe mine too, taking longer than was necessary over it. In one corner of the far side from the doorway stood a table and two chairs. They were made of white pine and had been kept scrubbed as clean as chalk. Old Boss sat on one of the chairs, his head bowed over the table. Jaillin was not there. Old Boss did not raise his head. Kaiser went up to the table and knocked on it with his knuckles. 'Ol' Boss,' he said simply, 'Mister Alan here.' Then Kaiser went on and opened a small door in the wall at the back of the table. He turned with his hand on the knob. 'I going lie down to res', he said. He went through to the room at the back, shutting the door after him.

Old Boss lifted his head and looked at me. For a moment I thought he was a blind man; his eyes held that white, steady, impassive look of blindness in them. Then the lids winked down heavily and a long second after uncovered new eyes blazing with a smile. The change burnt my skin and touched my heart. I smiled too and took an involuntary step forward. I wanted to shake his hand. He rose from his chair and stood straight. He was tall.

'Come an' sit you'self in this chair here.'

'Thank you, sir.'

'You jump up? You enjoy Carnival?'

'Yes, sir. I'm tired. I got tired quicker than I thought.'

'It is a good good thing how everybody does jump when it come to Carnival. It seem to light up a fire in the body an' dat is a good thing.'

'Did you ever jump up?'

'I never jump up.'

'Everybody seems to jump up these days.'

'They bu'ning up all the bad thing in they belly.'

'Well, I enjoyed it. I think Kaiser did too.'

'Kaiser tell me how he bringing you here. Man, I 'member when you was a little boy so, tall as a three mont' cane. Kaiser use' to talk 'bout you like a king.' I felt cold go through me. I had thought of him like a king. 'An' Jaillin talk to me 'bout you one time.'

'Jaillin?'

'Jaillin coming in soon. You going meet she again. She cooking up a curry an' roti an' bringing it here. Kaiser say you want to meet she.'

'I used to see her a lot. We used to walk up the river with Kaiser. We used to catch butterflies and take off our shoes and walk in the water. It was fun I remember.'

'You 'member that well, man, I sure o' that. It store up in you min' like a bit o' silver. That is what happen. That was a long time an' you 'member it after you long done fo'get a thousand things in between. That is how it is.' He was silent. I felt he was putting his thoughts together like pieces in a jigsaw puzzle.

'How is Jaillin?' I asked.

'I know Kaiser tell you 'bout she.' I blushed.

'Yes.'

We were quiet. I wished Kaiser would come back, but there was no sign of him. In the silence I wanted to hear a clock ticking, but there was no clock.

'When you grow up older everything get small that you think was big one time an' you never going have anything so big again as things was when you was young. I know 'bout that thing.'

'I think I see what you mean.'

'You can't think you see. You going see when you know.'

There was a noise outside, slight as the paws of a cat on straw, but I heard it.

'That's Jaillin, I think.'

'Yes, that is she. I think it mus' be she.'

Jaillin came in through the doorway quickly. She was carrying a long tray heaped with steaming tin pans and two bottles of rum and small one-shot glasses. Without a word she came over to the table and put the tray down. She did not look at me. She looked at Old Boss gravely. Then she went back to the doorway and sat down with grace on the mat that was decorated with the red cross and the four white fish. She did not look up at us. She arranged her skirt about her knees. The dark hair fell over a side of her face and she tossed it back: it was as if wire tightened across my chest.

'Hello, Jaillin,' I said. There was no answer.

'We will have a rum,' Old Boss said.

He poured out rum into three glasses. He walked over to Jaillin and handed her one of the glasses. Then he came back and gave me a glass. He turned his glass in his hand and took a sip. Then he nodded to us and that was the signal to drink. I swallowed the rum in the glass in one gulp; I felt like that; I was in fear of the girl who sat cold and aloof in the doorway against the sky of stars and would not turn her eyes on me. Old Boss murmured to himself, then he said:

'Jaillin, why you keeping a silence? This is a bad thing.'

Jaillin did not answer that. She sat on the mat as still as a stone. I began to sweat; I felt anger rising in me like a storm. Old Boss looked at me with impassive white, blind eyes.

'It is so she is.'

'I see that.'

There was no conversation. I began to feel secure in my anger and sat cold and quiet, waiting for what would happen. Old Boss poured out three more rums in the one-shot glasses. It was blond, good rum. I tossed the glass back in one swallow.

'People never know what is what wid each other,' Old Boss said.

No one answered. There was another silence. Jaillin did not move even a line of her face. I thought of the small brown house lizards that when they were frightened lay frozen still as if caught in amber. The kerosene lamp which hung above us sputtered incessantly. I strained to hear noises outside so that I could forget the silence in the hut. I picked out six sounds quickly: a boy not far away was whistling; frogs were chiming like a thousand horns in the ricefields; in the distance dogs were barking against each other; very near I suddenly heard the hoot of a jumby bird; occasional voices came from the huts on the edge of the patch of corn; carnival drums beat as if they were over the hills and far away. I counted the sounds up in my head. Old Boss bowed his head over the table again. Jaillin did not move from the doorway. I discovered noises in the silence more secret than the others. There was a light snap as if a lady's mirror held in a convoluted rim of silver had cracked. A heavy glove of leather thwacked against a cliff of rock twice. What was it? There was a very tiny scream, as from a cockroach crushed by a boot. Over all, my ears, examining the silence, gradually became accustomed to a hum which may have been traffic on the Eastern Main Road but which I interpeted then as the sound the world makes as it spins around the sun. My mind snapped back to attention. Old Boss still had his head bowed over the table. His rum glass had fallen on the hard earth but it had not broken. The spilt rum made a dark sign like a curved knife on the earth. I looked over towards Jaillin and for the first time noticed with pleasure that she was wearing the silver earrings she had worn that day up the river when I had given her the purple orchid for her hair. Her clean white blouse was low over her breasts and suddenly I felt desire mount in my belly and my testicles. She no longer seemed cold and aloof. I smiled at her averted face. 'Hello, Jaillin,' I whispered, not meaning her to hear. She was quiet. I leaned over and poured myself another rum. I held the glass up to the kerosene lamp and saw the liquor glow there, light as blond mead. There was no sign of Kaiser. The room was quiet, quiet, quiet.

Suddenly there was a movement and I turned my head sharply. Jaillin got up and came over to the table. She stroked me on the arm. My skin felt warm against her fingers.

'Come le' we go for a walk outside,' she said. 'Then we could come in fo' the food.'

I got up from the table and followed her. Old Boss remained quiet, his head bowed over the table.

'Perhaps he's dead,' I said idly.

'No, he not dead.'

We went out the doorway. I avoided stepping on the mat. The red cross and the four white fish gleamed like signals giving a direction somewhere.

'The stars look like bees,' I said.

We walked through the corn.

'You remember when we were young, Jaillin?'

'I remember dat.'

'How we used to go up the river? Kaiser used to come too.'

'Yes, man.'

'I wonder what happened between us. Something happened.'

'All right, Master Alan, I going tell you something. Don't close you' ears, eh. You say you remember so many years gone now when we use' to walk up the river free fo' so. You remember dat time well?'

'Very well, Jaillin.'

'All right, Master Alan. I was so sweet in love with you that time I could a gone to sleep to die.'

There was the silence of the centre of a stone.

'Indian girl grow up early, you know. I was loving you like a big woman then. You know how nothing could happen. An' you was white an' I was a brown girl an' things in every way was different. Boy, I use' to cry like a dam' stupid baby sometime. You ever hear that! An' I only going to Ol' Boss all the time so to tell he what happen. An' one time I go to he an' say this like I mad fo' something. I say, they shouldn't have a dam' t'ing like love in the worl' at all if it only bring girl like me to be unhappy as hell. I don't know if he hear me good, but he say quiet to me, I'm telling you, "You know how it is when the rice is heavy with paddy an' the water-fiel's are thick with those green, brown-head shoot, then the bird come over, all the bird, all the scissor-tail swallow specially, looking to get grain in their craw. You know how it is. An' the whole worl' good then. The sky blue as a blue-bird. The sun buil'ing up a whole house o' heat. Everybody happy

178

because the rice crop look so good there in the water-fields. You know how it is. People not even vex with the scissor-tail because they is a kind of sign that the rice is all that good, an' they racing those bird off with a big smile on their face. Yes. Racing them 'way off, saying shoo, shoo, shoo, loud an' happy like they was little chil'ren. Yes. You know how it is, chile. That is what mek a lan' good. Even the scissor-tail glad. You could see it. They going wil' up an' down over the rice-top. Dipping fas' like a woman's calabash bathing down a baby. Up an' down, up an' down, they giving that beauty from god's big han'. An' you know how it is sometime a bird in all those dipping an' dipping with the happiness come down smooth so an' lan' on the ground an' begin to sing like a whole heaven self tho' you know already scissor-tail can' sing fo' ten pennies even. Yes. That is the one bird o' the rice harvest. People don't chase she at all, chile. Don' min' how much rice she spoil an' she eat 'way, people don't try an' race she 'way. She have something particular, a kin' o' holiness, oui. Yes, chile. Without she, I'm an ol' man an' I'm still telling you, that worl' when everything seem good wouldn' be right at all. That is what after all. You know how by the ol' village befo' we come by here the river went sweet under the bamboos. You mus' remember. Well, that is it. That was a sweetness all o' we had from the bird. Yes. An' eating you' big paw-paw yellow like a bee dus' under that same samaan. Ah, man. Whe' from you think come the enjoyment o' that. An' carving pieces o' dice from hard guava, thinking in you' head the whole time 'bout the game coming up nex' day so. Ah, man, that was right, eh." '

She stopped suddenly. My throat was hurting.

'I wonder what he meant by that, Jaillin?'

'You wouldn' know dat. I would know that _tho'_.'

There was silence between us. We had stopped near a casuarina tree, chattering sadly in the night wind, to talk, and now we moved back through the corn towards the hut. I didn't understand what had happened. It had been quick.

Dazed and weary, I misjudged the mood of that walk and tried to take her arm. She shook my hand off furiously and walked apart. Desire for her dissolved into sickness in my stomach. Somewhere quite near a horse punched the ground with an iron hoof. I made my mind as firm as that clear, hard sound.

'I hear you hate white people these days.'

'Yes.'

I laughed.

Old Boss was bowed over the table still when we came back into the hut. He did not seem to have moved at all. His white shirt was stuck to his back with sweat. When we came in he raised his head and looked at Jaillin. Then he looked at me. His eyes were blind and white for a moment. Then his eyes burst into an amazing smile.

'You had a walk?' Old Boss asked.

'Yes,' I said. 'We walked outside to the casuarina tree.'

'How was the night?'

The lovely question hurt me but I did not answer. Jaillin did not say anything.

'Chile, serve up the food now,' Old Boss said.

Jaillin got out three plates from a hip-tall chest standing near the doorway and put them on the table. She pulled the chest over to the table to make a third chair. Then she uncovered the pans holding the curry, the roti and the rice. The steam came out of the pans in three white gushes. The curry smelled pungent and rich and hot; it was a cascadura curry. The brown roti, dusted with maize, was cut in long strips and Jaillin laid these strips out on the three plates so that they even overlapped the edges. Then she heaped the grainy white rice out on the roti and poured the curry over the rice. The food steamed on our plates. We tore off strips of roti in our fingers and ate the rice and curry in the strips. Jaillin poured out rum. The blond drink tasted sharp in my throat.

Old Boss began to talk. I hardly heard him at first because I was thinking of things far from the village. Pictures came into my mind and I thought hard about their perfect texture: a view of marbleus speeding down the river and the wild yearning of my boyhood for them; Jaillin giving me a polished shilling on my birthday; levels of beach burning like gold shields in the sun; the night above all my life towering like a black horse covered by shining bees. The voice of the old craftsman began to mingle with the pictures like a commentary. I heard what he said. Jaillin was silent.

'So when I was a small chile I use' to play gallant up in a little river by Arima. All we little boys was mad to fish an' jus' dance up so in the sun when there was nothing mo' to do. All that time finish up so soon so me head still heavy with thinking why it so that people to 'come people mus' kill a chile. You see that? When people small the worl' full o' richness. But, chile, you only have to get big an' this morsel of a worl' get cheaper. Look out fo' that. Big people saying that thing all the time but you don't know a thing till you pass t'rough you'self, an' all you now passing. You hear me?'

I did not say anything and Jaillin did not say anything. What he said seemed real to me and I had nothing to say.

'I been thinking 'bout all this a good long time now an' it look to me like something happen here going happen to a whole lot o' people. An' it not only growing up big that involve. Two other things add up the thing worse. One is colour, one is white, an' when you is chile that don' matter a ant's tit. But grow up an' the whole thing cheapen up like the pretties' bird rotting. An' another thing too besides. I say the whole worl' is only a dam' little morsel of a place. But besides Trinidad is a smaller place even. It all close up on itself, an' you have to look out fo' that with the bigges' eyes you have. When you lose you' firs' richness what you have to expan' to? You' min' get cheaper, Trinidad get cheaper, the worl' get cheaper. You have to fight that like hell. You see now what I saying. Everything mounting up to mek what you have in this lan' as a chile cheaper. I use' to watch all you an' what I watch was good enough fo' living.'

I could not think of anything to say. I had only half finished my plate of food and I began to pick at the curry and rice again. The food had got cold though, and I pushed the plate away. I knew it was bad manners but I could not help that. To look at the food now made my stomach turn with sickness.

'What you say is true,' I said, 'but there's nothing to do about it.'

Old Boss nodded his head. Jaillin looked at me and smiled gravely.

'Goodbye,' I said. 'Tell Kaiser goodbye for me when he wakes up.'

When I got outside I heard the horse snort and punch the ground with its hoofs. My mind came sharply to attention round that practical sound. I was glad to hear it. I began to think of the next day and what to do.